Emily's Wedding

Emily's Wedding

Patricia Fawcett

ROBERT HALE · LONDON

ISBN-10: 0-7090-8005-0
ISBN-13: 978-0-7090-8005-3

Robert Hale Limited
Clerkenwell House
Clerkenwell Green
London EC1R 0HT

2 4 6 8 10 9 7 5 3 1

Typeset in 12/15pt Times New Roman
by Derek Doyle & Associates, Shaw Heath.
Printed in Great Britain by St Edmundsbury Press,
Bury St Edmunds, Suffolk.
Bound by Woolnough Bookbinding Ltd.

*For my daughter-in-law Fiona
with a special thank you to Joyce,
who does wonders with a
needle and thread*

CHAPTER ONE

'Emily . . . why on earth are you *never* in when I call? You know perfectly well I will not ring that mobile of yours. Anyway, Mum here. It's about the venue, darling. I can get us in at The Spotted Dog or The Manor. Now I know The Spotted Dog is just a glorified pub but the food is out of this world and they have such a reputation and a rather lovely conservatory. The Manor on the other hand is very grand and the gardens are superb, although that will hardly matter in December. So, it's food versus scenic beauty and a considerable difference in price, of course, although you mustn't let that influence you in any way. What do you think? I'll leave you to mull it over and call you tomorrow.

'Bye.'

Emily Bellew pulled the car as far over to the side of the lane as she dared, wincing as she scraped the banked-up hedge with its splendid assortment of wild flowers, none of which she could put a name to. The unpalatable fact was these lanes had been built for horses and carts and a much more leisurely pace of life. She switched off the engine and sighed. Now, come on. Where was this village? The woman on the phone, Mrs Cooper, had made it sound as if you couldn't possibly miss it.

She could.

It was not a thing she would willingly own up to, especially not to Simon, but when it came to finding her way anywhere with the slightest whiff of confusion in the directions given, her senses deserted her and panic took over. It was nothing to do with dubious female logic, as he would undoubtedly say, it was just her. According to the map, this village seemed to be up a B road and then left up an unnamed squiggle. She'd done that, blissfully confident for a few misguided moments, ending up in a picturesque hamlet which seemed stuck in a 1950s' time-warp, straight out of a Miss Marple mystery. It was like a deserted film set with just one extra wandering round. Unfortunately, he didn't seem to understand English, or at least her brand of it. She might as well have landed on Mars from the absolutely blank look on his face when she asked for directions. He had, however, touched his battered cap in a gentlemanly gesture, which both surprised and enchanted her.

Thereafter, they had stumbled through an unsatisfactory conversation, which had only succeeded in allowing a pungent odour of pig into the car, which was now invading her nostrils and knocking out all traces of the gorgeous perfume Simon had bought her. She was certain, too, that the swine smell had seeped into the very fibres of her smart burgundy jacket making her wish she had opted for something more casual.

So much for wanting to make an impression! She would arrive flushed and smelling of the farmyard. Unhooking her seatbelt and reaching across to the back seat, she yanked over her bag, aware her stress levels were steadily mounting. This was not how it was meant to be. She had looked forward to today for it was supposed to be an enjoyable day out, the prelude to having the most beautiful wedding gown ever at a fraction of the cost of a shop-bought one. Her mother had offered to buy her the dress but she was paying with martyr-like determination for everything else so Emily had put her foot down and insisted – for some insanely independent reason – on buying it herself. That was before she had checked out prices, which very nearly made her faint on the spot because for this oh-so-special occasion she did not want to resort to budget alternatives. For once only, it had to be the best, the very best and nothing but the best.

Emily had inherited a mean streak from her father and it made her unbearably cautious when it came to making purchases of any kind. Before she met Simon, she had operated on an extremely tight budget, priding herself on being able to put something away each month from what was a not very impressive salary. In fact, skilful and efficient budgeting, dare she admit it, had become part of her life and she had derived great satisfaction from penny pinching until she met Simon and it dawned on her that she was becoming a budget bore.

Meanness was hard to shake off though and she wished she could be an impulsive shopper, instead of such a calculating one, but she couldn't help it. Comparing costs and constantly poring through home accounts trying to work out how they could save a few pounds here and there might be crucial to her existence, but it merely exasperated Simon, who argued, probably quite rightly, that life was too short to worry about stuff like that. Something would turn up, it always did, and the annoying thing was he was usually right. Although her salary was regular, he worked on a freelance basis, which meant they couldn't ever be sure of just what was coming in each month. Sometimes, they were incredibly flush and she had to watch him in case he blew the lot. At other times, a mere pittance trickled in from him. Privately, she accepted there had to be give and take in a relationship and she knew she had to learn to loosen up a bit when it came to spending money, before it began to assume a sinister importance.

Financially, it had to be said, they were incompatible, which, she was well aware caused many a split. It was just as well their sex life was in a class of its own. Simon was of the opinion that if that was fine, then everything else just fell into place, which was very nearly true, for she could forgive him most things when he turned on the charm, which he possessed by the bucket-load. Just thinking of him and that special look he reserved for her made her smile, but the truth was he could be incredibly moody and difficult to live with and she was destined, it seemed, to spend her life making excuses for him. Simon suffered fools badly and worse, allowed his feelings to show. You could say he was a bull in a china shop when it came to treading over people's finer feelings. Her mother, delighted she was to be married, was necessarily reserving judgement on her choice of husband. 'Interesting man,' she had murmured. As to her father, well . . . Emily was his only daughter and no man would ever be good enough. He had made no comment on her choice, which somehow spoke volumes.

She and Simon were facing expenses galore as the wedding and the buying of the house approached and cutting the cost of the wedding dress, even though it was a mere pittance in the overall scheme of things, was just one of her contributions to the cause. In any case, she liked the idea of having her dress fashioned for her, a one-off, an original.

The dressmaker, Mrs Cooper, had come highly recommended via her colleague Belinda, whose fabulous wedding photographs were the proof. According to Belinda, she might be a bit odd and scary but what Corinne Cooper couldn't do with fabric was simply not worth doing. She had a confidence that gave you confidence in turn and was a touch above your ordinary seamstress. Since Emily made heavy weather of simply stitching on a shirt button, she viewed even a so-called *ordinary* dressmaker with awe. Corinne, it would appear, was extraordinary, studying fashion design in London during the 1960s, a prize-winning student and one of the few to be offered a place in Milan at a couture house to study further although, with a baby in the offing, she had not taken it up. However, out of the top of her head and with the minimum of fuss, she could design a dress fit for a princess. Show Corinne a picture and she would not only make a similar gown but a superior one, somehow or other giving it a unique twist.

With a little howl of frustration, Emily tipped the contents of her handbag onto the passenger seat, looking for her mobile phone and managing to break a carefully painted burgundy nail in the process.

Manicure ruined and wouldn't you just know it. It was turning out to be one of those days when it went bottoms up from the word go. Stubbing her big toe first thing on entering the bathroom in a semi-dazed state should have set alarm bells ringing. Even now, just thinking about it, the toe, unhappily squashed into elegant shoes, had started throbbing.

Now what?

A tractor towing some sort of horrific-looking farm machinery lugged by, squeezing past with aplomb as she sat cringing, knowing she was as far over as she could possibly get, short of being in the hedge itself. The unseen driver must wonder what on earth she was doing sitting here but not enough to stop and ask. As he passed, a whiff of some other exotic country fragrance drifted through the window and a dollop of slimy looking muck dislodged itself from a metal spiral and spat against the windscreen.

Well, thanks a bunch.

She really didn't want to have to ring Mrs Cooper to confess that she was lost but she did not have any choice. As it was, she was late and that was extremely annoying, considering she had set out with time to spare, even to the extent of dallying on the way out of the city, taking a deliberate long cut off the A38, because she had not wanted to be guilty of arriving early and looking too keen.

She keyed in the number, thinking about excuses before she heard the woman's clear bright tones. Mrs Cooper's voice was low-pitched, efficient-sounding, confident and assured and yes, there was a touch of bossiness round the edge.

11

'Oh, hello Mrs Cooper, this is Emily Bellew . . .'

'Good morning, Miss Bellew. It's already a quarter to eleven. Are we running late?'

'I'm sorry but I'm lost,' Emily admitted, giving up on the excuses. 'I'm at a crossroads, looking at this signpost and nothing rings a bell and not one of the places is named on my map. There are lanes off, here there and everywhere, and I haven't a clue which one to take. I could take forever at this rate,' she added, trying a short laugh to which there was a worrying lack of response.

'What options do you have?'

Craning her neck and peering up at the offending signpost, she read out the quaint and faintly ridiculous sounding names and Mrs Cooper tutted.

'You are miles out of your way. I gave you quite clear instructions. How on earth did you get *there*?'

'I have no idea but obviously I took a wrong turning,' Emily said, irritated both at the woman's tone – she needn't be quite so disparaging – and because this was getting them off on the wrong foot. And to think Simon had suggested a quick reconnoitre last Sunday afternoon just to check where the place was and she had pooh-poohed that idea. She had Mrs Cooper's explicit directions and a tongue in her head so what was the point?

For goodness' sake, she was a supposedly intelligent woman. She had to be in her capacity as Clive Grey's secretary, acting as not only the first port of call for his complicated diary, but also nursemaid and chief-soother of his ruffled feathers. He might well have founded Greys, a company of distinctive auction houses, and was undoubtedly an expert in his own field but he often had a poor grip on reality. It was her job to keep him focused and stop all the meandering. She sometimes thought she was more important to him than his wife, so it ought not be beyond her to read a map.

Mrs Cooper did not bother to hide an exasperated sigh. There was a rustling of paper as if she too was consulting a map and then she said, 'It's no use. I'll have to come and get you because I can't begin to give directions from there. You're in danger of ending up in the middle of Dartmoor at this rate.'

She was told to sit tight and sure enough after what seemed an age when not a soul passed by, an enormous dirty 4 x 4 loomed up, driven by a woman who slammed to a halt beside her in a puff of diesel fumes, completely blocking the lane before leaning out of the window and saying, with cocktail party politeness, 'Miss Bellew? Corinne Cooper. How do you do?'

'Hello there.' Awkwardly, they gave each other a sort of wave.

'Follow me then,' Corinne ordered, revving up her considerable engine. 'Oh, word of warning, by the way. . . .'

'Yes?'

'There's a beggar of a hill just ahead so do give me some space in case I start to slip back. My clutch is playing up. But whatever you do, try to keep moving. If you stall, you are in the deepest mire. Bernard once got stuck there in the old Metro, half-way up, caused mayhem, and it was a devil of a job to get him started again. It may not look like much of a road but it's the only way in and out for these folk. You block it at your peril.'

Scared stiff, Emily followed her at a careful distance in her bright little car, a car that Simon referred to as her Noddy car, partly because of its colour red of course – but also the styling. She loved it, could squeeze it into the smallest of parking slots and weave her way like the best of them through city streets but bendy country roads and the single-track high-banked lanes in this area were something else. Having to reverse forever and a day if you met somebody coming towards you was not something she looked forward to, especially when there were ditches and horrendous-looking big stones at the edge, ripe for doing considerable damage to her car, her woman driver reputation *and* her no-claims bonus.

The hill was frighteningly steep with a hopelessly tight bend at the top where the vehicle ahead did stutter alarmingly but at last they negotiated it and, relieved, she followed Mrs Cooper at a fast lick downhill, having to keep her wits about her because the lady was disinclined to use indicators or brakes. They took several unmarked lanes, Mrs Cooper diving right or left at the very last minute, until at last a signpost appeared announcing that they were in Dapplestone and they were asked to drive with care through the village. On the edge of Dartmoor, it was larger than she had imagined with an impressive terrace of Victorian houses next to the pub, a few shops, a garage, a primary school and a church with a tower. Mrs Cooper kept right on and then, just as they left the village behind, she turned again, managing a careful signal this time.

But it wasn't over yet. In order to find the house it was necessary to wriggle through yet another ridiculously narrow lane, squeezing improbably onto an even narrower track and over a speed hump and then, just when Emily was giving up hope, there was the house jumping out at them from behind a corner.

Half-hidden as it was in the dip, the doll's house prettiness had the effect of making her catch her breath. She had not expected anything quite so grand. Its facing wall was covered in creepers, the circular rose bed at the front full of late pink and yellow roses and weeds in equal proportions. And, standing guard in one corner, a family group of palm trees. Close-up, the house had a vaguely neglected air, in need of a lick of paint, but was suffering it with muted elegance. Corinne Cooper slewed to a halt on pink gravel beside the entrance, getting out of her car and indicating where Emily should park. Somewhere, inside the house, a dog barked deeply but did not materialize. With her bruised toe suddenly stinging like hell, Emily stepped out into the pleasant mid-morning warmth. The leaves were on the turn, a few early ones already down, crunching under her feet, the soft autumn breeze ruffling her hair. She closed her eyes a second, letting the country air swirl around her face, hearing excited birdsong, feeling her stress levels dipping smartly as she did so.

It was hard to take that this deep Devon countryside was relatively close to the city bustle of Plymouth because the isolation and blessed silence was total. You couldn't see the village from here and, across a wooded valley, the moor stretched into the distance, blurring eventually into the misty blue of the still damp sky, a promise in the air that the sun was about to break through the light cloud. For a moment, as Corinne allowed her to take in the scene, Emily felt that she might have heard a pin drop in the farthest meadow.

'It's lovely,' she murmured.

Corinne nodded, her expression neutral, before turning and walking away briskly. This woman was not at all what she had expected. In her fifties, she was dressed in in-your-face orange, her ankle-length flowing skirt just showing off crimson suede boots. She was a busty and hippy woman, but with a definite waist accentuated by a broad gingery leather belt fringed with tassels. She was tall, so the weight sat easily on her, and her best feature must surely be her hair, a shining mass of coppery red curls. She reminded Emily of one of those deliciously rounded creatures in paintings beloved of Victorians, a naked figure reclining improbably outdoors with an overabundance of cherubs watching over her.

It was a near thing but she fell just short of being beautiful, perhaps had been in her youth, and, to Emily's enormous relief, she had detected, hidden in those large grey-green eyes, the one thing that might salvage this situation – a sense of humour! With a bit of luck, the formidable harridan was just a front.

Three wide, worn, shallow steps led up to the heavy front door, which Corinne, after inserting a key pushed at with some force. Someone had made an attempt to beautify the gravelled area with tubs and a stone trough but they were sadly neglected, the plants only just clinging onto life. Emily was no gardener but she couldn't fail to notice their sad state as she waited for Corinne, who was still struggling to open the door.

'I've told Bernard time and time again to get this sorted and I can see I'll have to see to it myself,' she said, almost falling in as the door finally gave way. 'It'll be the death of me,' she went on, cheerfully enough, holding it open and inviting Emily to 'come on through'.

The hall, with what must surely be the original tiled floor, was square, sunlight suddenly streaming in through a stained-glass window and splintering against the pale green wall into little rainbows of colour. There was a large striking picture – askew – of an elephant just about to charge. There was also a grandfather clock, scattered high-backed chairs and a side table with a phone and a heap of letters precariously balanced on top of *Yellow Pages*. The handsome desk opposite with a vase of dead flowers was the sort of thing that Clive would just love to get his hands on to put in the next sale.

'Must sort those flowers out,' Corinne said, following Emily's gaze. 'Blasted things only last five minutes from the supermarket.'

It was all vaguely cluttered yet charming, but Emily scarcely took it in, her eyes on the dark-haired man on his way down the grand curved staircase, a man in his thirties, casually dressed in jeans and a pale-blue, denim shirt.

'Got here then?' he asked, landing beside her. 'I understand you had a problem. You're not the first one, believe me, this place is hell to find. Everybody has trouble the first time.'

Emily shot him a grateful glance, glad that it wasn't entirely her own fault.

'This is my son . . .' Corinne said, very nearly ignoring him. 'Here's Miss Bellew at last, Daniel.'

They smiled at each other but did not shake hands.

For some reason though, Emily found herself giving him a backward glance, as she was ushered into what Corinne called her workroom.

Corinne reflected that she must really get that damned clutch seen to before she inflicted that panicky situation on any more nervous brides-to-be who found themselves lost in rural space. She put it down entirely to their state of mind. Bless their anxious hearts, but it seemed to her that the whole business of getting married was growing ever more complicated. In their day, back in the glorious 1960s, her marriage to Bernard was all accomplished with the minimum of fuss, give or take her mother's palpitations and her father's incredibly long-winded speech. They should have recorded it for posterity, a how-not-to-do-it speech. As well as warning Bernard that this flame-haired daughter of his would take some handling, he had at some point forgotten where he was and the speech had then taken on a distinctive scientific slant, as if he was lecturing his students.

As the guests' puzzled eyes glazed over, she and Bernard had not dared look at each other, knowing they would dissolve into giggles. She had been three months pregnant too, at the nauseous stage, and been totally unable to face the wedding feast. Being pregnant was the entire reason for the wedding, and unlike today, they tried their very best to keep that secret, the whole family seeming surprised by Stephen's eventual arrival six months later.

How different it was today when nobody gave a hoot which was somehow much more refreshing. She had recently created a dress for a girl who was eight months by the time the wedding arrived, pregnant and proud of it. Empire line had never been so welcome and looked so wonderful!

With so many essential strings to the wedding bow these days, flowers, venue, stag and hen dos, reception, the list, the cake, the favours, the theme, it surprised her that so few couples opted for what might have once been quaintly called an elopement, because the fuss and pressure involved was enough to get to even the most chilled-out girl. Add to that Miss Bellew's unfortunate misreading of the directions and it was no wonder she was quite pale and stressed. Her heart had gone out to the poor child, sitting in that little car looking so very vulnerable. Such a sweet face with big soulful eyes, quite different from the vision she had had in her head. She had sounded brisk and businesslike on the phone and she had therefore imagined somebody much more hard-edged. Belinda had recommended her and she recalled that young lady with affection. They may work together but they were poles apart. Emily was much more serious and the dress must reflect her personality. Unlike Belinda, no frills for her then.

Getting the clutch seen to on her car was just one of the many jobs she considered to be her responsibility because if she left any of them to Bernard they would never ever get done. Over the years, she had become rather adept at technical matters and could tackle things that a lot of women sweetly left to their other halves. She could turn her hand to almost anything, painting, decorating, fitting shelves etc, balking only at electrical work, which she thought wise to leave to the professionals in case she sizzled herself to death. She was completely prepared for widow-hood should the dearest man pop his clogs before she did.

Bernard was totally impractical, immersed in his work and was a marvel at half-finishing jobs. Far too easily side-tracked. After more than thirty years, they were toddling on, not completely happy with each other these days but not exactly miserable either – just toddling on. She wondered why she stayed with him some-times, because the romance as well as the sex had more or less fizzled out.

She stayed with him, of course, because of their past, because of Joe and their shared loss. Bernard had been her rock then and he alone had kept her from strangling Daniel. She knew the inquest had called it an accident but there had only been Daniel and Joe there at the time and Joe was dead so they had to take Daniel's word for what actually happened.

She knew he was lying. A mother knew such things. She had

her own ideas about what had happened. Daniel, who had become blasé about the whole business of climbing, had made a mistake leading his brother up the wrong damned path, which he didn't want to own up to.

She would never forgive him.

Bernard did his best, she supposed, to keep the peace between them. It wasn't in Daniel's nature to cause a complete bust-up, but Bernard knew she was on a very short fuse and that one day she might actually say it, accuse her own son of killing his brother, so he watched over them warily.

Daniel had spent the last few months over in South America, working this time for some sort of organization that ran dreadful-sounding climbing holidays in the Andes. During that time, there had been just the one phone call when he arrived and then silence until he turned up at Gatwick and rang to say he was on his way home.

Sooner and better Daniel found a girl and was off their hands, for this constant to-ing and fro-ing at his age was an irritation. He had struck a chord with Miss Bellew, for she had caught the interested backward glance the girl had given him and, even more surprisingly, the tell-tale blush when she first saw him.

Oops. And here she was planning her wedding.

CHAPTER TWO

'Emily . . . I despair, I really do, you're never there to pick up the phone when I call. Mum here. I hope you realize that this is all terribly short notice. We should have had a year's warning to do it justice, but I will do my best. Now, I've been speaking to various people and apparently we have to have a "theme". It's the done thing and it's all to do with colour, linking with the cake and the table decorations and the flowers and little gifts and so on. Helen's daughter had English Country Gardens, for example, as her theme although that won't work in the middle of winter, will it? December really is the most awkward time for a wedding what with Christmas looming and everything. It's going to be a choice of being bundled up to keep warm with thermals and what have you or not giving a damn and freezing to death. Anyway, think about a theme, darling, and let's have your thoughts.

'Take care.

'Bye.'

Corinne's workroom was also cluttered, a flamboyantly floral room with rose-patterned wallpaper, extravagant drapes at the bow window, swatches of fabric everywhere, a tailor's dummy positioned by the window as if looking out. A sewing machine sat on a table beside a huge box of assorted cottons and silks. There were heaps of embroidered cushions on the big old leather sofa, an alcove brimming with books, not artfully arranged but bunged in any how and, on the wall, pictures of Corinne's brides.

'Do have a closer look,' she said, and it was an order that Emily obeyed immediately. 'Beautiful, aren't they? I think of them all as my darling girls. And no, I don't have a favourite. There's only one who still lives locally.' She pointed out a slim figure in an eye-catching fish-tailed dress. 'She has three small children now and has rather let herself go. As for the others, one or two are now divorced, of course, and one poor darling is tragically dead, but there you are. That's life. One has to be pragmatic about these things.'

Wondering which poor darling was no longer with them, Emily glanced at the photos, trying to find some similarity, something Corinnesque, in the style of dress, but not finding any. One thing was sure, they all looked great, so it was a relief that Belinda's opinion was not rose-tinted but spot on, because, from these examples, Corinne Cooper was indeed something of a marvel.

'Sit down and calm yourself,' Corinne told her, giving a little shake of her head. 'What a fuss and bother! But it's over now, you're here at last so you can relax.'

Relax? Emily was feeling flustered from meeting Daniel and had no idea why. He was a good-looking man, certainly, but she was engaged to be married to Simon and her days of looking longingly at other men were definitely numbered. But, for a fleeting moment, confronted by Daniel, she had had a startlingly romantic vision of being held in those strong arms and being very firmly kissed by him and was quite alarmed that such a thing should cross her mind. She hoped that Corinne Cooper hadn't guessed as much, but looking across at her, she thought perhaps she had. She had always been hopeless at keeping a poker face and, wearing your heart on your sleeve as she did was a recipe for disaster.

On the other hand, why on earth shouldn't she look at another man? Simon was always eyeing up the girls, even though he strenuously denied doing it. Daniel Cooper was in magnificent shape and he looked sporty – outdoor certainly – with exactly the kind of rough-edged attractiveness that would be especially attractive to some women, if never before for her. Simon's looks were more classical, unspoilt, close to perfection in her eyes. He hated organized sport but he ate carefully, did not smoke and kept himself fit, had to for the sort of work he did.

'Daniel wanted to come and rescue you,' Corinne told her, the smile blessedly extending now to her eyes. 'But I thought you might not wish to be confronted by a strange young man in your hour of need. Please ignore him. He's without a girlfriend just now and I think he fancied helping out a damsel in distress. He's rather like his father. They can both be utterly charming but completely hopeless in so many ways. If I had known then what I know now about Bernard' – she rolled her eyes – 'I would have bailed out at the earliest opportunity.'

'Do you have help with the garden?' Emily asked, a little desperate to change the subject for she was not sure if Corinne was joking or not. 'It's huge. It's like a park.'

'Good lord no, we do it ourselves or rather, most of the time, don't do it as you can see. The leaves will be fully down soon and the picking up is so time-consuming. It makes me want to fell the damned trees but I always reprieve them because they look so wonderful in spring and summer. We ought to have known when we took it on that it would be work, work, work but we were taken in by it and we were terribly enthusiastic and didn't think about the problems but then when you're young, you don't. Everything seems possible then.'

'What on earth made you take on such a project?'

'We had romantic ideals, Miss Bellew, in those days,' Corinne said. 'We bought it for a song because it was falling to pieces and Bernard had inherited a little money that was burning a hole in his pocket, so we went for it, as they say. We did think about turning it into a hotel at one time but we talked ourselves out of it. It's not as enormous as it looks. It only has seven bedrooms. If we are to think of selling, we'll have to go to the ridiculous expense of installing extra bathrooms, a new kitchen and what have you.'

'It was very brave of you to take it on,' Emily said, thinking what Simon would say if she were to suggest such a project, even if they could ever afford such a thing.

'Stupid more like. Bernard earns quite a decent crust and we could afford a gardener but he has this problem with delegation. He much prefers to grumble like hell about mowing the lawn. We have an arrangement. He does that and I do the flower beds.' She flicked impatiently at her hair, a gesture left over no doubt from her youth. 'I make no apologies for them. I like to let them breathe, do their own thing, but I do pull up the odd weed from time to time, believe me. I hate regimental gardens, neat rows of colour. Town hall pomposity I call it. Polite perfection!' she added with a shudder. 'It's much the same with people when you get down to it. I like people to have one fairly obvious fault because perfect people are utterly depressing. I suppose that's why I married Bernard.'

Emily smiled uncertainly, relieved when Corinne smiled too. Even though she almost dismissed the garden as indeed she had dismissed her son and her husband, Emily thought it absolutely beautiful, a view that seemed so idyllic that sceptics might wonder just what was about to happen to destroy such tranquillity. The lawns dipped to trees and the unseen river in the distance and, from this angle, there was no trace of the bustle and confusion of the twenty-first century. This could be a scene from a dreamy, soft-focused Jane Austen adaptation, and didn't that seem highly appropriate given that she was here to discuss her wedding dress.

Perhaps the pace of life here was slower because Corinne seemed in no hurry to proceed with the matter in hand, looking very much at ease in this room that was clearly hers and hers alone, reaching out for a book that was on the small table beside her. Her arms were tanned and freckled, Emily noticed, and she took great care of her hands, the long manicured nails – surely incompatible with sewing? – painted a dark red. Conscious of her broken nail which had completely ruined *her* manicure, Emily folded her hands together, feeling stupidly nervous.

'I take a break occasionally, have to when I'm hand-stitching, and like to have a book handy. This is my current tome. Have you read it?' Corinne inquired, holding it out so that Emily could see that it was a serious looking volume about Elizabeth I. 'I can't get enough of biographies. I've just finished one on Samuel Pepys – what a rogue he was. I have to say I admire Elizabeth. She was a redhead, too, so I feel some link there and, like me, she could not stomach fools. I suspect she would have despatched my Bernard from court pretty damned quick. Not that my husband's a fool,' she added hastily. 'Far from it. In fact, he's one of the financial big-wigs at Pacsman. You know, the menswear chain . . .'

'Of course,' Emily said, recalling the distinctive blue-and-white striped bags. Pacsman was an expensive range menswear chain, catering for the middle-aged, the sort of shop Simon generally avoided, the sort of shop her mother might drag her father into when she decided he needed a new suit. It would seem that the aforementioned Bernard was something of a high flyer and would certainly be earning, as Corinne quaintly put it, a *decent crust*.

'Bernard studied history at university and that's his real joy,' Corinne went on. 'He's joined this Civil War re-enactment group but he hasn't much time at the moment. When he retires I expect he'll be off playing soldiers every weekend.'

Emily recognized this patter for what it was. Clearly, the woman adored her husband, this Bernard, but, for some reason, she felt the need to gently pull him to threads. She didn't do that with Simon. In fact, it was rather the opposite. She played on the positive side of his nature, never talking about his faults and his down-moods to others.

She glanced at her watch. She didn't want to hurry Corinne but she had been late arriving and it was getting on. Wasn't it time they started talking about the dress? Wasn't it time also that she took some control of this conversation? After all, she was the one wearing the business suit, she was the one forking out the cash.

'Coffee first I think, and then you must stay for lunch,' Corinne said, rising to her feet. 'Have a browse through the pattern books, Miss Bellew, and I'll be back in a moment.'

Daniel Cooper was in the kitchen, fully aware that his mother would be coming in to make her client a coffee before long. He hoped this poor girl knew what she was letting herself in for.

He hadn't meant to land at her feet like some sort of beached whale but, mind buzzing with other things, he hadn't heard the cars arriving. It was just pure chance he happened to be on the way down when he heard his mother fumbling with the door lock and by then he hadn't wanted to be seen creeping back up the stairs. He knew that his mother had been put out that he had put in an appearance, but then she was easily put out where he was concerned. He wondered sometimes why he bothered to come back home when he was so clearly not welcome, not by her anyway.

He could hear voices from the workroom or rather his mother's voice and he smiled slightly as he tossed a bit of biscuit in Bingo's direction.

'Don't tell her,' he warned the old black collie. 'Or I'll be in the dog house with you.'

He had baked some scones first thing in readiness for what he had now discovered was a delectable Miss Bellew. He was very into cooking and, when he was home, he was happy to take it over because his mum, though capable enough when she put her mind to it, was not interested. He might well have been a chef if things had turned out differently, but the climbing bug had bit

25

him in his teens and that was that. He had chosen Manchester University largely because of its proximity to the crags. He was regarded as capable and reliable, certainly one of the names that cropped up when an expedition was being considered. He did not regard himself as leadership material, was happy to be a team member, part of the élite climbing circle, and could no more give that up than sex, although, with the recent stormy break-up with Amanda, he got precious little of that these days. The recent trip to South America had been the final nail in the coffin of that relationship, even when he offered to take her along with him.

'And what the hell would I do?' she wailed. 'Sit and sweat it out while you're up one of your beloved mountains?'

The ultimatum had followed.

Give up the mountains or give up her.

No choice.

His mother's new client, unfortunately in a way, reminded him of Amanda. Miss Bellew was really something, a stunner in fact, his kind of girl, petite with dark-brown, glossy hair swinging about her face and she had blushed as she looked up at him. He found that charming, for he had imagined her to be a tough, no-nonsense business woman with calculating eyes and attitude. She had the smart suit certainly and the high clattering heels but her eyes gave her away, warm brown eyes that had quickly – too quickly – looked away from him.

It was tough that she was already spoken for, as his mother would say, so he had best forget her and keep out of her way when she was around, as she would be a few times more before her wedding. He didn't know what sort of frock his mother would conjure up but one thing was sure, Miss Bellew would look wonderful, being the sort of girl who would look good in any old thing.

On cue, his mother sailed in, in that way of hers, into the kitchen.

'Oh, good,' she said, seeing the scones already arranged on the plate and the coffee on its way. 'Thank you.'

'Not at all.'

You could feel the tension, always there, hanging between them like a thread. He wished she wouldn't make it quite so obvious to other people that she found him mildly distasteful, that he had disappointed her beyond words. He was aware that Miss Bellew had noticed the off-hand manner with which she had introduced him but, as he was unlikely to get to know her, explanations were unnecessary.

'I thought you were on your way out,' Corinne said, sliding plates onto a tray.

'Not yet,' he said, trying a smile. 'Do you want me to give you my itinerary for the week?'

'No need for that, and don't speak to me like that either, Daniel.'

'Sorry,' he said, seeing the glint in her eyes. She was a tough nut, but she had been broken by Joe's death and he would have given anything for it not to have happened. The hardest part was keeping the truth from her, but he had no choice. He couldn't tell her, couldn't tell anyone, not even his dad, what had really happened that day.

He sighed, turned away before she should see the sudden distress that was still capable of hitting him even after all this time.

'You took poor Miss Bellew by surprise, I have to say,' his mother went on. 'What do you make of her? I'm surprised she made such a mess of finding us. I gave her very clear instructions and look where she ended up. Can you credit it, but then she's awfully stressed, poor darling.'

'Aren't all brides-to-be?'

'Oh, yes. They like to imagine they have everything under control but it gets too much for them,' she said, doing a final check that she had everything on the tray that she needed.

'Shall I carry that in for you?' he offered, stepping carefully past a sprawling Bingo.

'I can manage, Daniel, I'm not entirely in my dotage yet,' she said. 'If you'd just open the door for me and then disappear.'

He did as he was told, managing to catch a glimpse of Miss Bellew perched on the sofa in the workroom. She was poring through a pattern book, wearing striking black-framed spectacles that somehow made her look very young and vulnerable. Why on earth he should feel so protective about somebody he had only just met he had no idea. He did not believe in love at first sight – what a stupid notion that was – and yet some of his pals, guys he had down as pretty hard-headed, had talked of it. Funny the things you talked about when you were stuck up a mountain. It was as if the higher you got up the mountain, the more your inhibitions loosened – maybe it was something to do with oxygen deprivation – and he and his companions talked about things that normally only women talked about, relationships and suchlike. When you were trapped in a storm on a ledge overnight for instance, only feet away from slipping into oblivion, you had to keep talking to keep your spirits up, stop yourself from losing it, talking about everything and anything, politics, religion, and yes, the subject of women and love had, of course, reared its head.

'Now, Mrs Cooper . . .' Emily began, once Corinne had returned with the tray and coffee. She had decided when Corinne was in the kitchen that she must proceed as she meant to carry on and take some control of the proceedings before Corinne swamped her. It had been an unfortunate start but it was not too late to remedy it. She was a busy woman, as was Corinne, and she couldn't afford to waste any more time. She had already taken her diary from her bag and it lay on her lap, ready and waiting, her pen poised.

'If I might just acquaint you with the facts?' she said, aware she was adopting her no-nonsense work-voice. 'My schedule is as follows. Our engagement announcement has appeared in the paper. We have booked the church and we're homing in on the venue for the reception and I have informed all my relatives and friends of the wedding date which is the 3rd of December . . .'

'And your fiancé? Has he done the same with his relatives?'

'Simon doesn't have any family,' Emily said. 'There are only a few working colleagues and I don't think any of them can make it, other than the one who's going to be best man, of course.'

'I see.' Corinne Cooper sat quietly but said nothing further so, after a quick glance at her, Emily continued.

'I'm sure you'll understand that with our working commitments and Simon being out of the country so often, I want to have everything organized as soon as possible, well in advance in fact and certainly before my mother starts on her Christmas preparations. There are only certain dates, for instance, when Simon will be available to come with me over to Kent to see the vicar. Even though my family have been regular churchgoers for years, Simon and I need to show our faces at a couple of services, spend some time in the parish and we have to have some sort of premarital counselling fitted in as well. It's becoming a nightmare finding space in our diaries.'

Corinne laughed. 'I'm sorry, do go on. It was just your mentioning counselling that reminded me of the so-called counselling we had. The vicar, bless his soul, was very embarrassed. He asked if I loved Bernard and I said yes and then he asked Bernard if he loved me and he said yes. That's all right then, the vicar said, and that was the sum total of it.'

'Perhaps there's more to it these days?'

'I don't see why,' Corinne said. 'It's a simple enough question and you should be able to answer it with a yes or no. People delve too deep, think too much these days and before you know what, they can very easily talk themselves out of things. It happened with Daniel and Amanda. I'm very cross with him because Amanda was perfectly suitable. It's not every girl who could take on somebody like Daniel.'

29

Emily smiled, waiting for an explanation if there was to be one.

'She knew what she was letting herself in for with the climbing and everything and seemed prepared to accept it,' Corinne said. 'They were close to getting engaged but they, or rather Amanda, started to consider all the implications of getting married and so on and having to cope on her own when he was off on one of his infernal climbs and before long it was all over. They did say it was a mutual decision and supposedly parted the best of friends,' she added with a rueful smile. 'However . . .' She paused, suddenly aware that Emily was hanging onto her every word. 'Excuse my being indiscreet but Daniel was hardly heartbroken, but then he tends to hide his feelings.'

'Does he?' Emily felt some sympathy. She supposed they were all capable of that, for wasn't she hiding her own feelings, trying to come to grips with her own doubts that were starting to trouble her more and more? 'I don't know if my time scale is all right,' she went on, worried slightly because her mother was doing her best to panic her.

'As far as I'm concerned, it's tight,' Corinne said, not helping. 'I can do it, although I can't start straight off because I'm in the middle of doing three bridesmaids' dresses and it's taking forever to sort out the fittings. You've given me adequate time but I would have liked longer. Most brides are planning for a full year and for some that's scarcely enough.'

'Oh. Well, I'm sorry,' she said, taken aback and feeling she had to qualify things. 'My mother's sorting everything else out. There's really only my dress for me to worry about,' she added, aware that she could at a pinch simply walk into a specialist shop and pick something off the shelves. 'Talking of my mother, she's pressing me for details of the dress so if we might discuss some styles now?' Emily said, concerned at what she saw as the lack of progress. 'I haven't really seen anything in the pattern book that I'm terribly keen on. But I have cut out a few things from magazines which I thought I might show you.' She rummaged in her bag.

'Put those away,' Corinne said, manner suddenly brisk and businesslike. 'It is not my policy to discuss the design of the actual dress today. I see today as a getting-to-know-each-other day. If I am to make your gown for you, Miss Bellew, then I must know something about you and your fiancé. It's essential. I'm not being nosy but without some knowledge of you both, some background, then I really can't begin to envisage how I want you to look on your wedding day.'

Emily frowned, as she felt control slipping away from her. She hoped Mrs Cooper wasn't going to try to dictate what she wore. It was her wedding, her decision and whilst she would appreciate advice, surely she would have the last word?

'I have no hard and fast rules,' Corinne continued, not noticing Emily's concern. 'I will do fancy and I will do perfectly plain. Whichever. But we have to marry the right dress to the right bride. There are certain styles, for instance, that only a model shape can carry off. A girl of five foot seven at the very least,' she finished, looking pointedly at Emily who could barely manage five two.

'Of course. I understand that,' Emily said, realizing that this was not going to be as easy as she thought. Nor did she want just another dress, like every other bride, she wanted *her* dress, the something special that Corinne was hinting at.

'From my experience, girls seem to go through life making only moderately poor decisions about clothes but come their wedding day, common sense often deserts them. If, in the end, we can't see eye to eye, then I would much prefer to lose the commission than make something that I feel does not flatter you.' Her eyes were suddenly hard-edged. 'I mean that. I'm not so desperate for money and I have my reputation to consider.'

'Why, yes, I do understand that, although I had hoped we might come up with some ideas today,' Emily said, irritated yet again that she was getting nowhere and that the woman opposite had the upper hand. Her take-it or leave-it attitude also irked and it was so tempting to storm out now and tell her to stuff the dress and go hunting around in shops, but the memory of Belinda's vision of a dress surfaced. Belinda, contrary to the general snide office assumption, had looked stunning. Quite simply, the dress took your breath away and was every bit as beautiful as any designer gown costing thousands, and so she held her peace.

'I thought a traditional design,' she ventured hopefully into a sudden silence. 'Big full skirt, maybe a strapless top . . .'

'You'll be shivering. Remember it will be December,' Corinne said. 'You may need a pretty jacket to cover up.'

'I'm open to discussion.'

'Are you having bridesmaids?'

She nodded. 'Two.'

'Children?'

'No. Grown-ups,' she said, thinking briefly of Stella and her tantrums. 'I thought turquoise perhaps or pale pink for them. Again, I'm open to suggestions.'

'Turquoise or pale pink? A winter wedding might need a stronger colour.' Corinne sniffed, making her feelings known. 'You do understand I shan't have sufficient time to do those as well?'

'Of course. You did say that. Anyway, they're over in Kent so it would have been difficult for them to get here for fittings. We thought they could get something off-the-peg but I would be grateful for your ideas on that.'

'Adult bridesmaids to me signal disaster,' Corinne said with a sigh. 'They are capable of torpedoing the bridal gown because one has to look at the whole picture. If I were you, Miss Bellew, I would settle for children. Stick to sweet little flower girls or little boys who add both character and humour and don't try to outdo the bride. Or, if they do, it's perfectly acceptable.'

'It's not as easy as that,' Emily said, privately agreeing with her but it was all arranged already. Her neurotic cousin Stella had wanted to be a bridesmaid for years and Yvonne was her one-time flatmate who had just assumed when given the news about the wedding that she was being asked to be bridesmaid. Given that situation and her flatmate's unexpected delight at the prospect, it had proved impossible to backtrack, even though Yvonne was a generous size 16, and Stella, a reformed anorexic and still skin and bone, so how would they find a dress that flattered both of them?

'Next time we'll have a look through some books,' Corinne said. 'And some sketches of mine that I shall rustle up now that I've met you. Do have a scone.'

'Thank you.' Emily bit into one. 'They're delicious.'

'My son made them,' Corinne said. 'Isn't it infuriating? I've always found scones a devil to make. Daniel has had no training but has this knack. He ought to have been a chef and have done with it. At least I consider that to be a proper profession.'

'Does he climb for a living?'

'That and things related to it. He seems to get by.'

'How interesting.'

'You think so? I think it's complete lunacy. He worries us sick when he's off on one of his silly expeditions. I think it's so very selfish of him, particularly as . . .' She stopped abruptly, face flushed. 'I'm sorry. There's a family problem and I have no right to burden you with it.'

'I wish my fiancé did something a little more ordinary to be honest,' Emily said, curiosity aroused. 'A nine-to-five job does have its advantages.'

'Oh yes. Dull but safe,' Corinne said, looking at her a little oddly.

'You have a lovely home,' Emily went on, delicately dabbing at her crumbly mouth with a napkin before looking round and out of the window. 'It's very grand.'

'Isn't it? It's worth an absolute fortune and I hate it,' Corinne

33

said. 'It's so empty these days and to be honest it always got on my nerves. It's so huge! As I said, we bought it for a song many moons ago because it was dropping to bits and nobody else was insane enough to take it on. We must have been quite mad because we had three small children at the time and Bernard had only just started out at Pacmans but, believe it or not, we had vision in those days, did an enormous amount of work to it before we got bored with it. Bernard adores it still, but it needs a battalion of staff to keep it up to scratch. To be honest we could afford to get people in but I like my personal space and staff do so intrude, so I make do with just one woman who comes in a couple of days a week. I want to move. What I would really like is a very modern apartment in the heart of London when he retires but Bernard won't hear of it. He's such a stick-in-the-mud. He's leaving here in his coffin he says.'

'I would give anything to have a house like this some day,' Emily said with a sigh. 'But you know how it is, you have to creep up the property ladder rung by rung.'

'Yes. Such a bore, isn't it? Now, Emily . . . may I call you that?'

'Please do.'

'And you must call me Corinne. I can't work with just anyone as I explained on the phone. I need to have a rapport with my clients and so I have to know something about them, about what makes them tick. Perhaps you can begin by telling me a little about yourself?'

Emily hadn't expected this. It was like a job interview and she did not feel prepared. She also failed to see what on earth it had to do with the making of a wedding dress. But Corinne was the one with the magic fingers so what choice did she have?

Digging in her bag, she pulled out some family photographs.

CHAPTER THREE

'Emily . . . I do so hate speaking to this wretched machine. Mum here. There's so much to arrange, darling, and so little time that it's giving me one of my migraines and your father's no help whatsoever. How did we ever come to ask Stella to be a brides-maid? Did you ask her? I don't remember doing it. Oh well, too late now. Anyway, I'm calling about the music because I've just had a thought. I thought perhaps Chopin's Nocturne in E flat whilst you sign the register. What do you think? You do know it, don't you? I'll let you think about it, discuss it with Simon. Your father's being an absolute bore. He wants me to draw up a budget. I ask you. Just ignore him if he rings you behind my back. Catch you later.

'Bye.'

'It was very nearly the third degree. I felt I was in the witness box,' Emily told Simon later. 'It really threw me. Corinne's a good listener, either that or very clever, all those little pauses that made me twitter on.'

He smiled. 'You don't twitter. I've always found you weigh up your words very carefully.'

'Do I?'

She glanced at him suspiciously, not sure that wasn't a veiled criticism. Yes, she knew she found it difficult to be spontaneous and she was certainly not given to impulsive gestures, but to be thought ponderous was quite another matter.

'You certainly do. One of the things I love about you,' he said, his cheerful grin sending her worries packing.

He was lying on the sofa, wearing a towelling gown after his shower, prior to getting ready for the latest overseas trip. This gorgeous man of hers was what might be called rakishly handsome, tall and rangy with fair hair and vivid blue eyes that were certainly capable of handing out a cold stare from time to time, when the description steely blue had never seemed so apt. She always laughed it off when she received that glare, told him not to look at her like that, but that look made her shudder inside and set those damned doubts wriggling.

Sometimes, for seconds only, he looked at her as if she were a stranger.

Sometimes, for seconds only, she saw him as a stranger too.

He'd been out shopping, bought one or two items in his favourite shops judging by the bags and receipts tossed casually on the kitchen table. For somebody who professed to be not the least interested in clothes, he had a natural flair for choosing the very best. She had glanced at the receipts, noted the prices with a sharp intake of breath, but was determined to say nothing, not when he was off to the airport shortly. She did not want to send him off after an argument about money because there'd been too many quibbles lately on that score, but she vowed they really would have to get things together soon or she would begin to feel worryingly out of control. Whenever she bought something on her credit card, she put the receipt carefully away in the file but he, as often as not, lost them and, as a result, she couldn't keep track. The rental for this place was at the top end of their budget and they needed to buy a property soon, before Simon started digging into their reserve fund that was put aside to pay the deposit on their dream home.

They had been together for over four years, living for two of them in a cramped flat in Windsor. She looked back on those days with a bit of a rosy glow, remembering them as the special times, concerned that they had slipped away and they were left now with just the residue. It was all becoming – dreadful to contemplate – rather humdrum of late.

She and Simon had met at a party hosted by a friend. She was on the rebound from a brief relationship with a prized bastard that ought to have put her off men for ever. So, wounded and wary that she should have made such a dreadful mistake, she was feeling vulnerable and not ready for anything new.

But she reckoned without Simon. She heard him before she saw him, finding his deep, lulling voice the stuff of sexy chocolate ads, hoping that when she turned round, he wouldn't be a terrible disappointment.

He wasn't.

Fortified by a glass of wine too many, she flirted outrageously with him for the rest of the evening, although, thank goodness, it hadn't got completely out of hand and she had gone home with her girlfriend and not ended up in bed with him. Next day, her girlfriend had given her the potted history of Simon Newell who was a freelance photographer and gaining quite a reputation for his photographs in the world's trouble spots, producing and selling pictures with the human touch that newspapers and magazine agencies worldwide were seeking. He was much admired in the profession, showing his versatility by exhibiting some beautiful scenic shots at one or two prestigious galleries, and was on the up. No girlfriend, but he's as straight as they can be and not a bad bet, her friend had also said with a knowing smile, and why on earth don't you give him a call because you're so obviously smitten?

But giving *him* a call, asking him out, being a very modern Miss was not her style and she hesitated, desperately afraid of a put-down, nervous, too, that any new relationship might be doomed. She needed time to recover from the last one. And then, just when she was telling herself to forget him, he rang, perhaps prompted by her friend, and asked her out to lunch. After that, it fairly ripped along and, although in many ways they had little in common, they had enough . . .

Two months ago, to her complete surprise, he had proposed. It wasn't an on-the-knees proposal, rather a throwaway question as they settled down for a cosy evening in front of the television.

'Marry you? Whatever for?' she remembered saying, realizing as she said it that it wasn't a very romantic reply. realizing also that if she'd known this was coming, she'd have made an effort with the meal instead of a couple of M&S lasagnes with packet salad. Wishing too that the shock hadn't made her dribble tomato sauce on her white top.

'Now look what you've made me do,' she said, rubbing ineffectually at the stain and letting the question settle between them, the most important question she had ever been asked in her life. 'Marry you,' she repeated, eventually raising puzzled eyes. 'I thought we were happy as we are. We agreed it didn't matter, not when there's just the two of us.'

'I've changed my mind,' he replied. 'Stuff what everybody else does. I want us to get married.'

She said yes eventually – three weeks later – because he wouldn't let it drop and immediately regretted it, for she worried that it might change things. They were happy enough as they were so why take a risk?

Her mother was predictably delighted and whizzed into immediate mother-of-the-bride mode, pulling out a planning list that Emily suspected had been lurking around for some considerable time. She was the much-loved, only daughter and of course, as such, her mum could be forgiven for making such an unholy fuss.

And now, with all the preparations panning out, she was already beginning to feel just a mite stressed with the wedding date booked, the reception to be held, after a great deal of debate, at The Manor, a chic country house. Her mother was on full wedding alert by now, forever leaving messages on the answer-phone, muttering about music and catering and the wedding theme. She was also fretting over the invitations, because Simon's side of the church was going to be practically empty as things stood just now.

'He must have some family, somewhere,' she said to Emily. 'Can't you get him to rustle some people up? Otherwise, I shall have to put some of our people there or it will look very lopsided.'

Why did seeing the light of excitement in her mother's eyes make her feel anxious? Why did she wish the wheels were not turning quite so fiercely, at a downward run now, powerless to stop?

How absolutely mind-bogglingly stupid. Why on earth should she want to stop it? It was just pre-wedding nerves that was all, the sort of thing all brides suffered from. Her colleague Belinda had very nearly called the whole thing off a week before the wedding and look how happy she was now.

She was, foolishly perhaps, leaving the honeymoon arrange-ments to Simon who was giving nothing away, other than checking her passport was up to date. She had faint misgivings that he might perhaps try to combine it with work and she might find herself in some war-zone, wearing a flak jacket and helmet. He wasn't the sort to relax easily and she couldn't imagine him booking a long, lazy fortnight in a comfortable winter hotspot, which was what she really hoped he would do. What bliss to get completely away from it all for a while. Do nothing but enjoy each other and have time together. Something that wasn't so easy on a day-to-day basis. It would really be a chance to recharge and to take stock of their lives, the perfect start, in other words to a lifetime together.

That was the theory anyway.

'Did you tell this Mrs Cooper we were living together?' Simon asked, glancing at his watch and swinging his feet off the sofa.

'Well, no . . .' Emily smiled a little. 'She didn't ask. She may have put two and two together. In fact she probably assumed we were, most people do these days. It's not a problem, is it?'

'Not for us. I was thinking more of her. I thought she might disapprove.'

'Good heavens no, she's not like that at all. She doesn't seem remotely stuffy. She chatted about herself and her poor husband, whom she complains about all the time. And a bit about her son, too. I suppose that was to loosen me up a bit. She was very keen to know all about you.'

He frowned. 'I don't like the sound of that. What did you tell her?'

'That you were just fantastic in bed and I loved you to bits,' she said, laughing as he looked horrified. 'What on earth do you think I said? I told her all I know, which doesn't amount to much,' she added, the little dig causing him to raise his eyebrows but make no comment. 'When I told her you were a photographer, I think at first she thought you did weddings and so on.'

'Heaven forbid.'

'She thinks you ought to be homing in on what you're going to be wearing,' she went on, remembering Corinne's eyes boring into her. 'She's very keen on what she calls the whole picture. She's a bit put out by Yvonne and Stella being poles apart size-wise. She didn't actually say as much but she did ask me to describe them and her face was a dead giveaway. She thinks they will be a disaster and I'm beginning to agree with her.'

He laughed. 'Sorry but you should have thought of that before you asked them.'

'Yes, well . . .' she sighed. 'I never did ask Stella and now mother's denying asking her, too, and I never meant to ask Yvonne either. It just happened and it's too late now. They're both like excited little girls and I can't upset either of them. As for you, darling, Corinne worries that the poor bridegroom can feel very neglected. And it is his day as well so he ought to feel involved.

So I'm involving you,' she finished with a smile.

'Thanks, but no thanks. Tell Corinne I don't give a bee's fart about arrangements. I'm happy to leave it to you. It's a woman's thing, isn't it?'

'Yes, but I must have some input from you,' she said, irritated that he was content to pass the buck completely, although that way of course if anything went wrong it was bound to be all her fault. 'For instance, have you given any thought as to what you are going to wear?'

'No,' he said, looking astonished. 'There's plenty of time for that. Do you want me to dress up?'

'Of course.' She laughed at the daft question. 'It's our wedding day. Is there another option?'

'OK. If it bothers you so much, I shall dress up. Let me think . . .'

'Nothing too way out,' she said. 'And there's no need to pay a fortune, either. We can shop around for the best deal.'

'Oh come on, sod the expense. It's once in a lifetime. Stop penny-pinching for once, Emily. I hope you're not going to go all stuffy on me when you find out where we're going on honeymoon. It's costing a bomb, I tell you.'

'Is it?' She smiled. 'Are you going to give me a hint?'

'Not likely. You can inform this Corinne I will be wearing a pale grey Armani suit with a black T-shirt. It's my favourite get-up and I feel comfortable in it. The last thing I want is to be togged up like a dog's dinner in top hat and tails or whatever.'

'T-shirt?' she picked up on that. 'Honestly, Simon, I don't think so.'

'Why not? Surely you're not asking me to be conventional?'

He made light of it but she caught the look in his eye and hesitated a moment before quietly suggesting that it might be better to hire something more appropriate, something for the best man too.

'Or is he going to wear a T-shirt as well?' she finished, feeling her voice rise. 'What on earth will people think?

'For Christ's sake, you're marrying *me*, darling,' he said, his eyes icing over. 'Not some bloody male model. I told you I am definitely not hiring a wedding suit and ending up looking like a tailor's dummy. OK, to please you I'll swap the T-shirt for a proper shirt but no tie. You know me, I don't do ties. How's that?'

'We'll see,' she said, hoping he was just trying it on but, if so, it was mean because he knew how much this meant to her, to her mother too and it would ruin everything if he didn't play his part. T-shirt indeed! Her mother would end up with one of her famous migraines if she told her.

She dismissed it because it was early days yet and she would win him round. Following him into the bedroom, she perched on the edge of the bed as he quickly dressed in the casual clothes he liked to wear for a long flight. It would be odd tonight with him gone and she knew she would sleep badly, as she always did the first night he was away.

She would lie awake listening to the clock chiming all through the night and very likely fall into a deep sleep about five in the morning, so that she would feel like death first thing. At least, there would be no excuse for not springing out of bed immediately without Simon gently coaxing her to stay a while longer. Knowing he was to be away for a while, they had made love last night, but they had been both tired and irritable and it had been ultimately unsatisfactory, although she had pretended otherwise. It was not a good send-off and she had determined to make it up to him this morning but by the time she awoke, lazily stretching out for him, he was already up and dressed.

'Corinne was very impressed when I told her you'd had an exhibition of your photographs and that you had been approached to do a book,' she told him now, passing him his watch.

'Do you need to impress her?' he asked, lifting his bag off the bed, together with his precious cameras.

'No. But I like to boast about you,' she told him, feeling her bad mood evaporating as he smiled at her.

'I don't see why you have to have your dress made,' he went on, not for the first time seeming just a touch miffed about the idea. 'You're always saying you haven't time to spit, so why give yourself all this hassle of driving all that way over to her house for the fittings? Why can't she come over here?'

She shrugged. 'She doesn't operate like that. And it was no trouble,' she said. 'Quite interesting to see the house and everything.'

'Find it OK?'

She nodded. 'No problem.'

'Look, Emily, I've been thinking about this. This is stressing you out. Why don't you just buy a dress like everybody else and have done with it? If it's a question of the expense then just go for it. If you can't find anything here then take a trip to London or even Paris.'

'Or fly out to New York?' she said, her sarcasm lost on him.

'Yes, if you like. Why the hell not? Have a weekend there. Pay what's necessary. As I keep saying, it's once in a lifetime,' he added. 'Or at least until the divorce comes through in a couple of years time when we hate the sight of each other.'

'Don't joke about it,' she told him, appalled at that and the easy way he said it. Of course he didn't mean it but he shouldn't have said it. 'It's not the cost,' she went on. 'Not entirely. It's because I have such a problem with being so small and I shan't be able to get anything to fit me,' she told him. 'It would have to be altered and altered so I might as well have it made from scratch. Anyway, I can choose my own design this way. It will be absolutely gorgeous, you'll see.'

'OK,' he said, holding up his hands in mock surrender. 'I can see I'm beat on this one. You do as you like. You always do.'

'What do you mean by that?' she asked, feeling her hackles rise.

Thankfully, the buzzer sounded just at that moment.

43

'There's your taxi. Take care, darling,' she said, relaxing as she kissed him goodbye. 'Don't take any unnecessary risks, will you?'

'Of course not,' he said, hugging her close a moment before giving her what was supposed to be a reassuring smile. 'You know me. I've got a charmed life.'

And his luck might run out anytime.

She hated this. The going away. It was necessary, part of his job, the job he loved, but she was beginning to feel she would never, ever grow used to it. Hers was just pencil pushing of a sort but his was dangerous. He was spending some time in the Middle East just now, but he could be found anywhere in the world where there was trouble, in the thick of it, revelling in that, but the truth was people were being killed at every turn and the situation never seemed to get any better, just lurching from one crisis to another. She worried he might be kidnapped – foreign journalists seemed a sure-fire target for terrorist groups – and her worst fear was that he would simply disappear and she would spend the rest of her life wondering where he was.

Living and working in London had been great while it lasted but she had grown bored with the job and the commute via bus and tube had eventually caught up with her. It was wearing her to a frazzle and the thought of doing it long-term appalled her. When she discussed it with Simon, he was surprisingly supportive, agreeing that she should look for something elsewhere.

'Where? Have you any preferences where we live?'

His shrug said it all so she widened the net to include the south-west which she had visited a lot when she was a child and when she saw this job advertised, she liked the sound of it, liked the idea of working in an auction house, and she particularly liked Clive Grey, the minute she set eyes on him, so that was that. When it came to the crunch, when she was actually offered the job, Simon was not quite as enthusiastic as she would have wished but, as he insisted it was her decision and he would go along with it, whatever the choice, she took him up on that. They were re-located in weeks before she had time to have second thoughts. Clive had been more than helpful, fixing her up with viewings for several flats they might rent and they opted for the first one they saw, liking both its location and the high standard of its interior.

She had settled in well enough, missing London a little, missing her parents a lot more. A trip down to Kent before had meant a busy but not too long journey, but it was now a substantial one, a real effort, and her mother acted as if she had moved to the end of the earth.

It had been a momentous year and soon she would be married to Simon and living in her own house, if they had found one. Or would she? After months of looking, of being on every estate agent's books, of viewing house after unsatisfactory house, it was all becoming a bit of a nightmare. She dreamed about it sometimes, this magical house, and, in the dream, it was so perfect, a chic combination of old and new, but then something disturbing happened in the middle of the dream and she woke up with her heart pounding, never able to remember just what had happened.

It was just an anxiety dream and something she should simply toss aside before it started to become important and meaningful. Nevertheless, her anxiety had led her to question the way her life was heading and not just in the job stakes. It was such a momentous step, getting married, committing to Simon, and she had better snap out of this mood shortly or she would never survive until the wedding date. Three months to go and it felt suspiciously like they were dragging their feet towards it, shuffling ever onwards, to the day when they would stand side by side in St Mary's church and finally make the commitment they had been avoiding for such a long time. As of now, her feet felt leaden and she was fighting to shake off those little persistent doubts that seemed to be sticking to her like glue on cotton wool, certainly they were as difficult to shift.

She dared not tell Simon, who was such a pragmatic soul, but she had given details of her birth time and date to a colleague at work who did under-the-counter natal astrology charts. Angharad, who flitted round the various auction houses in the group, had managed to con everyone she knew into having them done which had caused some confusion as people tried – sometimes in vain – to pinpoint not only the date of their birth but the exact time, that particular information being crucial. It was amazing how many mums seemed not to know that to the nearest hour, not having the foresight to check their watches as they gave birth. Somewhat surprisingly, her own mother had instantly supplied the information, which had pleased Angharad because she said it made it so much easier to come up with an accurate picture.

At the moment, Emily was awaiting her personal chart and feeling just a touch nervous for it appeared that Angharad, regrettably honest as the day is long, was sparing no punches, reducing a couple of the girls to tears with her predictions. Angharad had been unrepentant. If you can't face up to the truth then forget it, was her philosophy.

All utter garbage but nonetheless some of the girls had been amazed at how disturbingly accurate she had been, talking about the personality traits they sometimes tried to hide. Emily knew better than to believe any of it and couldn't think now why she had ever agreed to it, other than not wanting to be thought snooty by the others who had initially regarded it as a bit of a laugh.

She prided herself on being able to walk under ladders without thinking twice, do something without crossing her fingers and touching wood and so on. She was not superstitious and she never bothered to read her stars which were complete mumbo jumbo. She liked to deal in facts but had not known how to let Angharad down by casting any doubts on the unscientific procedure. In any case, although she was reluctant to admit it, Angharad was a little strange and it didn't do to mess around with people like that. She might cast a spell on her for heaven's sake.

She had already told Angharad, laughingly, that if it was bad news, she really didn't want to know.

So far, no news.

CHAPTER FOUR

'Emily . . . it doesn't matter what time I try, you're never, ever there. Mum here. Are you getting any nearer with your dress? Far be it from me to offer advice because I made an utterly atrocious decision with my own but I really do feel you would be better keeping it simple. Stunning lines, that sort of thing. I need to know because of the flowers, darling. I think we should go for a fabulous bouquet. Apparently hand-tied bunches are very in at the moment, so Victorian, and would be perfect the florist says for a winter wedding. And we must get away from pink and white carnations for the rest of us. So passé. Roses would be lovely. What do you think? I'll try again later.

'Bye.'

When he was at home, Daniel Cooper slept in his old bedroom, the one he had shared with Joe and it smelled just the same, a faint mustiness from a damp problem that they had never got round to fixing.

Sometimes if he woke during the night, smelling the darkness, momentarily unsure where he was, he imagined Joe to be there, above him as he always was in the bunk bed. Once, quite recently, he had even lifted his arm to touch the upper bunk before he came to and realized it was not there. And nor was Joe.

He and Joe had leaned out of this very window, far far out of it, seeing just who could lean out the farthest in fact before they fell out. They had knotted sheets together once, tied one to the bedpost and thrown the cotton ladder through the window. They had held for Joe but not for him but it was a soft landing into the flower bed below and he damaged nothing more than his ego. Without the sheets, he remembered in turn hanging onto Joe's arms and then his wrists. It was, of course, harder for Joe to hold onto him because he was older and bigger but Joe was wiry and deceptively strong and had never let him drop.

As kids, they had also climbed up to their room from outside, using the solidly clinging ivy as a grip and finding all sorts of interesting foot-holds on the way. Maybe that had started him off on the climbing. Who knows? Joe, younger, slighter, had been the ringleader in many of their childhood games but, because he was older and supposedly wiser, he always got the blame when things went wrong. It had been the two of them against the world. Even with all the rooms in this house, they chose to share, chatting into the night, sharing their hopes and dreams and, as they got older, talking about sex and girls. Joe had been pretty intense about girls, popular with them, good-looking and yet with a vulnerable edge that appealed to their maternal instincts. Whatever it was, he had it, that elusive *it*.

Their brother Stephen, who definitely did not have it, had never been part of their games; only a year older than Daniel but much more than that in practice, a bookworm and to them a bore, not on their wavelength at all. He and Stephen had never been close and, even after Joe's death, they did not grow any closer and now with Stephen firmly and happily entrenched in Australia he supposed they never would. There was an invitation to visit of course, any time he was in the neighbourhood, as if he might just casually drop into Australia but he hesitated, remembering Stephen's accusing eyes at Joe's funeral, eyes that echoed those of his mother. Nothing was said but a mountain was left unsaid.

Joe's stuff was still up in the loft, stuff that should have been thrown out long since. Growing up here had been great and, even though there had been a considerable water feature once, nearer a mini-lake than a pond, their mother had never been unduly concerned about the dangers of water games and allowed them to do pretty much as they liked. Her laid-back approach had been the envy of their friends and sometimes during the long summer holidays they would disappear for the entire day and she wouldn't know where they were until they turned up, usually in time for tea. It meant a raised eyebrow and a casual inquiry as to what they had been up to, but nothing more than that. He was grateful for that, for that freedom that today's youngsters seemed to lack.

During one summer holiday, they built a raft, the two of them, and rowed out into the middle of the lake where it was easily deep enough to drown, before they were spotted and yelled at. Sure enough, the precarious craft capsized on cue but they were both strong swimmers and, even though hampered by clothes and the giggles, they had no problem getting back to shore. Those had been good days, days when he hadn't noticed that he came third in his mother's list of favourite sons. Joe, the only one of them with creative leanings, was first, of course; Joe who looked so much like mother, Joe who had so pleased her by being accepted onto the textile design course to follow in her footsteps. Without doubt, he was the favourite son and then came Stephen who was so terrifyingly bright you needed sunglasses to look at him.

He was piggy in the middle and going nowhere.

His was a large room at the back of the house, looking out over the orchard, and, although when he first came back home he had thought it a bad idea to have this particular room, he had soon realized that it was important he did have it because how otherwise could he lay this particular ghost? He had got rid of the faded carpet and sanded and varnished the floorboards himself.

50

Instead of the childhood bunks there was a big bed in the corner, and he would have liked to put his stamp on the room, do something different, maybe have a tented ceiling effect to remind him of sleeping out in the open, but his mum had put paid to that idea, saying there was no way she was asking Mrs Henderson to dust a tented ceiling as the poor woman had vertigo if she looked up too long. When you have your own place, she told him with that familiar rebuke in her eyes, you can have as many tented ceilings as you like.

OK. He wasn't going to get in a twist about it. It was just an idea and, when he thought seriously about it, a crappy one at that. You could not create the outdoors indoors. Not possible. He'd once had a girlfriend who was into interior design and he supposed some of her fairly madcap ideas had rubbed off.

He'd messed around without a nest to call his own for too long for it to matter much where he lived, and how he lived come to that. It was the same with all his climbing friends, somehow they found it difficult to settle. Living rough as you did on a trek made it hard to adjust to the soft life of comfortable sofas and hot baths whenever you felt like it and yet, conversely, when you were on a trek, up a mountain, you dreamed of such things. Dreamed also of candlelit restaurants with a lovely woman sitting opposite smiling at you. Dreamed of making love to her in a big bed with clean sheets.

He had been in love once, not the interior designer, but it fell apart because Amanda wanted to change him, wanted to make him the man *she* wanted him to be, so that was that. Maybe he was better as he was, footloose and so on, although even as he considered that, he knew it to be a nonsense. He was more conventional than he might appear. He wanted a woman, a wife in fact and he wanted kids too. He knew that would please his mother because, with Stephen and Co so very far away, she felt she had missed out on her grandchildren.

Daniel was in his room sitting at the old desk in the corner going through his accounts. His money came from various sources, drips here and there, and surprisingly made a manageable whole. He paid no rent whilst he was here because his mother refused, absolutely refused, to take any money from him and he drove an old estate car, much too pragmatic a soul to be remotely concerned about his image or serious lack of it. He knew what Stephen and that stuck-up wife of his thought about him and no, he didn't like being thought a sponger but it really wasn't like that. He just had his own way of doing things and at the moment he was contemplating putting some of his savings – serious money that his paternal grandmother had slipped him before she died – into becoming a full partner in the adventure centre one of his climbing friends had set up a few years ago. Harvey had had a near do on a mountain and had lost his nerve, or maybe Harvey was just sensible enough to realize that, with a couple of accidents under his belt, including watching as two of his best mates perished in an avalanche, the odds were shortening. Harvey was keen for him to commit more to the business and, so long as he was still free to say yes if he was offered a climb and go off for up to six months at a stretch, it was a good idea to have something behind him.

The business had started off as a kids' holiday adventure scheme but they had branched out now to other areas. They still did kids' weeks in the summer, based on the Camp America idea, but parents were increasingly nervous these days and the compensation culture a serious threat, so their main income now was derived from doing recreational courses for jaded professionals, team-building for want of a better word, and although the majority of the said professionals hated and feared it, the employers were dead keen.

Bingo scratched woefully at the door and Daniel let him go on a few minutes before getting up to let the old dog in. He dreaded the day they would inevitably lose him, not just because he was so affectionate but because he was a link still with Joe. Joe had known him as a puppy and he knew that losing Bingo would bring it all back to his mother.

'Sorry, old lad,' he said, apologising for thinking the thought as the dog bounded in, a bit grey now round the muzzle, eyes a little glazed, going to sit on one of the big cushions on the floor, pawing it in circles a minute before subsiding in a tired heap.

Asleep and snoring in seconds.

Life was so basic for dogs. A good run, a full tummy and somewhere to sleep, that's all they needed.

It was like that on the mountains, Daniel thought, where you had to adjust quickly and set yourself new goals, the main one being to survive. Survival was what it was all about and he'd come pretty close – closer than he dared admit – to not surviving. Misjudgements mattered. Misjudgements, mistakes, could mean death. He'd lost a few mates over the years and that never got easier. After Joe died, he'd gone off in a daze and, entirely out of character, taken chances galore on the climb as if he was challenging somebody up there to despatch him, too. He'd been brought up sharp when the expedition leader took him aside and warned him to toe the bloody line before he caused a major incident.

He put his papers away, checking his diary for next month when there were a couple of speaking engagements, one hundred pounds each plus expenses, chicken feed but that was how he worked. He had been told he was a good speaker, generally talking to a mixed audience and managing to win over the uninterested ones by the end of it. He supposed it must be his enthusiasm that carried the day as he always felt sick to the stomach just before he went on 'stage'. He regarded it as a necessary evil, enjoying it once he got going. He had also checked today how much he had in savings, the current share price relating to the shares that nobody else knew about, and the cash in his various accounts.

Not bad. Not bad at all.

'Is Bingo in there with you?' his mum's voice came from the landing. 'I thought I'd take him for a walk.'

She tapped on the door before coming in, standing just inside the room trying to rustle up an unenthusiastic dog. Daniel looked at her, his redhaired and voluptuous mum, and wished she was not quite so honest. It wouldn't hurt her to pretend she at the least liked him. All his life, it seemed to him, she had blamed him for everything. Especially Joe's death. He knew she thought he had lied at the inquest.

He wanted her to accept his story, hug him and tell him that it *hadn't* been his fault. He also wanted her to be proud of him, of what he did, and not puff up so much like a contented peahen when Stephen was mentioned. It was just as well he was in Australia, because the constant comparing she did was beyond a joke. He did not need to be reminded that Stephen had acquitted himself well, was a partner now in an advertising firm, had married a beautiful if slightly weird doctor and had two perfect kids, boy and girl two years apart. He lived in a well-heeled suburb of Sydney with no intention of returning permanently to the UK and all was fine and very dandy.

'Do you remember Miss Bellew the other day? She was called Emily. Very nice young woman. What did you think of her?'

'OK.'

'I thought she was pretty. In a quiet sort of way.'

'A knock out, I thought. But she has a fiancé, hasn't she?' Daniel said, smiling, for he could see through her completely. This was the cue for a chat about any other young women there might be in his life. Well, she could whistle for that. He wasn't going to discuss anything like that with her, preferring to present her one of these days with a *fait accompli*. Preferably already quietly married so that she wouldn't get in a tangle about the frock.

His mother shook her head thoughtfully.

'If you ask me, that wedding's never going to come off. I shall still make the dress of course but it will never be worn. How very sad.'

'Ever the pessimist . . .' he laughed.

'Mark my words. I'm rarely wrong, Daniel.'

CHAPTER FIVE

'Emily . . . Mum here. Emergency, darling, I've had to ditch the photographer after all that trouble getting him in the first place. I'm afraid I stormed out of his studio – I really can't go into details – so I absolutely can't go back there. No way will I grovel. Can Simon not help? Surely he knows somebody who can do decent wedding photographs? I've tried two others and they're both booked already. Isn't it ridiculous? Anyway, don't you worry. I'll sort it out and call you later. If it comes to the crunch, we can always call on your Uncle Alan who would be better than nothing so long as we keep him away from the booze. Speak to you soon.

'Bye.'

Once a month, her branch of Greys held a general sale, lots from house clearances mainly, bits and bobs of household paraphernalia that had often been somebody's treasures but were now reduced to sitting on a cataloguing table. One of the assistants checked through the items and anything interesting was of course passed on to Clive for a further look. One or two impressive pieces had come their way via a house clearance. Most of the stuff though was harmless miscellany, often producing a surprisingly large amount of money for the next of kin.

Emily was busy helping to sort the list out, spending the morn-

ing in the saleroom with one of Clive's assistants, who was sift-
ing through some newly arrived boxes of stuff, pouncing on a
particular item with a yell of delight from time to time, but she
was finding it difficult to focus, her mind on the astrology chart
that was sitting back in the office.

'According to Angharad,' Michael grinned at her as he carefully unwrapped ornaments, 'I'm coming into money. Very soon
she thinks. At least I think she's saying that, the whole bloody
thing is so oddly put together that it's difficult to decipher. You've
got to have all your wits about you to work it out. But, reading
between the lines . . .'

'Dangerous,' Emily said, casting an amused glance his way.

'I like to live dangerously,' he said with a shrug. 'Now the
point is, knowing this, should I book that fortnight skiing in
Colorado for the family, the one I can't afford, or should I hang
fire for a while?'

Emily smiled. It was well known that Michael's financial
commitments were fraught, with him effectively running two
families, older children coming up to college and two younger
ones with his current partner.

'It depends on whether or not you believe her, Michael.'

'Ah, there's the rub.' He lifted out a figurine, took a moment to
give it the once over before setting it aside with disdain. 'She told
Henrietta she had better prepare herself for a problem and the
poor child ended up in hospital after that accident. What do you
make of that?'

'Coincidence?' Emily ventured, wishing he hadn't reminded
her of that.

'Sod it. I shall book it at lunch-time,' he said, having apparently convinced himself. 'And then if it doesn't happen, I'll sue
Angharad for the lost deposit. Although, when you get your chart,
you'll see she puts a disclaimer in. If you get your time of birth
wrong then you might as well be out by a thousand years. Clever,
eh?'

She left Michael heading for the travel agents at lunch-time, and before she set off herself to get a sandwich, she finally opened the envelope and peeped in, making sure it was the chart she had been expecting, even though it was addressed to her in Angharad's distinctive arty writing. She sighed as she slipped it into her bag to read at leisure tonight. She was alone and bored with solitary television watching and it would give her something to do. Why she had ever asked Angharad to do her chart signalled a momentary blip in commonsense. She supposed it was because peering into the future, just a little bit, even through your fingers, was too much to pass up and Angharad was a qualified astrologer with certificates to prove it.

The interesting thing was that some people, like Michael, were very talkative when they received their charts, letting others pore over them, giggling at certain things, oohing and aahing at the accuracy of some aspects of it. It was uncanny some of the things Angharad unearthed about their backgrounds when they swore blind they had never, ever mentioned it. It was also hard to come up with a satisfactory explanation and even the most sceptical people seemed to come round grudgingly to the fact that there was something in it. Other people, however, took their charts home and never spoke of them again, and it was quite obvious that Angharad had put the skids under them, possibly scared them out of their wits.

Emily wondered which category she would fall into. Indeed, she wondered if she should shred it now whilst she had the chance. She could simply stuff it into the shredder with a load of sensitive papers and Angharad would never know. Even as she thought it, she knew she would not because quite simply her curiosity had got the better of her. If it was good then it would give her a bit of confidence which she was sorely lacking just now but if it was bad, she would ignore it.

Either way, she was not going to let Angharad get to her.

The lady herself turned up later in the morning, drifting in as was her wont. Emily was never quite sure what she actually did but, whatever it was, it was apparently essential liaison work between the different branches of Greys.

Catching Emily's eye, she came over to ask if she had received her chart.

'Thank you. I'll look at it this evening,' Emily told her, dying to ask what was in it, just a quick precis would do, but she kept her curiosity under wraps, not wanting to show any concern.

'I've put a note in the margin,' Angharad told her. 'I can go into it further if you wish but it will mean a private session and a great deal more work. I can let you have one for half price as you're a friend. Only fifteen pounds.' She caught Emily's aghast look and, with a hurt look, hurriedly explained that, if she ordered a natal chart from anywhere else she would have to find at least a hundred pounds, so Angharad really was offering a bargain.

Well, honestly.

Barely keeping her temper, wondering just how much in total Angharad had raked in, she thanked her politely, telling her that it was most unlikely she would need that.

Angharad smiled, fingering the jewelled cross that lay across her chest. She favoured low-cut tops with dainty little cardigans to show off her ample bosom. 'The chart I've prepared for you is just the tip of the iceberg, as it were,' she said. 'But don't hesitate to ask me if you feel the need for any deeper delving.'

Emily watched as she walked off, wearing an ankle-length black skirt over black boots and a favourite red cardigan, a matching ribbon caught round her dark plait. Giving her a final despairing glance, Emily tried to concentrate on what she was doing, which was having a quick check at what was happening within the company and whether there was anything about which Clive should be informed. As a trusted auction house they had a reputation to live up to and were therefore scrupulously honest. Clive was liked by his clients, a good auctioneer with his own informal friendly style, a bit jaunty, fond of quips, and if anybody could get the bidders going, he could.

As an employee of Greys, it meant that she could not bid for anything and that ban extended to Simon too, which had annoyed him in the past when he had seen a couple of fine prints he wanted to bid for. However, it had resulted in their fine-art specialist Geraldine having a chat with him and, in the end, she had visited a few galleries with him, offering advice and pointing him in the right direction.

That had annoyed Emily in turn because, investment or not, she did not see how they could afford to pay five hundred pounds for a limited-edition print by some American artist she had never heard of. Simon had accused her of being a philistine where art was concerned and, trying in vain to like the said print, she had not bothered to deny it.

Ah well. On the wedding front, she had another meeting with her dressmaker next week, the woman operating on an extremely loosely based schedule. Emily wanted the dress ready as soon as possible, one thing, one major worry, one important decision out of the way and she was not concerned about losing or gaining weight, for she never did either. And she had no intention of becoming pregnant as had some of her friends in the run-up to their weddings.

Staring at the computer screen, where she had switched to preparing next month's general catalogue for the printers, she took a few minutes to daydream about the wedding. With that wonderful thing hindsight, December was maybe not the best choice weather-wise. It would probably be grey and gritty with the rain veering from light drizzle to torrential but she allowed herself to dream of soft silky snowflakes gently floating down as they posed for photographs in the quaint porch of the little coun-try church near Canterbury where they were to marry. She might need thermal underwear, but a Christmas card idyllic-Victorian snowy theme might be an idea with a velvet wrap over her dress and the bridesmaids in dark blue which might slim Yvonne down a touch and bulk up Stella at the same time.

Corinne was right of course, it would all be a lot simpler if she could just restrict it to little ones but, with Yvonne already coming up with madly impractical ideas and Stella with something to look forward to at last, how on earth could she disappoint them? Again, she worried about Simon and what he would wear. She had briefly brought up the subject again but he was being annoyingly pedantic about this tie business and wisely she was leaving it for the moment. She would win him round. It was just a matter of catching him at the right moment.

There were so many things to think about and it was going to be very expensive for her parents, who were insisting on footing the bill. Simon had lost touch with his mum years ago and he refused point-blank to discuss it, the reasons why it had happened and the reasons why he was not going to try for a reconciliation, nor indeed inform his mother of his intended marriage. She had an idea he knew where she was but trying to drag information out of him was like pulling teeth and always ended with him telling her to leave it alone. She knew that it was a single-parent set-up and he never talked about his father and she thought it wise not to question him. Time enough for that, but it was on the agenda and she would find out before too long. Again, it was just a matter of picking the right moment.

'I've snipped the apron strings, darling,' he told her. 'That's that. Believe me, it's the best thing to do.'

She did not want to snip her apron strings, only extend them. As an only child, she was close to her own parents, even though geographically she was now many miles away, which made his attitude to his mother doubly difficult to understand. Not understanding amounted to not knowing him, the real him, and she was concerned at the gaps, felt she ought to know every little thing about him so that she knew precisely what made him tick. He knew everything there was to know about her, about her family, her friends, her life at school and the stuff she did at work. He knew as much as she did about Yvonne and Stella, about her colleagues and friends Belinda and Geraldine, and her boss Clive. There was only Angharad she kept quiet about because she didn't want him to know about her. To be honest, she was a bit ashamed at how gullible she had been where Angharad was concerned and half-amused at the superstition attached to it.

When it came to her and Simon, the fact was she was the chatterer, he the listener. She wanted him to feel he could talk about things with her, any old thing, things from the past that worried him, things she might be able to help him with, things she would try to understand. But, he would not talk about it even with gentle pressing; it was as if he had suddenly emerged fully grown with no childhood, no background. There were no reminders of his young life, no photographs, no letters, nothing and she determined to find out, but was approaching it with caution so as not to receive one of his icy stares. It felt suspiciously as if he were excluding her from his past and she found it hard not to feel miffed at that. It was almost as if he didn't trust her and that was unforgivable. They needed to be able to talk to each other about anything and that included finance of course, which she would have to bring up sooner or later.

'Have you heard there's been another bomb explosion at a bus stop? Tel Aviv,' one of her colleagues said, putting some papers on her desk. 'Carnage again. Ten killed including a foreign journalist,' she added coolly.

A journalist or maybe a *photographer*? God. Oh, God. Staring up at the woman, Emily felt her body temperature plummet, was suddenly aware of her rapid heartbeat. Instantly, a vision of her Simon flooded her head. Body broken, the life gone out of him, dying all alone, without her. She always had a mental bag packed when he was off on an assignment, ready to drop everything and fly out to be with him.

Over a relieved cup of coffee later, when it was established the casualty was not Simon but some other poor soul, she glanced crossly at the woman who had delivered the news. She knew that she was a mite envious, for she had not been slow to spot a few looks his way when he had, on the odd occasion, picked her up, dispensing his boyish smile in every direction, oozing a lazy and undeniably sexy charm. Oh yes, and his job did have a certain glamorous ring to it, even though that was the very last thing it was. It seemed a heroic thing to do, a touch headstrong and devil-may-care, and that was probably the reason for the envy.

That, and the antique diamond ring he had given her when she had finally accepted his proposal. Quite – no, *very* – extravagant. Lovely though it was, and it certainly attracted a lot of interest from the visiting jewellery expert, it jarred that her reaction, after the initial delight, was marred by the thought that they really could not afford it, his credit cards already stretched close to the limit. Penny-pinching about her own engagement ring! As one of her friends told her when she was gently protesting, 'For goodness sake get a life, Emily.'

That terse remark shut her up and she complained no more. Of course she was pleased. It was just . . . oh, what on earth was the matter with her these days? It was as if getting engaged and planning the wedding had brought all the doubts bubbling to the surface, doubts she might have kept suppressed in a previous life.

She and Simon were renting this spacious unfurnished apartment in a prime area of town and it had happily provided a bare canvas for their, or rather *his* collection of fine antique furniture – one of his little foibles – and her more mundane modern classics, a combination of new and old that worked brilliantly, or so she thought. Simon was always on the look-out for other things and always pored through the catalogues when they were doing a collectibles and furniture auction, making himself cross because of the no-bidding rule.

Emily sighed, staring out of the window where sheer cream drapes were tied back either side of a roman blind, the view of the ever-changing harbour calming. She was glad of the air conditioning this evening because they were experiencing an Indian summer. It had been a hot day, the air thick, headache-inducing but, although she had taken the packet of aspirin out of the bathroom cabinet when she got home, she had decided to leave it awhile and see if it wore off on its own.

She had spoken to her mother last night and was increasingly concerned that this was all getting too much for her. She knew mums got a little harassed with wedding arrangements, but her mum seemed to be excessively so and Emily wondered if a quick civil ceremony, arrangements concluded in the wink of an eye, might not have been kinder to her. Her dad said no, she was absolutely in her element for it was what she had been working towards for years. Nothing must go wrong and, if it was up to her mother, nothing would.

She was on about flowers now. And the bridesmaids' dresses. It would mean a trip sooner or later over to Kent to fix them up with something that she herself actually liked. Talking to Simon was out of the question, for it was as if he had wiped his hands of all the planning. She was well aware it was all very much a female thing, this anticipation, but for goodness sake he might help a bit. His nonchalance verged on apathy and that bothered her because it was his wedding, too.

Oh heavens, the possible catastrophic combinations of things that could send it all crashing in a heap were mind-boggling.

Having deliberately delayed looking at the astrology chart, wondering in fact if she should bother at all, Emily ate her meal at last sitting at the breakfast bar in the narrow kitchen. She liked this apartment, top-notch and pricey, but it was very much a stopgap and she looked forward to having her own home, a whole house. Ideally, a big old house in the country, a toned-down version of Corinne Cooper's gorgeous home. Not to fill with children necessarily, the jury was out on that one, and she was not going to be rushed. No, she simply wanted to have lots of space so that they could escape each other.

Thinking about escaping each other when they were not yet even married seemed disturbing, and at last there was nothing else for it but to look at the chart.

CHAPTER SIX

'Emily . . . this is your mother leaving a message. How about a heart-shaped theme? Doesn't that sound romantic? I got the idea from looking at invitation cards with little golden hearts on them. We can carry it through to the cake and everything and you could give the bridesmaids' silver lockets. What do you think? Your father is being a perfect pain – I can't seem to drum up any enthusiasm in him whatsoever but don't worry, he'll be fine on the day. I'll see to that. Speak to you soon, darling.

'Bye.'

Bernard Cooper lived and breathed the retail world, the financial branch of it anyway.

People, the general public that is, the bane of his life, simply had no idea what went on. They just sailed into a store, usually turning right and expecting to home in on whatever it was they were on the look-out for. It was part of the job, of course, to make sure they were waylaid at every turn with tempting displays. They prided themselves at Pacmans on the personal touch with great attention to detail from the salespeople upward. They aimed for just the right combination of not too pushy but not too laid-back either. That concept was difficult to get just right and he always advised his salespeople to stand back a moment and try to gauge how a particular customer might wish to be approached.

Bernard had worked his way up, starting as a graduate trainee on the shop floor, so that nobody could get away with fobbing him off. As far as sales techniques went, he had been there, done that. If a customer bought a suit then he ought to go away with a shirt and tie as well. The first flash of the credit card was the hardest bit and after that customers were often on a buying roll.

Quickly showing an aptitude for figures, Bernard had found his true vocation in the finance department. Ten years ago, having served his apprenticeship here in the south west, he had been widely tipped to get the top job based in London but that bloody man Malley had stepped in from nowhere and swept him aside.

The humiliation, the sympathetic glances, had been tough to take. Corinne, already planning a move to London, had been thoroughly gutted and had never quite forgiven him, even though it was hardly his fault that Dickie Malley's new-broom philosophy had done the trick at the interview. Playing safe as he had done was a no-go and, if he got the chance again, he was going to be as aggressive as the next man.

Although he was desk-bound for most of the time, he still liked to get into the stores, out amongst the troops as it were, even though he knew it irritated the hell out of the shop managers, smacking as it did of interference. So what? He needed to keep a close eye on things. They weren't out of the woods yet, still suffering from the downturn in sales due to a large-scale cock-up in strategy. The powers that be, a few misguided board members led by the infamous Malley, were trying to woo a younger clientele. Bernard had never been convinced of the wisdom of it for, in his judgement, they must take care not to offend their solid client base. Look at M&S, for God's sake.

There was a bit of a crisis in store today with one of the lifts playing up. Thank heavens it was only a member of the sales staff and not a customer who was stuck between floors. Unfortunately, Dorothy was claustrophobic and close to panicking, but in that case why the hell was she using the lift in the first place? There was only one set of stairs, it wasn't as if they occupied a skyscraper. Not a leg to stand on if she got in a huff about it. He had somebody sitting by the lift shaft uttering soothing words as the engineers worked on it and so far word had it that she was holding it together – just.

Most of the staff liked him well enough, although privately a lot of them wondered how he got away with it because, for a man who worked for a top-notch menswear chain, he couldn't get his own act together. What Bernard could do with an expensive suit was nobody's business. As for the shirts . . . he seemed to have an endless supply of plain-coloured shirts, not exactly crisply laundered and certainly no advertisement for the shirt department, and he always wore his old school tie, a minor public school in the Midlands of which he was inordinately proud and fond. The ties were narrow and striped, maroon and dirty gold, cleverly managing to clash with every single shirt. Why the chief executive Malley didn't pull him up about his appearance was a mystery, but then Dickie Malley went his own sweet way, due for retirement soon and letting a helluva lot slide. Anyway, he seemed pinned to his London office and only deigned to appear in this area about once or twice a month when, with his entourage, he made a regal progress through the stores.

New salespeople were surprised to find Mr Cooper was married, having assumed from the unironed shirts and general air of neglect that he was a crusty old bachelor of the old school. They were even more surprised when they met Corinne at the little dos that were arranged from time to time, for she outshone him all ends up. Imagine Bernard being married to such a flamboyant redhead. *His* hair, long at the collar, was wispy grey and unruly, whitening further each year, the result Bernard said of the disturbing sales figures of late. It was all very well him trying to juggle all the financial balls but they were landing in everybody's court. It was pulling socks up time, cashmere or otherwise, time to ditch this damned fool idea of becoming trendy, but try telling that to Malley who seemed to have lost all his retail marbles of late.

Bernard supposed, with some regret, that, like Malley, he wouldn't be greatly missed when he retired. He would miss, in a bizarre way, the getting up early business, the drag of the commute, the workaday atmosphere, the buzz, the excitement, the ups and downs of it all and then, at the end of the day, the slog back home through the traffic when the high of his day gradually collapsed as he neared home. He loved the house, but it was time for a move. The upkeep of the sodding garden was becoming horrific and he was loath to pay somebody to do it for him, for that would be admitting defeat.

At work, some new fellow would take over from him, young and keen, very likely somebody with a barrelful of bright ideas, somebody who would cope with all the damned paperwork that drove him crazy. Sometimes he longed just to get back on the floor and sell.

He supposed, coming from a shop-owning family, albeit of a small variety, that he was destined to go into retailing, going to college first though to study history, something his family found faintly amusing because it was no help at all in his career. He never regretted those years though, and his own fierce love of history remained as brightly lit now as it had ever been, perhaps even stronger. His love for his wife, on the other hand, had certainly mellowed of late and, if the flame, the passion, was still there, it was sadly diminished, a mere flicker.

He knew Corinne thought he was winding down at work, marking time now, but not a bit of it. Recently, with retirement in a few years or so looming, he had found a new lease of life, a new purpose, a bit of urgency was creeping in. He had never worked so hard on new promotions and management strategies. Privately, he was writing a book, a new slant – he hoped – on the Civil War, a period of great interest to him. He was keeping it quiet because telling Corinne would put the kiss of death on it. She would be thinking bestseller when the most he could hope for was that some publisher would like the end result and, if they didn't, he would bloody well publish it himself. He was working on it whenever he got time, shutting himself away in his study at home.

Malley, five or so years his senior, was retiring at the end of the year and he fully intended to step into his shoes. Second time lucky. He had been a solid second-in-command for a long time and it was his due. He was owed it. There was a long tradition of the chief executive coming from finance. He would make it this time round if it killed him and frankly, he couldn't cope with another let-down if they passed him by again.

He was cautiously proud of what he regarded as his success here, the way he had solidly climbed up the financial ladder to his present position, but increasingly worried about his personal life. Right from the start, he'd wondered what the hell Corinne saw in him, wondered why she'd picked him when she could have had one of the more handsome students. She'd been a stunner in the early days, the sort of girl who caused a silence when she entered a room, particularly a room full of young men whose testosterone levels were at full strength. Something a colleague had said recently had reminded him that Corinne was an attractive woman still and probably ripe for an affair while she had the chance. Not that there was a lot of scope round here for an affair and it wasn't as if she went out to work so chance would be a fine thing and that was some consolation for he knew he couldn't bear it if she ever left him.

They were drifting aimlessly, bickering too often, and he didn't know where they were heading. When he was passed over all those years ago, he had needed her support, needed her to tell him that it wasn't his fault, needed her to come up with some reason why. Instead, she had blamed him for giving a poor interview and he supposed, in his turn, he had never quite forgiven her for that.

It wasn't perfect, then, but the thought that she might suddenly announce she wanted to leave him appalled him, for how on earth would he survive without her? She had proved she wasn't exactly the sort of wife who supported him through thick and thin and she did precious little for him in terms of looking after him, but he didn't want that sort of creepily contented wife. He wanted her with all her faults.

The truth was their marriage needed a shot in the arm. He needed to drag Corinne away from those frocks of hers, that infernal stitching, and take her off somewhere, get back to where they used to be in their marriage when every day had been something to look forward to. He had once been impulsive and he recalled the excitement when they first saw this house, deciding within the hour, within the first few minutes, to buy it. Corinne had told him to calm down, think it through, but he had swept her misgivings aside and he knew that, secretly, she loved that.

An expensive whim and one she, if not he, had lived to regret. He knew she wanted to move to town and by town she didn't mean Plymouth but London of all places. Why there he had no idea. London was no place to retire. People retired here, didn't they? They would be doing it backwards, if they did go and they would if he got the promotion. They could get a fortune for the house, enough to buy a little *pied-à-terre* with no garden to look after and no Mrs Henderson trailing round like a lost soul with her duster. And yes, on the plus side, it might be rather fun to be near to the good museums and art galleries and it would be heaven for Corinne. She didn't have friends here but that was hardly his fault. On their arrival here all those years ago, she had started how she meant to go on, having no truck with village life, so that she was regarded as snooty. She said she couldn't give a fig what they thought of her, but he knew differently. She did mind but it was too late now to change.

He would keep quiet about the promotion. He would also make some inquiries about selling this place, buying an apartment in

London and spring the whole bloody lot on her when the deed was done.

It came to him that he had neglected his wife lately, neglected her for years in fact, but that couldn't be helped when he had been so caught up with his work and she with the children and her sewing.

Being the wife of the chief executive with a house in London to boot would be just the ticket to boost their sagging relationship. He might have to call upon Marian to help him keep it quiet, which was a bugger because he didn't care to involve Marian in his private life. For reasons known only to herself, his secretary admired him, for want of a better word, lusted after him maybe, and, whilst he was flattered of course, her attention to his every need with eyes as loopily devoted as Bingo, made for an uncomfortable situation. He knew it was regarded with some amusement by the rest of the staff and he had to be careful not to do or say anything to inflame her pent-up passion, and had to avoid serious eye contact at all costs. In a tipsy state after three or so gin-and-tonics, she had once collared him in a corner at the Christmas do, mistletoe in hand, and it had been a bloody close call that he had got away with the quickest of pecks on the cheek. She did nothing at all for him, never had, never would, and it was time she resigned herself to it. He felt sorry, of course, but it was no great secret for Corinne knew all about it, treated it like the joke it was, which somehow made it all the more sad.

The day at the store, the one in Truro, ended with Dorothy rescued, pale-faced, from the lift, having been trapped for two long hours. Somebody had the gumption to go out for a bunch of flowers which was pushed under her nose directly she was out. He had personally put his arm round her shaking shoulders and given her a comforting squeeze before passing her over to the store manager, who was anxious to do his bit. He didn't think, after all that, there would be any come-back, any whisper of compensation for personal suffering or what have you, although

some bright spark had muttered things about her needing counselling. In the event, the flowers, a cup of tea and a custard tart in
the staff-room smoothed things over and she was sent home
early.

It was a relief to get into the car and drive home. Parking round
the back of the house, Bernard picked up his piles of paperwork
and some research papers for his book, and whistled in, stopping
to pat the old dog who came out to meet and greet him and escort
him indoors. He noticed the lawn needed cutting – again, damn it
to hell – and wondered if Daniel would oblige, as he had last
week. Might as well make use of him whilst he was here. The last
time he'd gone off to Chile to run climbing holidays in the Andes
they hadn't heard from him for six months. Not that that had
worried Corinne, although he had started to fret himself, hoping
that all was well. Bad at communicating, Daniel, but then you
couldn't take a mobile phone up a mountain and post offices were
few and far between.

'Where's your mum?' he asked, coming through to the kitchen
where Daniel was cooking.

'Out.' Daniel looked round. 'Don't know where. She should
have a mobile, then you could keep in touch.'

'She doesn't want one. Says it's good to be out of communi-
cation sometimes. Like you are as often as not,' he added
pointedly, hanging his suit jacket up, loosening his tie and rolling
up the sleeves of his shirt, before pouring himself a cup of tea
from the warm pot. He liked this kitchen. It looked like the before
picture in those makeover slots. None of this built-in stuff, just
big old cupboards full to bursting with pots and pans and a deep
pantry whose shelves were groaning with jars and tins. A cook's
kitchen, someone had once said, someone who obviously didn't
know Corinne. She could cook, but just chose not to.

'Doesn't it worry you? Not knowing where she is or what she's
up to,' Daniel asked, that nice smile of his lighting up his face.
Good-looking lad, Daniel, Bernard thought, genes nicely distrib-

uted in this son. Bloody good-natured too and it was such a pity Corinne had taken against him.

'I trust your mother implicitly,' Bernard said, irritated because that very thought – what the hell was she up to? – had just occurred to him too. But then he knew Corinne. She liked a bit of mystery. Bet she wouldn't say where she'd been when she got back either. She'd just smile her enigmatic smile and leave him to wonder. He kept a close eye on movements in the village but so far as he knew there was nobody new, no interesting middle-aged man for her to be swooning over.

'I know you trust her. I'm just joking,' Daniel said, turning away to do some chopping. He did it with the ease of the expert, big sharp knife that could slice your finger off if it had a mind to.

'What are you making?' Bernard asked, cooking a mystery as ever to him. 'Is that our supper?'

'It will be. It's a spicy stew.'

'Excellent. You can't get a decent lunch anywhere in town any more. It's all fast food. Bloody disgrace. Marian's taken to bring-ing in sandwiches. Has her lunch in the office.'

He thought briefly about that, the neatly cut ham sandwiches, half brown, half white, the little tub of low-fat yoghurt, the banana. Same lunch every day, but then that was Marian. He could talk about Marian to Daniel because he did not know her, did not know about the stupid crush.

Bernard glanced affectionately at his son, the one that Corinne had never truly loved. Daniel had been conceived in Spain at a lovely old farmhouse in the hills on a balmy August evening. They'd had a wonderful day out, baby Stephen being a little angel as usual, had a fantastic meal rounded off with a nice bottle of wine before finding themselves in the bedroom in the antique bed without contraceptives and deciding – big mistake – to risk it.

Daniel was the result.

Corinne hadn't wanted another baby so soon after Stephen but that was no excuse to forever take it out on the poor lad, which was what she did. It hadn't been his fault that she had such a bad pregnancy and difficult birth and suffered post-natal depression afterwards. It was a miracle they'd ever tried again but they had, although she had two late miscarriages following Daniel, both girls, before the pregnancy with Joe, which had been surprisingly easy. Even though she was disappointed he was another boy, she loved him obsessively from day one. Later, with her tubes tied – it was that or a vasectomy or, horror of horrors, complete abstinence – Joe was destined to be the last child. Maybe that's why she never stopped treating him like a baby.

After Joe's death, it was left to him to try to make it up to Daniel and he did try but he wasn't sure if he ever got through. He'd always felt awkward with his children when they were children and it was no better now they were grown up. He didn't understand this business about hands-on dads. He'd always been too busy at work and Corinne had liked a routine for the children so they were always in bed before he got home. He'd always gone up to say goodnight but as often as not they were asleep or as near as. He remembered standing at the door of their rooms, looking at them silently, smiling to himself, but they never saw that.

He hadn't a clue what went on in his eldest son's head but Stephen seemed to be happy enough even though Bernard didn't get on with that wife of his, but then nobody did. Damned strange woman, doctor or no doctor. They were better off in Australia, out of the way. He tried to understand Daniel too, but it wasn't easy to get through to him either and he clammed up whenever the accident was mentioned.

'What happened?' he had asked, the first time they were alone afterwards. 'You can tell me. I won't tell your mother.'

'You know what happened,' Daniel said. 'He was following me and he slipped. It was the only part of the path where you have to take extra care but it's a path ramblers use, Dad, that's

75

how dangerous it's considered to be. Nine times out of ten there's no problem. He was just in the wrong place at the wrong time. It had been raining and it was slippery. Just a moment's lack of concentration, that's all it was.'

'That's the truth?'

Daniel nodded.

He knew he was lying. Corinne was right about that.

As for Joe . . . how he missed Joe. Oh, how he missed Joe.

He was the one son so like Corinne with the same eyes and that wonderful colour of hair. There must have been some of his genes mixed up in there somewhere, but it had been difficult to spot where. Even now, the agony of that awful day often reared its head, at inconvenient moments such as in the middle of a meeting, stopping him in his tracks, interrupting his chain of thought and causing everybody to look anxiously at him. Even now, there were moments when he forgot and, in a confused muddle, imagined he saw or heard his son again. One of the trainees last year had been Joe's double from the back and he had needed to steel himself so that, when he did turn round, it was not so much of a disappointment that it was not Joe. Of course it wasn't Joe. For one, Joe would not be seen dead wearing a suit like that, but then he reminded himself Joe *was* dead, his body smashed to smithereens. How quickly had he lost consciousness as he fell? He was assured by the medical people, very quickly, and sincerely hoped that was true and they weren't just palming him off. It was desperately important to him that Joe would have known nothing by the time he plummeted face down into that rocky outcrop.

'I need to talk, Dad,' his middle son said now, interrupting the unhappy thought.

Bernard looked up in surprise. 'Fire away,' he said.

'I wanted to let you know that Harvey's asked me to go into full partnership with him at the adventure centre. It's doing well, and now that we've moved into adult activity courses and team appraisal as well as the kids' centre, we don't have all our eggs in one basket. It's a growing market.'

Bernard looked closely at him, watching as Daniel ferreted around in the cupboards, ostensibly in search of dishes. This was a turn up for the book and no mistake. Daniel acting responsibly for once and something he ought to encourage. After all, he couldn't go on climbing for ever and he needed a back up, a proper job.

'Have you told your mother?'

'No. I thought I'd tell you first.'

'Do you need capital?' he asked, a bit embarrassed to be suggesting such a thing. 'You only have to say and I'll sort something out. I've got a bit put by for a rainy day. It would be just between the two of us,' he added quickly, knowing Corinne wouldn't care for the idea.

'Thanks, but it's all organized,' Daniel said. 'And I'll be moving out, of course. Maybe as early as next week. There's the cottage at the centre going begging so that will be my base. It's a bit basic but that won't bother me.'

'Good.' Bernard waited until Daniel was finally finished, the meal cooking in the oven, before he carried on.

'You're not to let it get to you . . .' he said.

'What's that?' Daniel said, as if he didn't know.

'Your mother . .' Bernard grimaced. 'She's a stubborn old so-and-so. Always has been. I blame what she does, that damned sewing. I mean to say, does she seem the sort of woman to be satisfied doing something like that. Stitching!'

'She likes it. Therapeutic she says. I think it's good that she channels all her creative energy into it. She needs it. We all need something,' Daniel added thoughtfully. 'That's why I cook. It's practical and it takes my mind off things.'

'And I suppose that's why I like the re-enactments,' Bernard said. 'They're my steam-hole. You can't think about much when you're going hell for leather across a field, yelling blue murder.

You don't think it's daft, do you, me doing that?'

'No. Each to his own, Dad.'

They shared a quick grin.

'Why don't you get yourself a nice girl?' Bernard asked, surprising himself at the question. 'Settle down like Stephen?'

'For one, Dad . . .' Daniel smiled, 'nice girls don't grow on trees no matter what Mum seems to think and two, I'm not sure it would be fair on a girl. After all, I'm not giving up climbing, not yet, and wives and girlfriends have a tough time of it when we're away.'

'The right girl would understand,' Bernard muttered, although on reflection Corinne never seemed to understand him. Nor he her.

'Leave it,' Daniel said, awkward but firm. 'Stop trying to hold my hand. I'm a grown-up, Dad, hadn't you noticed?' he added with a grin.

Bernard looked at the big handsome lad who reminded him so much of his own father and smiled too.

Daniel could take care of himself.

CHAPTER SEVEN

'Emily ... message timed at ... let's see ... six-thirty-two, Monday. Where are you, darling? Mum here. I have news. Aunt Louise phoned today to ask about your list. Are you having one? I told her I thought you probably were because it seems to be the done thing, although I can't get over the feeling that it's such a cheek. Aunt Louise agrees with me. We never had lists and you just had to lump it if you got landed with three toasters. Anyway, let me know so I can let her know. She's panicking already about her hat, but then she's like that. Stella is worrying her sick. I do hope she picks up for the wedding.

'Speak to you soon.

'Bye.'

The first page of the astrology chart was a Map of the Heavens, totally inexplicable with masses of figures that Emily made no attempt to understand, believing that in all probability it was complete fabrication anyway, a product of Angharad's over-imaginative mind. It all looked very scientific, however, with the planets' positions plotted and lots of symbols.

She struggled to understand it and the various asides that Angharad had written in the margin. The universe was apparently in constant motion, never still and forever presenting a new picture. Composing a chart therefore was a bit like taking a photograph – a moment captured forever and Angharad was keen to point out that, contrary to popular belief, astrology was not guesswork. The chart would provide Emily with the opportunity to choose for herself the right moment to make momentous life changes, in other words to make the very best of her life and avoid the possible pitfalls. It was detailed and she supposed, in fairness to the composer, it had taken some considerable time to do.

'Huh!' Emily chuckled to herself, seeing for a minute Angharad bent over the chart, working on it. Angharad with her distinctive green eyes peered at things, papers, computer screens, people, as if she were short-sighted which, as she wore neither glasses nor contact lenses, seemed not to be the case. There were other rumours about Angharad too but it was her own fault for, not content with supermarket shopping like any ordinary mortal, she often spent her summers sweeping through the fields near her Cornish home collecting things for herb teas, wild mushrooms and a selection of dubious greens for salads. With home-made remedies for every ailment under the sun and a pursed-lip attitude to conventional medicine, a thoroughly modern witch had to spring to mind. More worryingly, perhaps, Belinda had confessed to consulting her about infertility, before joyfully announcing her pregnancy. Since Belinda had only been married five minutes anyway, it seemed premature, even though she was thirty-nine, to think about infertility and Emily reserved judgement on the role Angharad's foul-smelling potion had played. Belinda was convinced though, and Angharad had already been invited to be godmother to the child when it arrived.

Quickly turning the page, she discovered that two planets in particular dominated the ascendant and 1st house – whatever that might mean – and there followed an attempt to explain about the planets, the transiting ones of Jupiter, Saturn and Uranus, ending by saying that for the next few years Jupiter and Saturn would be the main forces in her life. It would seem, according to Angharad, that she had a protective instinct towards those closest to her but might have to learn to let go of those she becomes attached to. She was a homemaker and would feel lost and lonely if she did not have a home of her own once she had left the family home. And she liked to keep an eye on the finances and was unhappy when they were out of control. Oh well, there was something in that and so far as she knew, she hadn't admitted as much to Angharad so where had she dredged that one up from?

Strangely enchanted by it, enthralled when she knew she ought not to be, she spent an age reading the chart line by line, taking it all in, amazed at the absurdity of it, wondering how on earth Angharad had the nerve to charge them all for what amounted to entertaining twaddle.

As Emily contemplated marriage and the resulting tremendous change in her life, the chart issued a stark, strangely worded warning that something momentous was just about to happen. Emily smiled, thinking of Michael and his *coming into money*. Angharad had placed a red mark on the page and put a corresponding pencilled note in the margin to say that she would go into deeper detail about this, but only if Emily wished to pursue it. The signs were perfectly clear and she was not going to shirk her responsibility by omitting it. And then followed a veiled reference to a death.

Oh, for heavens sake! Emily had never thought of herself as superstitious, but nonetheless her heart gave a sudden pound at the idea.

Annoyed at herself for allowing it to get to her, Emily put it down a moment. She ought to tear it in two, fling it, but one or two things that some of the other girls said, the uncannily accurate things, even Belinda's blooming pregnancy, made her read on.

The chart then went into another flurry about the sun in relation to Mercury and how she was coming into a period of great change. She was not at a happy point in her life just now but she would be happy eventually, although in order to be so she would undergo a huge upheaval.

Well, would you believe the nerve of the woman? Where had that come from and how dare Angharad say she was not happy now? What did *she* know? She was very happy, blissfully so, engaged to be married to a wonderful man, everything going for her, so how could she not be happy?

She had seen the way Angharad looked firstly at her engagement ring and secondly at Simon and she would be prepared to swear that half of this was coloured by plain jealousy. So far as she knew, Angharad was not in a relationship nor would she be until she changed her tune and stopped being so doom-laden. Perhaps it was time she did her own chart to check the state of her own life before she started offering snidy comments on others.

According to Angharad . . . the number of times she had heard people say that over the last few months, say it in an awed whisper at that, as if she had some sort of special powers.

Emily put the chart down, disturbed by it. Oh yes, you could laugh it off but it was too late for it was said and there was always going to be the nagging worry that she was right. One thing she knew. She would certainly not be saying anything to Simon about this.

'There's a house you might be interested in, Emily,' Clive said, standing by her desk, bringing with him a strong smell of expensive aftershave. He was, as usual, immaculately turned out in crisp blue shirt with toning silk tie, beautifully cut dark suit and highly polished shoes. The suit was one of several top quality numbers, one that she had collected from the dry cleaners only the other day.

Emily knew her job description did not strictly include collecting her boss's laundry and keeping a private social diary for him, reminding him about family birthdays, anniversaries etc, but that had quickly become part of her duties, and she knew she ought to have put her foot down at the start if she had wanted it otherwise.

Now, it was set in stone and far too late. He relied on her and she was beginning to feel a fierce loyalty to him, quick to defend him if the need arose.

'A house? In our price range?'

He nodded. 'A bargain. Fantastic place out in the country. Period cottage. I can't guarantee a thatched roof but it's got a history. Elspeth got a whiff on the grapevine. You'll love it. You can snap it up if you like before it gets put on the market. It's a friend of one of Elspeth's friends who's had a bit of bother with her marriage so she's having to sell up. Obviously if you can agree a sale without involving agents, it will be good news for you and her. I've put a word in for you already.'

He tossed her a scrap of paper on which was written a name, address and phone number and she thanked him and popped it in her bag. She could not make any decisions without consulting Simon but at the same time, time was of the essence and Clive was quite right, a quick sale by-passing the estate agent was the dream scenario.

'Pop in my office and we'll go through next week's list,' he told her and she picked up her notebook and followed him in, taking in the views of the boats in dock, the sun streaming in silvery flashes across the water, Torpoint clearly visible. She loved the business of Plymouth, the smell of the sea, the screeching of gulls as they swept overhead, the strong maritime tradition, the historical links with Francis Drake. Born and brought up as she had been near the sea in Kent, she supposed a love of it was in her blood.

Clive had definitely made it, in spacious office terms, the desk wide and empty, the seating area in the corner filled with two large sofas and a coffee table, the walls dominated by large modern paintings by local artists he liked to promote. Emily had never seen his home but she imagined it would be similar, certainly uncluttered and, although she had never met his wife

Elspeth, she looked, from the silver-framed photograph on the desk, as if she would not tolerate a mess either. They lived in a converted barn and, from what Clive had let slip, they had gone for a distinct modern style. Even though he dealt day-to-day with antiques, they apparently had no room in his home.

Looking out from the wide window, clouds were gathering today, gloomily bulking up, and a few days of lower temperatures were predicted. She thought briefly of Simon out there in the thick of it under brilliant blue skies, hot and dusty, and sighed. She knew it was difficult to communicate, but it surely wasn't beyond him to ring her once in a blue moon and let her know how things were.

Leaving Clive with a morning's worth of phone calls to make, she returned to her desk, which occupied a corner position in the smallish outer office. Removing the jacket of one of her workday suits, not quite rolling up the sleeves of her blouse, she opened up a file and set to work. As always, when she was focused on work, time flew and before long she noticed people drifting off to lunch and, with some surprise, glanced at her watch.

Geraldine Grainger was heading her way, slipping her jacket on. Geraldine was a porcelain and fine-art specialist, appropriate for in some ways she was like a delicate china doll herself. Older than Emily, she earned considerably more but it was her additional private income that had helped her buy a small thatched roof cottage in a sought-after village in the beautiful South Hams, a mere snip at close on three hundred thousand. She drove a large powerful sports car and wore designer clothes, the very stuff of life for the successful business woman. She had been very welcoming, making every effort to become friends with Emily and she liked her, even though she could see through the confident exterior. She had the feeling that Geraldine would give her all for a man like Simon. She was thinking of asking her along to dinner and Simon was quite happy for her to do that, but it would mean finding a man for her. Simon was no help and, as it couldn't be anyone from work, she was a bit stumped.

Geraldine was tall and thin, a gene thing and not from dieting, with a fine-featured prettiness and a certain restless grace. Her short blonde hair was expertly cut into a serious wedge and she was wearing a cream skirt and a long silky cardigan that almost reached the hem of it and terrifyingly high heels of the kind that she cheerfully admitted crippled her. She might be accused of dressing a mite sexily for the office but that was Geraldine and they were used to it.

'Fancy a spot of lunch, Emily?' she asked. 'I need to step outside and get some fresh air. My head's spinning.'

'It will have to be quick,' Emily said, reaching for her bag. She had intended to have an apple and a mineral water at her desk but lunch would be very welcome and Geraldine was normally good company. 'I have to be back by two.'

Once in the café, Geraldine waited patiently whilst Emily made a hasty phone call to arrange an appointment that evening to view the house out in the sticks. It was all very well Clive raving about it but she wished she could have seen a picture of it first. What if she hated it? How awkward that would be especially as Clive's wife had gone to such trouble on her behalf. On the other hand, that was no reason to buy a house, was it? It was purely business and Clive would understand that. She would be polite but firm if necessary and he would understand. She almost wished now that she hadn't told him about their hunt for a house, passing on the criteria to him which he had in turn passed to his Elspeth.

'You look very worried,' Geraldine said, glancing at her. 'Would you like me to come with you to see the house? I'm free if you want.'

Emily considered. She was, of course, perfectly capable of forming an opinion for herself on the property but a second one would not come amiss and she could then report back to Simon – if she could get hold of him – with a bit more confidence if

Geraldine okayed it too.

'Thanks. I would like that. We can stop off at the flat for a quick bite before we set off.'

'Don't go to any trouble.'

'I shan't.' She glanced down at her suit. 'I need to change.'

Geraldine smiled. 'She won't be the least bit interested in what you're wearing, believe me. All she cares about is whether or not you can come up with the goods. You're in a strong position with nothing to sell so we can do some negotiating. I've had a bit of experience in this house-buying lark. I can spot the faults.'

'Oh, dear. You won't put me off if I fall in love with it, will you?'

'Of course not. When I saw mine, the first time, I admit I over-looked all the little faults just because for me it was so perfect. Opening my curtains and looking out at the sea is worth so much to me.'

'Lucky you,' Emily said, meaning it. 'It's such a hassle trying to get ourselves sorted out. I want to be settled, to put down proper roots,' she said, remembering what it said on the chart and reflecting that Angharad had been spot-on there.

'I know,' Geraldine said, oozing sympathy. 'Even if it isn't the forever house, you want to feel some sort of permanence about it.'

'That's right. Although we do intend to move back to Kent eventually,' she said, wondering if that would ever come about. The fact was, the longer she was away, the less likely a return was on the cards.

'Poor you. And you have all the worry about the wedding, too.'

'Oh yes, there is that. My mother's going to have a heart attack if she doesn't slow down. She's pushing me to come to a decision about the wedding cars. I didn't realise there was so much choice. What do I want? What do *we* want? Simon says he's not bothered so that leaves it all to me . . .' she laughed. 'I feel like tearing my hair out. There shouldn't be so many choices. Do I go for a stretch limo, a vintage convertible, a Rolls Royce or even a horse and carriage?'

'Horse and carriage definitely,' Geraldine said. 'That sounds so very romantic.'

'Yes but a horse is an animal . . .'

'So?' Geraldine smiled. 'He will be well trained. He's hardly going to bolt, is he?'

'Yes, but from a purely practical point of view . . .'

Geraldine laughed but there was a sudden edge to her voice.

'We've been through all this with the engagement ring, Emily. For once, stop thinking practical. Be adventurous. Dare to be different. Go for the horse and carriage. It's fairytale wedding travel.'

'That's what their brochure says,' she said. 'You know, I just might. It will certainly surprise Simon. Oh Geraldine, if I'd only known there was so much involved, I'm not sure I'd have said yes.'

'Oh come on, you don't mean that,' Geraldine said. 'I know I already have my house and pretty much what I want but I don't mind saying, Emily, that I envy you finding your Mr Right. You seem very suited to each other.'

They smiled, Emily struggling to think of something positive to say. Geraldine, from a comfortable upper-class background, was successful, attractive and there seemed to be no reason at all why she shouldn't find a man to share her life with.

'The problem is I've got very choosy in my old age,' Geraldine told her, pausing to order a cheese-and-pickle sandwich on rye. 'It's difficult when you're earning a fair whack like I am. I'm determined I'm not going to end up supporting some layabout just because I want a man about the house. So, I've drawn up a check list and, if he doesn't tick all the right boxes, he's out after the first date. There's no point in prolonging the agony. I'm going to be ruthless.'

'Check list?' Emily smiled. 'Now who's being practical?

Whatever happened to romance?'

'Finding a man these days for a woman like me isn't about romance,' Geraldine told her, adopting a serious voice. 'I've done the romance bit, believe me, and it hasn't worked out. The way I see it is this . . . it isn't about falling in love, it's about choosing the right man for you. A man with prospects, somebody who is going to suit your lifestyle, somebody who is going to be a good father. You can laugh all you like at arranged marriages, but I think they have something going for them, Emily. I'll settle for that any day rather than have the earth move.' She bit into her sandwich. 'As a matter of fact, Angharad says I haven't long to wait. He's just round the corner, according to my chart. In fact, she suggests I might already have met him. I'm racking my brains to think who it can be but I can't come up with anything. All the really hot men have already been nabbed.'

So, Geraldine had coughed up her twenty-five pounds, too.

'Don't tell me you believe that nonsense,' Emily said. 'Although I have to confess I've had mine done, too.'

'Angharad is very persuasive.' Geraldine glanced at her. 'What did yours say?'

She shrugged. 'Something and nothing.'

'Maybe it is nonsense but it's given me a boost,' Geraldine said. 'There's going to be a lot of soul-search involved apparently . . .' She raised amused eyebrows, 'but by Christmas, she says, I will have my man.'

'I hope she's right,' Emily said, thinking that it was more likely that Angharad was trying to keep in Geraldine's good books. 'Check list, eh? I went for Simon simply because I fancied him.'

'And look where it's got you,' Geraldine said. 'That man neglects you dreadfully. Think about it. You spend most of the time alone.'

'I knew it would be like that when I first met him,' she said. 'It's the job, Geraldine. He can't do the job and be at my side constantly.'

'That job of his would have sunk it for me. Bye bye, Simon. I need somebody who works locally, or ideally somebody who can have an office at home, so that we can tie in when we have children. I'm thirty-five so I need to get on with that soon if I'm to have my two.'

'My, we have got it all worked out,' Emily said, a touch irritated that Simon should be thus dismissed.

'You know me, I have to apply a certain logic in my work and not get carried away,' Geraldine went on, keen to explain. 'And I don't see why I can't apply the same sort of logic to finding a man. I'm not going to let my heart rule my head, not this time.'

'But you still have to meet him. How will you do that? At the delicatessen counter in the supermarket? Or the gym?'

'No. That's old hat,' she said with a smile. 'I don't do the gym anyway. I wouldn't want it to be widely known, Emily, but I'll tell you.'

'What?'

'Don't laugh but I've joined an agency.'

'A dating agency?'

'Yes. And there's no need to look like that. The lady who runs it is extremely discreet and you have to reach a certain standard and earn a certain salary before she accepts you on her books. Why not?' she said defensively, catching Emily's expression. 'I must be practical about it. I'm looking for a marriage of equals.'

'Be careful, Geraldine.'

She laughed. 'Oh come on, I'm a big girl. And the first time you meet a client it's in public so there's no chance of ending up with a serial killer. It's no more dangerous than getting to know somebody you meet at a party. I've got a date lined up,' she said, her eyes crinkling as she smiled. 'He's called Philip and he's an architect. Sounds great on paper.'

'Best of luck,' Emily said, wanting to know more about this but, glancing at her watch, she finished her sandwich quickly. 'Sorry to rush you but I've got to get back.'

'What time have you fixed to visit the house?'

'Seven.'

'If you don't mind, it will be easier for me to meet you there rather than come to the flat,' Geraldine said.

'Fine. See you there then.' Emily wrote the address down on a piece of paper and passed it over.

'Be ten minutes late,' Geraldine said. 'Just long enough for her to get worried that you're not going to turn up but not too late that she thinks you're rude.'

Emily smiled. 'You have done this before, haven't you?'

'There are tactics you should observe when you're looking round,' Geraldine told her as they made their way back to the office. 'Don't look too keen, obviously. Try to keep a neutral expression.'

'Like this?' Emily assumed what she thought of as a poker face.

'On second thoughts, just be yourself. Make pleased noises but don't be scared to say if something's not quite right either. It does no harm to let buyers think that you're not absolutely smitten even if you are. Rather like handling men in fact.'

They exchanged a rueful smile.

CHAPTER EIGHT

'Emily . . . Mum here. Are you having children or not? At the wedding I mean. There's a school of thought that suggests adults-only is easier but if you want children there then it might be an idea to have a créche or an entertainer to keep them amused during the speeches, otherwise they'll be running wild and disrupting everything. My preference would be to exclude them and never mind what the parents think, but your father says we must be careful not to offend. God knows why he suddenly feels the need to stick his oar in. Anyway, I need to know your thoughts before I start sending out the invitations. Have you got Simon's list yet? He really will have to come up with some names. By the way, your father has a cold. He's taken to his bed anyway and I'm up and down the stairs like a yoyo administering to his every need. Men are such babies as you'll soon discover. Speak to you soon, darling. Take care.

'Bye.'

'I don't know why the hell we have to go to these things?' Bernard said, standing in the bedroom in his underpants, vest and socks, looking through his wardrobe. 'What am I supposed to wear for this damned function?'

'It is not a damned function as you well know, Bernard,' Corinne told him patiently. 'It's a little welcoming do for the new

91

man and it will look very odd if we don't attend. Anyway, I'm looking forward to it even if you're not. Going to a Pacmans do is better than nothing, although a weekend away in London and a visit to the opera would be so much nicer.'

'You don't like opera,' he said.

'I most certainly do. Some of it anyway. In any case, going to the opera is a wonderful excuse to dress up and be seen.'

'We haven't got the time for a weekend away,' Bernard said, wobbling on one leg as he stepped into his trousers, leaving them unzipped as he reached for a shirt.

'Not that one,' Corinne said, leaping forward to retrieve it before it slid off the bed. 'Good heavens, Bernard, are you colour blind?'

'Which one then?' he asked, frowning at her. 'I don't see that it matters, anyway. After what Marian says, I'm not going out of my way to impress this new chap.'

'Meaning what exactly? What has Marian been saying now?' Corinne asked, intent on putting the finishing touches to her make-up. One had to be so careful as one grew older not to look like an actor on stage but she knew what suited her, always had, and she still used the same mix of eye-shadow she had used for years because they were simply right for her. Behind the eyes, in her head, she felt pretty much as she had felt at thirty, well maybe thirty-five. Bernard, she recalled, had started to get on her nerves about then. 'What has Marian been saying?' she repeated as Bernard fell suddenly silent. 'Oh, come on, Cooper.'

She called him that when she was annoyed with him and his tone had irritated her. He made such a palaver about going out that in some ways it wasn't worth the effort.

'This new chap is a marketing wizard from all accounts, somebody who's supposed to get us out of the shit-hole Malley thinks we're in,' he said. 'He's too bloody impatient that's the trouble. We are getting there – slowly – but he wants a miracle and he thinks this chap will produce it. I doubt it.'

'Don't be so defeatist,' Corinne said. 'He'll certainly be an improvement on the last man. His ideas were hopeless, you said so yourself. You've got to play to your strengths, darling. You won't get young men going into your shops unless you have some nubile wench half-naked just inside the door. And your loyal clientele don't want to see jeans and sweatshirts hanging up or, God forbid, hear pop music pounding away.'

'I know that,' he said. 'Anyway, Marian reckons this new chap is as camp as they come.'

'So what?' she laughed. 'Is he good at his job?'

'Not bad,' he conceded. 'He comes highly recommended. Pacmans poached him, of course. Malley offered him the earth, plus all the usual inducements.'

'Well then. Being gay doesn't matter, does it?'

'In theory no but I can't get my head round it. Marian's seen him in town buying flowers.'

'Oh really, darling, what's wrong with that?' she said with a sigh.

Marian was a real old boot who always looked at Corinne through pursed lips. She had bought Bernard a silk scarf for Christmas and even though it would have been purchased from the accessories range with her staff discount, Corinne still thought it was a bit of a liberty and far too extravagant when Bernard had presented her with a box of After Eights. With Bernard completely clueless at Christmas, rushed off his feet, Corinne had bought the chocolates, wrapping them and reminding him to give them to Marian, reminding *her* of the times she used to buy little gifts for the boys to give to their teacher at the end of term. Same thing really. Marian, it had to be said, was a pain. She lived alone, though she didn't seem to have a home to go to and rumour had it that she slept in the staffroom and had Pacmans tattooed across her heart. 'Marian is so very provincial, bless her heart. Can't a man buy flowers without it meaning anything?'

93

'He bought them for *himself*,' Bernard said, as if that explained everything. 'He's renting a flat until he can find a house and his room is full of them. Marian went round with some papers he needed to see and he invited her in for a coffee. Flowers galore and he arranges them at that. Bragged about it. Now I ask you, what man in his right mind would ever think of buying flowers for himself?'

Silently, she reached for her lipstick, having satisfied herself that her eyes were done to perfection. 'How petty-minded, Bernard,' she said, feeling a deep irritation that it should bother him at all. What had happened to the liberal-minded man she had married? 'Gay or not, I am very much looking forward to meeting him. What's his name again?'

'That's another thing that gets on my nerves. It's all bloody first names these days. This new initiative. They've changed all the name tags on the shop floor. I can't be doing with all this familiarity. You used to know where you were when you stepped back a bit. Anyway, for what it's worth, he's Cuthbert.'

She grimaced. 'Good grief, although he can't help his name, can he? Do we call him Bert?'

'Absolutely not. Full title. He made that very plain. I feel sorry for him with a name like that. I sometimes think if you get given the wrong name, it can get you off on the wrong foot for life. Parents have a lot to answer for. At least we gave our boys good solid names. Stephen. Daniel. Joe.'

'Yes.' The vision in the mirror blurred an instant and she quickly took hold of herself. Why oh why had he mentioned Joe, just when she had applied a second coat of mascara? Joe, cut down in his prime as he had been, just when the offer of his place had been confirmed. He had got excellent grades in his A levels and his future was assured. His offer of a place on the textile design course was secure and she just knew he would have followed in her footsteps exactly, apart from getting pregnant, of course, which had shot all her dreams skywards. 'I've always rather liked my own name,' she said quietly, taking a deep breath. 'Do you like it, Bernard?'

'Corinne?' Bernard asked, looking surprised, as if hearing it for the first time. 'It's a bit flash but all right.'

'Well, thank you,' she said with a faint sigh. 'I happen to like Bernard very much indeed.'

'Do you? I always thought it was a bit airy fairy. I wanted to be called Frank, but that was my brother's name. On the plus side, it should be a good spread tonight, I suppose, they've got decent caterers in,' he went on, searching now for his cuff-links. 'Where are the gold ones you gave me for my birthday?' he asked, looking at her in much the same way the boys had looked at her when they were small, expecting miracles to happen, expecting Mummy to know every damned thing under the sun. These days she was feeling ever-more maternal when it came to Bernard.

'Side drawer in the red box where they always are,' she said, regaining her composure. 'Wear the blue tie,' she said as she saw him pulling out one of his damned old-school ones. 'It's time you threw those out, darling.'

'They're no longer available,' he said with a puzzled look. 'Annoying, isn't it? So I'm rationing the ones I've got left.'

'Quite right,' she said, giving up on that one. 'But tonight is not an old-school tie night. Wear the blue. It will go with the shirt.'

'Will it?' He seemed astonished and she smiled, feeling a moment's fondness for him. He was utterly hopeless. Without her, he would be well-and-truly lost and, in an odd sense, so would she without him. After all, who could she complain about if he wasn't here?

'I'm ready when you are,' she said, standing up and smoothing the satin skirt. Was all this a bit over the top for a small welcoming reception, she wondered, looking at herself in the full-length mirror. Calf-length black skirt, sparkly black vest and a crimson hip-disguising jacket that was fighting with her hair. Marian would be there, her lumpy body bunged into the shapeless floral frock she had been dragging out of her wardrobe for the last goodness knows how many years, looking daggers at her as usual, jealous as hell. She couldn't seriously be interested in Bernard, could she? It seemed extraordinary. Bernard had never been what you might call handsome, even in his youth. On the other hand, there had been a certain devil-may-care charm. She had, she was delighted to remember, tried flirting with all the boys on his corridor and without doubt, Bernard scored the most points. He was the only one with the gumption to take up the bait she offered and with just one touch from him, she had well and truly melted. He could kiss like nobody else and set her pulse racing like nobody's business. It had started out as a bit of fun and falling deeply, seriously in love had not been part of the equation.

Once upon a time . . .

'How do I look?' she inquired of her husband, noting that, after all the palaver, he was moderately well-turned out himself for once. He scrubbed up well when he took the trouble.

'Lovely,' he said, scarcely glancing at her long enough to form an opinion.

With a sigh, she followed him out slowly, a little wobbly in her new high heels. If there was anybody there to flirt with tonight, and chance would indeed be a fine thing, then she would be doing it.

The evening passed more pleasantly than Bernard had anticipated. In a social context, Cuthbert was a nice enough chap, personable and presentable. As to whether or not he was gay, he had no idea. They didn't yet put that question on the job form, although it was just a matter of time before they did. Sexual orientation? It wasn't the sort of thing you could ask outright. Although it was possible to ask a few gentle questions.

'Got a girlfriend, Cuthbert? Is there going to be a Mrs Innes?'

Corinne gave him a look as Cuthbert smiled and said not yet but you never know. He was still waiting for his Miss Right.

'You're a wise man,' Bernard said, ignoring Corinne's exasperation. 'Let me tell you, man to man, that, with the exception of my wife of course, the ladies are best avoided long-term.'

'A fine state you'd be in, Bernard, without me,' Corinne said with a sidelong despairing glance at him. 'He didn't tell you, Cuthbert, that I gave up a promising career for him.'

'Preggers at university,' Bernard explained with a quick grin. 'I nearly got shot down in flames by her father. Bloody awkward all round when she was planning to go abroad after she graduated. She was a cracker in those days, Cuthbert.'

'Still is, surely?'

'Well, yes of course she is.' Bernard felt a puff of pride, revised his opinion as he caught the appreciative look the fellow aimed at his wife. Marian was wrong. This chap was no more gay than he was.

'What were you going to do, Corinne?' Cuthbert asked, seeming most interested and looking straight at her. 'Before Bernard . . . er . . .' he grinned, lost for the right words and with a smile she put him out of his misery.

'Before Bernard impregnated me? I was studying fashion and I wanted to go somewhere where the action was,' Corinne said, turning her back on her husband who was stuffing himself happily with bite-size flaky pastry savouries. 'Paris. Milan. Maybe New York.' Her smile was slight. 'And this man, Bernard Cooper, ruined it all for me.'

'Hey, not quite,' Bernard dashed pastry crumbs off his shirt and accepted a small glass of sherry from the tray that was doing the rounds. He knew that Corinne's remark had been said in jest but there was an awkward element of truth in it that worried him. Corinne had set their landing alight, having a bit of a fling with all the other guys, stopping just short of going all the way as they

97

called it in those days. Until she met him that is.

A quickie, that's all it had been, that's all it was meant to be, and wasn't it just their luck that they'd struck gold first time. But once it was done, it was done and he would never have dreamed of trying to get out of it, even if her father hadn't been behind him brandishing the mythical shotgun. In fact, all in all they'd had a bloody good marriage. Going a bit stale now but they were no spring chickens. You couldn't keep that pace up, all that sex and stuff. Things mellowed.

Cuthbert was definitely not gay. In fact, Corinne was thrilled with the way they had flirted with each other. He was years younger of course and it was rather disgraceful of her but such fun even allowing that she was woefully out of practice. Mischievous eye-contact had prevailed all evening and surely she had caught him looking at her breasts, which were looking pretty good in their push-up bra. He was definitely not wearing a Pacmans suit, which was rather naughty of him, but she liked the hint of rebellion in the gesture. He was good-looking in a Hugh Grant sort of way with a lovely sense of humour and she suspected he would not have been overly concerned if she had suggested they sneak away for a few moments for a quick snog.

And then, at the end of the evening, after the mercifully brief speeches of welcome from Bernard and another senior figure and a rather good return one from Cuthbert that had the audience in gales of laughter, he had done the one thing that truly delighted her. He kissed her hand as they said goodbye, brushing her fingers ever so lightly with his lips.

And so, buoyed up by that lovely gesture, she was feeling in a distinctly playful mood when she and Bernard returned home. She couldn't hold her drink these days and was most definitely the worse for wear, swaying just a fraction as she stepped out of the car into the cooler evening air. It was a romantic sort of night, the sky at its theatrical best, a sliver of a pale moon hanging in the velvet midnight-blue, stars twinkling, and, quite enchanted by it all, she gazed up a moment before dizziness overcame her and she clutched Bernard's arm for support.

'Good chap that,' Bernard said. 'I'll have to have a word with Marian. Starting bloody daft rumours. He's as straight as the next man. Mind you, he's very young and inexperienced, never mind his little bit of success at the last place. Bit wet behind the ears as regards retail know-how and I will have to have a session with him on figures. I don't think anybody's explained the true facts to him. We are in the process of climbing out of what was deep shit.'

'Language, darling,' she said, laughing at his indignation.

'And as for the kissing hand bit . . .' he added with a puzzled shake of the head. 'Going over the top if you ask me, but you seemed to enjoy it.'

'It was charming,' Corinne told him, looking at her hand where dear Cuthbert had pressed his lips against it. 'I wonder why gentlemen don't do it more often? Have you ever kissed a woman's hand, Bernard?'

'Good God, no. Why would I do that?'

'Exactly.' She fired him an exasperated glance, pulling her jacket closer, feeling a chill. 'You're far too English and hand-kissing is so . . . so *European*. Maybe he has French connections.'

'Fancy a nightcap?' Bernard asked, undoing his tie and scratching under his arm.

'Oh, I think I might have had enough to drink,' she said, stepping out of her shoes and feeling the cold of the kitchen floor under her feet, which brought her down to earth with a bump. 'I feel a bit tiddly, Bernard, if you must know. And you know what I'm like when I'm tiddly.'

'I meant a cocoa,' he said, quickly pulling out a chair for her before she melted onto the floor. 'Or a malted milk.'

She yawned. 'I can't believe you, darling. Time was you'd have had me by the hat-stand in the hall after a night out. Time

99

was we'd be tearing our clothes off directly we shut the door. And now you're offering me cocoa.'

'We can go up to bed then,' he said, catching on. 'And do without the cocoa, although on your head be it if you can't get to sleep.'

She laughed, seeing for a minute something of the Bernard of old. Slowly, realizing what he'd just said, he smiled and ran his fingers through his hair.

'Mrs Cooper,' he then said, picking his words carefully, 'did I forget to tell you how ravishing you look tonight?. No wonder that new fellow couldn't keep his eyes off you. He'd better not try anything or he'll have me to deal with.'

'Enough talk,' she said, picking up her shoes and carrying them upstairs. She knew exactly what would happen, knew there would be no surprises, knew that it would be pleasant rather than earth-moving, knew also that afterwards Bernard would hop into his Pacmans blue silk pyjamas with the navy piping and navy dressing-gown and trundle down to the kitchen to make his blasted cocoa.

Sitting at her dressing table, she took off her make-up as Bernard pottered about downstairs doing goodness knows what. Minus make-up, she shuddered at her reflection. She would have benefited from a face-lift ten years ago. In her make-up drawer was a silver box, a heart-shaped box, and she took it out now and opened it.

Joe . . . the last photograph.

Taken by her.

She savoured it a moment, looking closely at it, at Joe posing for the camera with a lopsided smile on his face.

'I have a couple of photographs left in the camera,' she heard herself saying as he and Daniel loaded up the car for their five-day trip to the Lake District. 'Stay there and I'll get it.'

In the event, by the time she got back, Daniel was already in the car, raring to go and Joe was waiting for her, anxious too to be off.

'Now, you will be careful,' she told him when she had snapped him, peering in the car then and adding 'Look after him, Daniel, you know how clumsy he is.'

Joe hugged her then, holding her just a fraction longer than she expected because he was like Bernard in that respect, undemonstrative when it came to goodbyes.

'Bye, Mum,' he then said, eyes on a level with hers.

'See you soon,' she said, waving until they were gone.

It was meant to be a break for them, a spot of brotherly bonding. Joe had worked so hard, had been under a strain what with exams and a recent break-up with a most unsuitable girl, a tarty piece who had thankfully if rather despicably taken up with his best friend. He was dreadfully upset and she had been unable to console him, but that was what first love was all about and he was over it now and it was good to think he could now look forward. Once he got to college, he would soon find another girl and forget all about his first love.

Hearing Bernard finally coming upstairs, she stuffed the photo back in its box and closed the lid.

CHAPTER NINE

'Emily . . . are you there? You should be at this time or are you still working all hours? You should tell your Mr Grey if he's taking advantage. Mum here. I've seen this fantastic outfit in a sweet little boutique in Canterbury, darling. A suit edged with fur and it's just so elegant. A bit of a neat fit but if I lose just one stone which I fully intend to do it will be perfect. It's a Betty Barclay and far too expensive of course but I shan't tell your father how much. The only teeniest thing is the colour. It's winter white. Do you think that would be all right or will it look odd for the mother of the bride? If you really really think it will, do say and I'll get something else. But it's just so beautiful. Speak to you soon.

'Bye.'

When Simon got back from the latest assignment, things were rather cool between them, taking up where they left off with the wedding plans and his now trenched-in determination not to wear a tie. Whoever heard of a bridegroom without a tie? Surely to please her, he would bend what was a daft principle?

She dare not tell her mother, who had enough on her mind getting her own outfit, but she did mention it to Geraldine whose advice was to stick tight and not make a fuss. He would see sense eventually, she said, and it was probably only attention-seeking, anyway.

That irritated, the idea that Geraldine thought him childish and, even though she shared the view, she vowed to be more circumspect in future and not say too much about her private life because Geraldine seemed to have closed the door on hers. Since admitting joining the dating agency, she had side-stepped questions about it and Emily had finally got the message that she was in no mood to talk about it. Reading between the lines, she must have suffered one or two very forgettable dates.

As to her own love life, the doubts were escalating, but still she hesitated to bring things to a head and confront Simon with them. If she kept these silly doubts to herself then they would go away. It was important to remember the good times and she kept harping back in her mind to the first time he kissed her, held her, whispered that he loved her, and the way she had floated on air for days afterwards in such a romantic swirl that she could not hide it from her girlfriends.

If this was it, then it surely was fantastic. And although they had sadly got over that initial euphoria, there were still plenty enough times when it was just great. If she let him go, and recently she had found herself sadly contemplating life without him, what then would she have to look forward to? She would be like Geraldine, searching for a man with her little pathetic list, ticking boxes, being so very clinical and unromantic and she wasn't sure she wanted that.

Wisely, she left the tie business for the time being, wavering indeed and thinking that perhaps after all it wouldn't be the end of the world if he appeared tie-less at his wedding. If he was still adamant, then she would back him and they would face her mother together. Compared with the awful things he faced up to daily in his work, whether or not he wore a tie at his wedding was a mere triviality. That decided, she felt better about it.

She needed him to be in a good mood anyway before she showed him the house that the owner was kindly holding for them before putting it on the open market. The lady owner was in no hurry to move but, if they wanted to buy, then she could quickly arrange something and they could be installed in the weeks it took the solicitors to flutter around with the paperwork.

Geraldine had given the go-ahead on it, considering it to be an excellent buy at the suggested price, a house with potential for them to put their own stamp on it. It would need money spending on it, of course, to bring it up to scratch, but then that applied to most properties and surely that was the fun of it. Thinking of builders and so on traipsing through, knocking holes in walls and disrupting their life for weeks, possibly months, was a bit of a downer but Emily determined she would face that if it happened.

On the very first visit she had already decided she wanted it before she reached the garden gate and, once indoors, it indeed proved to be the house of her dreams, oddly similar in many ways to the one she did dream of. She could already visualize herself there on a winter evening in that cosy lounge before a log fire, legs stretched out, Simon beside her, sipping a glass of wine, listening to music; could see them waking up in that lovely bedroom with its views of the countryside. With nobody over-looking them, they could sleep with the curtains drawn back so that the morning light would gently wake them, that and the sound of the birds. There was, she acknowledged as Geraldine gently pointed it out, a distant hum of traffic from the main road but she assured herself that it would not trouble them.

Not able to put it off any longer, she arranged a further visit with Simon, driving them in her little car, talking nervously all the way. She knew he had had a bad field trip last time, witnessed a few things that he preferred not to talk about, although he professed to be excited about some of the photographs he had taken, photos she had not seen, images she suspected he was deliberately keeping from her. She knew that it was his job to take photographic records of macabre and grisly events but that the necessary intrusiveness of it, of putting the picture first, sometimes got to him. She would be worried frankly if it did not because that would show an utter disregard for human emotions and she knew him well enough to know he cared deeply about others. He didn't always show it, could be quite flippant on occasions, but underneath she knew he cared.

As to the house, she had made it perfectly clear that, whilst she adored it, if he really didn't like it – for whatever reason – then that was all right and he wasn't to feel too badly about it.

And wasn't that a complete lie?

If he didn't like it, if he pulled the rug out from her romantic dream, she would never quite forgive him. She had done all she could to put him in a receptive mood this morning, even to the extent of making him a cooked breakfast as a very special treat. To her surprise, on his arrival home late last evening, he had been a little brusque as she kissed him a welcome, not exactly pushing her away but at pains to tell her he was completely knackered and just needed to get into bed and sleep it off. It was a surprise brush-off because, after being apart, sex was usually the first thing on both their minds and she had felt hurt and disappointed, going into the bathroom in a huff and blowing out all the little scented candles that she had arranged round it.

As she stopped outside the house, she felt a sharp anxiety, an actual pain in her chest, watching his reaction closely. 'This is it, darling,' she said. 'What do you think?'

'Give me a chance,' he grumbled mildly, peering out. 'The roof's shot, for a start.'

'Is it?' She hadn't given the roof a thought, other than that it was not a thatched one, but that first negative reaction from Simon did not augur well, and she flashed him a sharp glance. 'That can be put right, can't it?'

'For a few thousand and a lot of hassle, yes.'

It was raining stair-rods this time so the effect she and Geraldine had of golden sun on warm stone was lost, and the far-reaching views were completely switched off under the heavy grey rain clouds and the misty steam rising from the fields. It

105

gave it a surreal quality and they had to make a dash for it or sit all morning in the car. By the time they made it to the front door, sans umbrella of course, having clattered through a stiff gate, brushing past shrubs and skirting the worse of the puddles, they were wet through themselves, shaking themselves dry like dogs as they were shown into the hall.

Emily, apologising, looking down at the wet marks she had made on the carpet, noticed for the first time that the carpet, the light-coloured carefully neutral one that was laid throughout the house, was way past its best. Her hopes faded a fraction because she knew Simon had keen eyes and would have spotted that at once.

It also felt chill in spite of the fire that raged in the wood burner in the hearth and, worse, there was the slightest whiff of damp. And this time her more critical eyes took in the glaring faults, faded wallpaper, the cracks in the ceiling, the worrying dark patches on the ceiling, the badly arranged kitchen, the grim avocado bathroom. Funny she had not noticed them first time around but she had been completed bowled over by it but then, she hadn't noticed Simon's little idiosyncrasies either when they first met. They came much later, were still coming in fact.

They declined, because of the rain, to go into the garden even though the owner offered them the use of wellies and a golf umbrella, settling for a quick look from the kitchen window.

'You can't see all of it from here,' the owner said, cross that they weren't going out to see it, pointing vaguely through the mist. 'But as Emily knows, there's a separate bit beyond the hedge where I grow vegetables and fruit. I was very nearly self-sufficient last summer.'

'I've never quite seen the point of growing your own vegetables,' Simon said smoothly, smiling to show he was not being vindictive. 'Isn't it much easier to grab them at the supermarket?'

Emily could have killed him as they laughed, the owner insisting that the taste was the thing.

'Isn't that always the case?' he went on, seeming determined to be awkward as hell today. 'In the end it all comes down to individual taste?'

Emily, seeing a doubtful look appearing in the other woman's face, tried unsuccessfully to shoot him a deadly glance but he was oblivious and, now that he was in his grumbling stride, spent the remainder of the time picking faults.

She could not speak seriously to him, not with the owner standing beside them, chattering rather desperately into the silence that finally descended, but she had no need to speak to him because his feelings were obvious for anybody to see.

It might well be her idea of heaven but it certainly was not his.

And that made her all the more determined. To hell with him, she would be living here much more than he would so surely that had to count for something. And count for something it would.

All right, so it wasn't perfect but it could be made so, but she was going to have her work cut out to convince him.

They drove back in silence for most of the way until she could stand it no longer. The rain had settled to a steady drizzle and the windscreen wipers flicked away as, beside her, Simon began to hum the catchy tune they had heard on the radio on the way over.

'I can't think why you're so cheerful,' she said. 'That couldn't have gone worse.'

'Oh, I don't know. You wanted to show it to me and now you have. Mission accomplished, surely? Another one bites the dust.'

'You think so? You were determined not to like it from the word go.'

'I was not. I was perfectly prepared to love it.'

'You needn't have been quite so dismissive. I felt quite embarrassed. How could you, Simon?'

'Oh, here we go. This is supposed to be a joint decision. Remember? Remember how you hated that place I liked, the one over in Kingsbridge?'

'That was different,' she said staunchly, not quite sure how. For somebody who professed not to be bothered one way or another, he had gone overboard a few months ago on a house she had really disliked. Tall and narrow with a garden to match, there had been three floors and a mountain of stairs to climb and clean and, to top it all, the kitchen was in the basement, the view from its window of a high stone wall and nothing else. The practicalities of living there were just too outlandish and she had told him as much. He had not been convinced but to be fair to him, he hadn't put up much of a fight. He had, she acknowledged, been a darned sight more graceful than she was going to be.

'Did you think I would lie to her?' he went on. 'Tell her how wonderful her house was? Build up her hopes? It might be a cliché, darling, but honesty in this case is definitely the best policy.'

'But we haven't had the chance to discuss it,' she howled. 'You needn't have said anything. You needn't have picked up on every little thing. Couldn't you see she was practically in tears? I felt so sorry for her. She's had a really miserable time lately, having her husband walk out on her and everything.'

'Oh, come on, she'll have to learn to take it on the chin,' he said. 'This is business. You don't buy a house because you feel sorry for somebody.'

'Most of the work is just cosmetic.'

'Not so. It's dropping to bits. It will need complete re-wiring, new gutters, roof and that's just the obvious things. We can do better than that. She'd have to knock twenty thousand off the price before I'd even consider it.'

'She won't. The price is fixed.'

'I see. So she can be all business when she wants to be. If she won't, then that's that. We forget it.'

'Geraldine thought it very sound,' she persisted as her hopes tumbled all around.

'And why on earth should we take any notice of what she thinks?'

'Because she has a good head on her shoulders,' she told him. 'You've met her. You couldn't meet a more sensible woman. You were more than happy to take her advice about your paintings.'

'That's different. That's her job. She knows what she's talking about there, but when it comes to houses, you ladies do tend to go starry-eyed.'

'We do *not*,' she huffed, controlling her anger with difficulty. For two pins, she'd stop the car now and push him out. Let him find his own way back. A good walk in the rain might bring him to his senses, stop him being so damned insensitive to her feelings. She knew the house was dropping to bits but it didn't matter. She loved it and that was that.

'And didn't you hear the traffic noise?' he said, his voice lighter now, with just a hint of amusement in it. 'I thought you were after complete peace and quiet?'

'There has to be some compromise,' she muttered, knowing only that she wanted the house, that she'd already moved in in her mind and it was too bad of him to put such a damper on it.

'Can we talk about this later? You'd better concentrate on your driving,' he said, as she cut in on somebody who hooted.

Talk about it?

What was there to talk about? He'd made his feelings perfectly clear.

Recklessly, she overtook another car on a bend, heard him draw his breath sharply as she just managed to scramble back before an oncoming lorry bore down on them.

'Sorry,' she muttered, feeling her nerves jangle. All right. Calm down and think.

But . . . if he thought he could win her round on this, sweet-talk her and dare to try to make love to her this evening, now that he wasn't quite so knackered, he could think again.

CHAPTER TEN

'Emily . . . we shall have to re-think the theme, darling. Uncle George is due to have a triple by-pass on Thursday and as Auntie Grace has also been diagnosed with angina, it seems just the teeniest bit insensitive to have a heart theme, don't you think? Or am I being too sensitive? Your father won't be drawn either way. It's such a nuisance when I was getting on so well with it. Mum here, by the way.

'Let me know if you have any sensible ideas.

'Bye.'

It was sheer chance that Daniel happened to be in his mother's house when Emily arrived for her appointment. He was installed in the shabby cottage at the Centre now and, although the state of it should not bother him unduly, he found, curiously, that it did and had set about decorating throughout in a simple fashion that pleased him. It was deceptive in size, Tardis-like, with a couple of extra bedrooms doing nothing, which would be a useful over-flow if they ran out of rooms for guests in the main building.

He was taking his belongings there in dribs and drabs, having acquired a huge number of books and CDs over the years that he couldn't bear to part with. His mother was threatening to take the lot to Oxfam if he didn't move them soon, so when she suggested he pop round on Wednesday to pick them up, he had rearranged his diary to cope with it. They were in the thick of a kids' adventure week, nine- to eleven-year olds, but their staff were well in tune with that and he was on top of organizing a weekend for tired executives although, having taken charge of the kids on their climbing course, he was pretty tired himself. It wasn't so much the climbing, which was of necessity gentle but the responsibility of looking after the more anxious children and trying to coax the shy ones to join in. Insurance was sky high and they had to make damned sure the kids got back in one piece. The compensation culture being what it was, they daren't return a child with so much as a bandaged finger, let alone a broken bone. It meant, regrettably, that they had had to do some careful reorganizing of some of the activities, taking out as many elements of risk as they could, which was a pity for surely that's what life was all about, but they had to comply with regulations or be shut down, for that was the way of the world just now.

He was thinking of writing an article about it, about the dangers of wrapping children in cotton wool, of depriving them of some risk. Risk, in a carefully controlled environment such as theirs, was not only necessary but hugely beneficial.

It was funny having the house to himself, but at least it meant there were no distractions. He retrieved his books from his old room and put them in a box, carrying them down to the car. As he slammed the boot shut on them, he heard a car approaching, turning to watch as it made a steady progress down the drive towards him. It was a chill morning with a cool north wind, the thick clouds scudding darkly across the sky. Used as he was to watching the weather closely when he was up a mountain, he knew they would have rain, a good relieved sky-full, before the day was out.

'Hello, there,' he said, when Emily stepped out of her car. 'Lovely to see you again. Day off?'

She nodded. 'I worked Saturday as a favour,' she told him. 'Is your mother about?'

'I've no idea where she is. She tends to take herself off on a whim,' he said. 'I've no doubt she'll be back in time, she's never late for her appointments, but would you like to come inside and I'll make us a coffee?'

'Thanks.'

He showed her into the kitchen and set about making coffee, chatting about this and that, trying to put her at ease. She seemed abnormally tense, casually clad today in tight jeans that showed off her nice bum and a fluffy pale blue sweater, her hair bunched up somehow and held together with a colourful scarf. He liked women with their hair like that, liked it even better when they allowed him to let it all loose. He liked her hair. He liked the colour and the texture, not that he had yet had the opportunity to touch it. It just looked good. She didn't look as if she messed about with it too much, unlike Amanda who had been fearsome if he ruffled it in any way.

'How are things going?' he asked, tense himself now as he handed her the cup. 'Are you and your fiancé still on speaking terms?'

'What do you mean?' she snapped, eyes suddenly glittering. 'Of course we are.'

'Sorry. I didn't mean to be personal. I just know how stressful this all is. I've seen one or two of mother's brides in tears before the big day arrives. That's all I meant.'

She shrugged, pushing at her fringe. 'If you must know, it's not really the wedding preparations that are the problem, it's finding a place to live once we are married. We rent an apartment in Plymouth just now, you see, and we want to buy something in the country. We've been on the look-out for ages. The estate agents are beginning to sound desperate when I ring them. The thing is, I've seen this gorgeous cottage that I really love but Simon's not keen. He's being terribly practical and I know he's right. It's going to cost thousands to put right, and it's usually me who thinks about money so I suppose I'm letting my heart rule my head. I love it, you see, and I can see us living there.'

'Hmm.' He stirred his coffee. He wasn't too good at this sort of thing and he wondered quite why she had told him. He hadn't meant to pry, he had just been making polite conversation that's all and now, as she looked at him, pleading for help and encouragement, he suddenly felt involved. 'I wouldn't really know never having bought a property with somebody else but I suppose you both have to like it. I know both my parents were dead keen when they moved here. Mother's fed up with it now but I think they'll carry Dad out feet first. He won't move. He's much more attached to the old place than she is. Funny that, don't you think? I would imagine it's usually the other way round.'

'Me, too.' She sipped her coffee. 'Are you moving out?' she asked. 'I saw you shifting boxes.'

'I've moved into a cottage at the Centre where I work,' he told her. 'It's been neglected for years and it's grim,' he added, thinking of the cleaning out he had done.

'Centre?'

'Sorry. That's The Harvey Head Adventure Centre a few miles down the road. We do courses for both children and adults. Team building stuff for them . . .' He grinned as she grimaced. 'I know. People are scared by the idea but it's very informative, tells you a lot about the way people's minds work. The people who shine, come through, are sometimes the ones you would least expect. We scratch the surface most of the time,' he went on, getting into his stride, recognizing she was genuinely interested. 'I've found you have to be in an extreme situation with somebody before you really get to know what makes them tick. Danger brings out the best or the worst in people. The trouble is it really brings it home to some people, finding out what makes them tick and sometimes not liking it.'

'Where have you climbed?'

'Where?' He smiled. 'Most places. All over the world. Wherever there's a mountain to be climbed in fact. I wouldn't

113

bore you with it all.'

'You wouldn't bore me. Have you anything planned at the moment?'

'Not just now. In fact I've just declined a climb over in Austria. I was tempted but I don't have the time. I need to stick to the Centre for a while, get some of my ideas up and running there. But next year . . . who knows? I get itchy feet and I'm jealous as hell when my friends are out there and I'm not with them.'

'Simon, my fiancé, is a photographer. Wherever there's trouble in the world, he's there. One of his pictures recently made it into all the main papers. He sold it overseas, too.'

'That sounds interesting. I'm a terrible photographer. Always cutting people's heads off, that sort of thing,' he said, doing his best to lighten things up, trying to make her smile her lovely smile.

But it didn't work.

She sighed, refusing the offer of another cup of coffee. 'I wish he'd give it up, but he won't. Not yet anyway. But I worry about him when he's away. I worry he's not going to come back one day.'

He nodded, understanding. He'd had to tell the wife of one of his best mates that he hadn't made it and he would never forget doing that. She was a climbing wife and she understood what he was there to say even before he said it, but it was still tough. It was starting to come home to him that maybe some day he would have to make a choice. It wasn't fair to put a woman through what this woman was obviously going through. What a dilemma though, when climbing was your life and how the hell do you solve it?

'That sounds like my mother,' he said with some relief, hearing the car arriving. 'We'll go to meet her.'

'Thanks for the coffee. Look, Daniel . . .' she hesitated, 'would you do me a really big favour?'

'If I can.' He smiled, watching as she fiddled with a bit of her hair that had come loose, finding he quite wanted to fix it for her. 'Go on then,' he prompted. 'Don't keep me in suspense.'

'We're giving a dinner party next Friday evening,' she said quickly, as outside a car door slammed. 'There'll be me and Simon and a couple called Brian and Belinda. And we've invited my colleague, Geraldine. She's lovely. She's a fine-art specialist. Would you like to come along?'

'And be the lovely Geraldine's blind date?' he asked, feigning horror. 'Oh, I don't know about that.'

'Sorry, I shouldn't have asked,' she said, the faintest of blushes on her cheeks. 'I can't think why I did. It's quite all right if you're too busy. I understand.'

'No, you don't. I'm only teasing. Of course I'll come,' he said as his mother heaved against the front door. 'Give me directions how to get there and I'll see you then.'

'That damned door.' Corinne exploded into the hall, carrying bags of shopping, smiling as she saw Emily. 'Hello there. I saw your car outside. Were you very early?'

'A little. Daniel made me a coffee.'

'Good.' She threw her jacket onto a chair where it stayed a moment before slithering off onto the floor. 'Hang that up, Daniel,' she instructed, turning her back on him as she led Emily through to the workroom.

CHAPTER ELEVEN

'Emily . . . this is me, your mother, leaving a message. I've had Yvonne on the phone. What a chatterer! I couldn't get a word in. The point is, you can't let Yvonne dictate what she's going to be wearing. She's on about a purple dress, says she can't get a straight answer from you. You really will have to come over and have a discussion with both Yvonne and Stella. The news is not good about Stella but Aunt Louise thinks she'll be fine by the wedding. But I think we ought to start thinking about a replacement just in case. What do you think? I'll speak to you later, darling.

'Bye.'

'Do you want me to pop round early and give you a hand?' Geraldine offered, seeing Emily staggering back from lunch with some supermarket carrier bags.

'No, it's all under control,' she said, knowing she would probably regret turning down the offer. She was leaving early this afternoon, courtesy of a very amiable Clive, and she had to clean the apartment thoroughly, as well as get the food prepared for the dinner party. After that, she had of course to find a few minutes to do her hair and make-up and get herself kitted out in something smart and sexy. She could cook, she told herself, but she needed time, and time, having fussed and fiddled endlessly with the menu, was something she was spectacularly short of.

Simon was no help and, in fact, she preferred him to be out of the way whilst she got things ready. The apartment had never felt like home, a stop-gap that had gone on for longer than they had intended. It was classy and a good address, but totally lacking heart.

When she got back, she realized she had forgotten the flowers. It meant a hasty trip into town, another scooting round looking for a parking space near the florists, followed by indecisive minutes she could not spare before she was back with the flowers that she didn't then have time to fuss with. So, it was bung into vase time and hope for the best.

It was not a good start and she wondered if she had time for a long scented soak in the bath. On second thoughts, the way she felt she might well drift off completely and there was far too much to do. First of all, she had to employ herself briefly as a quick and efficient cleaner. It was clean for they were fairly tidy souls, but not quite clean enough for guests and certainly not clean enough for the pristine Geraldine, whose floor she was sure you could eat off. With the bathrooms shining eventually to an inch of their lives, fully aware she would have to whip around once more after Simon had had his shower, she concentrated at last on the food.

By the time that was organised, Simon was due back and she had time for herself. A bit of much-needed pampering.

'You look harassed,' Simon said, wandering in with a couple of bottles of wine. His contribution to the event.

'I am. Go and have your shower now, then I can clean up after you,' she said, hating herself for saying it but knowing it would be quicker by half that way. 'What are you wearing?'

'Casual,' he said. 'What else?'

'Well I'm dressing up,' she said tartly, pointing to the little black dress hanging there. 'I forgot to say anything to Daniel.'

'Does it matter? He can come dressed as Santa Claus as far as

I'm concerned. I can't think why you invited him? We don't know him. I like to be amongst old friends when I'm dining.'

'I invited him for Geraldine,' she said, tired of saying it. 'You know this is for her. She's having no luck finding a man.'

He laughed. 'Tough. I never realized you fancied yourself as a matchmaker.'

Slipping into the dress, she just knew that tonight was going to be a complete disaster. The casserole was missing a vital ingredient which might or might not make all the difference and she still had all the last-minute stuff to do. Emerging from the folds of the dress, she saw that she was flushed already.

But more worryingly, and the thing she was reluctant to admit even to herself, was that, for the entire day, from waking up this morning, she had been thinking constantly of Daniel.

Not Simon.

But Daniel.

Daniel found the apartment without any trouble, sliding his old estate car between two upmarket models, taking the trouble to lock it, although frankly anybody was welcome to it. It had done ninety-six thousand miles in its lifetime and he would have to think of changing it someday, but on the plus side, it had loads of space and he needed that for all his gear when he went off for the weekend on practice climbs.

Once in the building, having buzzed their number and been told by a male voice to come right up, he took a silent lift up to the fourth floor, stepping out onto a deep carpet. There was the smell of fresh paint, maybe the corridors had recently been done in a toning Wedgwood blue colour, and definitely no graffiti, rather some modern bold prints. Holding the bottle of Australian red wine he had brought along, wishing now he'd pushed the boat out and gone for a more expensive variety, he headed for the end of the corridor and their door.

Handing over the bottle, seeing the look on Simon's face as he glanced at the label, Daniel took an instant, unforgivable dislike to him. It was because, despite uncharacteristic dithering about what the hell to wear tonight, he had apparently blown it.

Big mistake.

And Simon's quick glance, a smirk no less, had silently underlined that. Daniel had opted for his good suit and a decent shirt, even wearing the gold cuff-links in the shape of a D somebody had bought him last Christmas. Frankly, he didn't possess much of a wardrobe, not having the need for it and he couldn't think why this party this evening had assumed such an importance to him.

Yes, he could. It was Emily, of course, the delicious Emily. Forget the lovely Geraldine for whom he was officially here, it was Emily he really wanted to impress and God knows why, because she was going to be married to this cool-eyed guy called Simon, whom he didn't trust from the moment he set eyes on him. This guy called Simon who had called him Dan from the word go and had taken no notice of his quiet insistence that it was Daniel. This guy called Simon who was looking – wouldn't you just know it? – unbelievably casual in jeans and a polo shirt with a designer logo.

You had to make quick judgements in climbing, because sometimes your life might depend on them and he carried that over to his private life. It was an instantaneous thing and he was seldom wrong. For some reason, a sharp memory surfaced, a memory of one of the times he had been truly scared stiff when he had to put all his trust in the guy he was roped to. He had been aware of his heart beating, his breath painful, when one false move or rather one inadequate ice-screw could have sent them tumbling hundreds of feet to their deaths. They had abandoned that climb that time but then, the next day with both their egos deflated, they had tried again and succeeded.

He knew one thing. He was glad it hadn't been Simon he'd had to rely on that day.

He noticed some of Simon's harrowing photographs on display, prominently positioned on the lounge wall, hardly the sort of image you might like to stare at night after night.

A talking point, he assumed, but he certainly didn't want to talk about them and he wondered why they were there. A picture of somebody spilling their guts out in a street was not something he would have on *his* wall.

Oh God, this promised to be an evening to forget, particularly when he was introduced to Geraldine, knowing at once that she was as much attracted to him as he was to her. There was about as much spark as two sticks over a damp wood-fire could produce, but catching Emily's little look of hopeful inquiry, he managed what he hoped was an interested smile.

'Emily tells me your mother is making her wedding dress,' Geraldine began, making room for him beside her on the sofa as Emily plied him with an aperitif. 'That's how you met apparently.'

'We did.'

He noticed her hands toying with some delicate nibbles, elegant, very pale hands with silvery fingernails, a ring on most of her fingers, plus a jingly bracelet on her thin wrist. Added to that, silver earrings *and* a silver choker and she was definitely labelled as a woman who was frequently ambushed in the costume jewellery section.

'And Emily also tells me you run an Adventure Centre for professionals. I hope to goodness we never get sent there,' she went on, her light laugh directed at everybody except him. 'I shall refuse to go. I believe those sort of courses are downright evil. You might know they started in the States. They are designed purely to humiliate the people who are not into that sort of thing. Isn't that so?'

'Oh, come on,' he said, taking a few peanuts out of a little glass dish and wondering if she was after an argument straight off. 'You've got it all wrong. We don't force anybody to do anything they don't want. I don't know where that idea came from. You never know, you might enjoy it.'

'Absolutely not,' she said with a shudder. 'I hate everything to do with sports of any kind. I really can't understand people's obsession with it. And what on earth it has to do with business skills completely baffles me.'

'They call it team-building,' Simon broke in, overhearing them. 'Isn't that so, Dan? What it really is of course is a means of scaring the shit out of good managers and bringing about all sorts of doubts. Fear of failure and all that. And when you consider that companies take the results seriously and it counts towards your next salary appraisal then I'm with Geraldine on this one. Sorry, Dan, but there it is. All I can say is thank God I'm freelance.'

Daniel smiled slightly, seeing he was out-numbered. He could explain at length just what was entailed, how bloody good it was for the individual, how it helped people to re-assess *themselves*, how very often the plus points outweighed the minuses, how sometimes it provided people with a completely new and refreshing outlook on life and business, how it made managers look at underlings in a new light. He could argue all these and more but, looking at Simon's smug face, he wouldn't give him the satisfaction of knowing he was riled.

They were saved by the bell, by the noisy arrival of the remaining guests and for a while there was much activity as they were introduced and settled down. Emily appeared now and again but was noticeably absent, mostly in the kitchen. When at last she did reappear, she was flushed, brandishing a ladle, looking ravishing in a black wraparound dress, a tiny blob of cream on her lips about which nobody offered a comment.

'Oh good, you're getting to know each other,' she said with a smile, seeming to miss the distinctly chill atmosphere that even giggly Belinda, the other female guest, had failed to warm. 'It's all ready, so, if you'd like to sit down . . .'

Emily had produced an excellent meal although she looked harassed as she sat down with them. She explained at length, as if they didn't know already, how she came to know him, via his mother who was making her heavenly wedding dress.

'I never met you when I was there,' Belinda told him, stating the obvious. 'But I have to say, Daniel, your mother is quite a woman. When she suggested peach and ivory taffeta I told her no way. I wanted cream. But then, when she showed me the material . . .' She rolled her eyes theatrically. 'Well, I just died. It was perfect. Just that important bit different. Wasn't it, darling?'

'Perfect,' her man agreed with a grin.

'So, how come I didn't meet you, Daniel, when I was being fitted?' Belinda went on. 'I would certainly have remembered you,' she added with a sidelong, mischievous glance at her husband.

'I was away,' he said briefly, ignoring what he supposed was a compliment. 'On a trip.'

'Up a mountain I expect,' Simon said, sharing a smile with Geraldine. 'Tell us about it, Dan.'

He didn't want to talk about it. It had been a bad trip. The team leader had made what was in hindsight a crap decision and they'd gone ahead on near vertical loose ice, taking a chance on the screws holding and they'd lost a guy as a result, a good friend. Whatever their personal feelings on the leader's decision, they stood by him. It had brought it all back of course. Joe. Joe hadn't fallen nearly as far as Martin, but the end result was the same. They'd tossed a coin at the end of it and he'd been the one who had had to break the news to Martin's pretty, pregnant wife. She'd just stood there, dry-eyed, nodding as if she had been expecting it. It had been bloody awful.

'No shop talk,' Emily said, giving him a quick understanding glance. 'Strictly forbidden. Is this OK?' she went on, pointing to the food. 'Not too spicy?'

There were general murmurs of approval and she subsided

122

gently back into her chair, looking across at him and smiling. 'Daniel's a good cook. He can make scones.'

'Scones? Good lord!' The lovely Geraldine said, cool in mint-green. She was like a preying mantis, all angles, Daniel thought, and would look a lot better with a bit of weight on her.

Belinda was four months pregnant and inclined to talk non-stop about it. Daniel caught Emily's eye at one point, shared a moment's amusement with her, as she valiantly tried to stem the baby-talk. What on earth would Belinda be like when the baby actually arrived? They had been subjected already to a picture of the first scan, a blob with a distinct resemblance to ET, over which they all made encouraging noises, even though he suspected he had looked at it upside down or back to front or something.

Simon was an attentive host, having a few words to say about each bottle of wine he produced. That figured, a guy like him had to be an authority on wine. They sat in this trendy apartment with its curious mix of styles and made polite conversation, all of them knowing that the little attempt to palm him and Geraldine off together had failed dismally, the lady herself at pains to point out the obvious.

With a little laugh, she produced a list from her handbag of the criteria her man must match and, as she calmly recited them out to great guffaws from Simon and the others, it quickly emerged that he couldn't tick any of the required boxes. It was pretty obvious, too, so perhaps it was meant as a put down or maybe he was being too sensitive. But, with the exception of Emily and Belinda, whom he liked despite the giggles and baby obsession, these were not his sort of people.

Belinda's cheerful chat saved the day, but it was hard to find time for a private moment with Emily, who spent the entire evening fluttering from kitchen to table and back again. When she was at the table, she seemed nervous, spending a lot of time tucking her hair behind her left ear, a little gesture he was beginning to recognize and love. Unlike Geraldine, she seemed content with just one item of jewellery, her very flashy engagement ring. Seeing it sparkling on her finger, seeing the looks she occasionally cast at the lucky guy, he felt a deep jealousy that was close to physical pain.

Making his apologies at last for breaking up the party, he left. Emily escorted him out ostensibly acting the polite hostess but he suspected she really wanted a quick word.

And so it proved.

'Sorry. . .' she muttered, out of earshot in the hall but lowering her voice just the same. 'Bit of a shambles that. I can't think why Geraldine's been so bitchy.'

'She wasn't bitchy, just honest,' he said, although he supposed she had hit it on the head. 'But I don't think we'll be seeing each other again.'

'No. Well, then . . .' she paused, doing that hair thing and drawing sudden sharp attention yet again to that whopping diamond on her finger. 'Thanks for coming along, anyway. Sorry it was such a long drive for nothing.'

'Hey, stop saying sorry,' he said, drawing closer, so that she was momentarily pinned against one of Simon's treasured pieces of furniture, a delicate desk. 'Forget Geraldine, I enjoyed it. The food was great.'

She pulled a face and he felt his heart give a great tumble. Her make-up was a little shiny by now, eyes shining, too, as she dared finally to gaze at him. And that gaze told him everything he wanted to know.

'Emily . . .' he found it difficult to say what he wanted to say in about ten seconds flat. 'I . . .'

'I know,' she said quickly. 'Bit of a silly situation, isn't it?'

Although the urge to hold her was immense, her nervousness made him draw back at once and, after a brief goodbye kiss on the cheek, he made his escape.

Driving back, completely sober because he had barely touched the wine, he found he was as down as he had been for some time. After the failure of his last relationship, he had told himself to give himself a proper breather before embarking on another but recently the fond memories of Amanda and what might have been were fading as Emily Bellew – what a wonderful name! – exploded into his life.

Even before the little moment in the hall as they said goodbye, the funny feeling had persisted all evening that she was also attracted to him, or was he just being daftly optimistic? He had no qualms about booting Simon into touch if it came to it, wedding or no wedding, and indeed hadn't his mother said she thought it would never happen?

What the hell did a bright, thoughtful girl like Emily see in Simon who, from what he said, wouldn't let anything or anyone get in the way of a good photo shoot? He had, during the pause between the main course and dessert seen fit to pass around some recent photographs that Daniel had found not only offensive but insensitive, with poor Belinda going quiet and paling as she looked at them. They had for a moment talked earnestly about the state of the world and the plight of some unfortunate people, but it wasn't the sort of stuff to bring out at a dinner party and they certainly didn't need that before they started on the meringues.

He had caught the glint in Simon's eyes and, although he certainly recognized the professionalism, he did wonder where the compassion was? Emily hung onto his every word but once, with Simon absorbed in chatting with Geraldine, their eyes had briefly locked and he saw the momentary sadness and confusion there. She was fighting hard to deny what she felt, because her life was neatly mapped out, and changing course now, would lead to a lot of heartache all round.

Should he say something, do something? He should maybe have given into his feelings at the last and kissed her properly, given her something to think about, told her also to stop the hell worrying about it all. If all she was worrying about was hurting

Simon's feelings, well, tough on him. He would survive.

Was he being a complete and utter arse for even thinking these things? He ought to stay well away from her, but he just knew he would be finding out when she was next due over and somehow or other make some excuse to be there yet again.

Oh, hell.

Complications.

Didn't he have enough of those already?

'That went well,' Simon said when their guests were finally gone. 'Although I don't think Geraldine hit it off with Dan. You should leave well alone, let her find her own man.'

'I know. It was a mistake,' she agreed, remembering Geraldine's wry smile as she said goodbye. 'I thought opposites might attract. Maybe not. I don't think he was that impressed, either. And I could have died when she pulled out her little list. I mean, does she carry it around all the time? Was that meant to be a joke?'

'I'm not sure. It's hard to tell with her. She seemed very uptight. What's she like at work?'

'Fine. Good at the job. She has a terrific eye according to Clive, and what she doesn't know about art isn't worth knowing.'

'I know that. She left me behind when she took me off to that gallery in town.'

That made Emily glance towards the five-hundred pound print on the wall that he had been persuaded to buy. 'She's just a bit intense just now. I think she's making too much of it, this looking for a husband. I mean, how hard can it be? She's pretty, isn't she?'

'I suppose she is for some blokes but she's not my cup of tea,' he said. 'Too tall, too thin and too blonde. I like my ladies little, dark and worried-looking.'

'Am I worried-looking?' she asked with a little smile.

'All the time, darling. And it's got worse recently. You look like you carry all the worries of the world on those sweet little shoulders.'

'Do I?' He followed her into the kitchen as she started on the task of loading the dishwasher. So he had noticed then. At last.

'He's a funny guy, that Dan bloke,' Simon said. 'I can't think why you asked him. Didn't have much to say, did he? And the suit! You should have mentioned the dress code, darling.'

'There isn't one. I thought he looked nice,' she said. 'Sometimes it's good to dress up properly.'

'Don't start on that. I am not going to start wearing a suit in my own home, Dan or no Dan.'

'His name's Daniel and perhaps he didn't get the chance to say much,' she said, watching as he placed glasses on the tray. 'Careful with those,' she warned, 'they're crystal. I'll wash those separately.'

'What do you mean, he didn't get the chance?' Simon asked, coming over and nuzzling her shoulder. 'You smell gorgeous,' he murmured, lifting her hair and trailing little kisses along her neck before cupping his hands around her breasts. 'How about we leave all this and go to bed?'

She shrugged him off, feeling herself surprisingly unmoved. Normally, she might not have noticed how he monopolized the conversation when they had guests, normally she might have been pleased that he took over so ably when Belinda threatened to swamp them with all the horror stories about the start of her pregnancy. Thank heavens she hadn't mentioned Angharad and the chart. She had asked her not to, but Belinda was so preoccupied with her coming child that she had an awful memory these days.

'You didn't give Daniel a chance to speak,' she went on, aware she was treading into dangerous waters. 'And everybody was very negative about what he does at his Adventure Centre. We didn't get to hear his point of view. It might have been interesting to hear what he had to say.'

127

'He could have spoken if he had wanted to,' he said, moving away suddenly, eyes icing over. 'Bloody hell, what is it with this guy? Why do you feel you have to defend him all the time? And why did you ask him to come to dinner? You don't know him any more than I do. If you'd asked me first, I'd have told you he wouldn't wash with Geraldine.'

'You don't know Geraldine.'

'And neither do you if you think a woman like her would be interested in a man like him.'

'Oh. So, suddenly, you're an authority on relationships?'

'No, but I think I know Geraldine a bit. She doesn't go for that sort of guy. Our Geraldine is clever and no fool. She goes for a bit of sophistication. And success. She doesn't back a loser. Surely you know that?'

'Are you saying he's a loser?'

'Too true I am. Mountaineering? What sort of career is that? Anybody can climb a mountain, darling. It's all done with equipment nowadays. I'm told that even climbing Everest is child's play. The ropes are already in place and all you have to do is climb the stairs and take a whiff of oxygen from time to time.'

She laughed, but it was forced. 'You do it then,' she said. 'I don't think it's quite as easy as that.'

Washing up forgotten, they had wandered by now into the bedroom where the lamps were lit, sending out a warm pink glow, the curtains already drawn. Their large comfortable bed beckoned. It was very late, more than time for bed, and she was exhausted by the effort preparing and serving tonight's meal had taken out of her. Thank goodness, at least the food had been fine, the vital ingredient not so vital after all, the wine excellent. She sat wearily on a chair, rubbing the stiffness from her neck as Simon undressed, his upper body bronzed and taut, certainly attractive enough to warrant a few envious glances on the beach.

By the time he was down to his boxer shorts, she was still fully clad, although she had kicked off her heels as soon as they were alone. She knew from Simon's manner that he expected this little current flare-up to be over in a flash, that by the time he got her into bed the row might even have excited the both of them enough for it to be one of their more memorable lovemakings.

But this time she was far more on edge than she had been for some time, and she knew why. She was trying to close her mind to it, but she was having these daft thoughts about Daniel and this evening there had been more than enough meaningful looks for her to have no doubt of *his* feelings. For two pins, she could have made an excuse halfway through dinner, lured him into the kitchen and let him kiss her as she knew he was dying to do. And then, in the hall, he had backed her into a corner and a first kiss had been a mere whisper away.

Simon was right. She knew nothing about him, but then she did not know much about Simon either, and she had not let that be a reason for not falling in love with him. She had loved him. Once. But, did she now?

'Hey . . . come here,' he said, voice low, sitting on the edge of the bed. 'You shouldn't bother with entertaining, darling, if it gets to you like this. We're not alone often enough these days so we should make the most of it while we can.'

His tone was warm and sexy and, looking over at him, she remembered the good times, the times when they laughed and loved each other, and wondered where they had gone. More importantly, would she be able to lift herself out of this depression and stop being so critical of him all the time?

'It's just . . .' she felt the tears welling up, told herself it was only because she was exhausted. 'I'm not sure any more. About all this. About us. About our getting married.'

He came across and took her in his arms, where she rested her head on his shoulder, calming down as he stroked her hair gently. What a fool she was. Of course she loved him. It was just a case of extreme wedding nerves that was all.

The phone rang just as he was unzipping her dress and, for a minute, it seemed they might let it ring. But a phone call at this time was so unusual that of course neither of them could do that, so Emily pushed him gently away and said she would get it, pulling her zip up as she went to answer it.

'Oh hello . . .' It was a woman's voice, a voice she did not recognize. 'Is that Emily?'

'Yes,' she said, feeling her heart thud and immediately fearing the worst. Her mother or father maybe or somebody really close. Remembering that astrology chart and its little note of doom, she sat down quickly in case her knees buckled when she received the news. If it was her mother, she would go completely to pieces. Her mother might be trying her best to be the mother from hell just at the moment but she loved her to bits. 'What is it? What's wrong?' she asked.

'Nothing's wrong,' the woman said quickly. 'And I'm sorry to ring so late but I'm so excited to find him at last that I couldn't wait until tomorrow. Is he there? Simon?'

She caught his eye, shaking her head in puzzlement.

'Yes. He's here,' she said. 'Who's this?'

'I'm Heather. His mother. Tell him it's his mother.'

CHAPTER TWELVE

'Emily . . . it's your mother ringing at 6.35, Tuesday. I know you said you didn't mind but I can tell what you're thinking so you'll be pleased to know I shan't be having the white suit after all. I might still buy it but I won't wear it for the wedding. As for you not having a list, I'm not sure what I think about that. Whose idea was that? Asking for cash seems so cheap. I've looked it up in the *Debrett's Etiquette Guide* for 1965 and it states categorically that it is a non-starter. However, having said that, with couples living together before they get married these days then it is apparently acceptable in the modern world. So, I'll pass the word round even though it pains me to do it. Speak to you soon.

'Bye.'

She and Emily had reached a decision about the dress, bearing in mind that it was a winter wedding, opting for a cream silk dress with a strapless boned bodice – Emily having a lovely shape – and a figure-hugging slim skirt. With it there would be a short, sharply designed cream jacket edged with colour, as yet undecided, to take care of the winter chill. Corinne found herself thinking about Emily quite a lot, wondering why she was becoming so fond of a girl she scarcely knew.

It was a little worrying although hardly surprising to Corinne, that Daniel seemed to have become involved with Emily, albeit acting as a blind date for a friend of hers. She gathered it had been a disaster, his silence on the subject when she next saw him the proof of that. She and Bernard did not see so much of him now that he was living over at the Centre and this morning she was taking the opportunity of a break in sewing to clear out his room in the hope that he would not be coming back.

It was hard living in this house.

There were too many memories of Joe.

Maybe that was the reason she wanted to move away from here, so that she could escape them, and yet how could she ever escape them? Moving away would make no difference as Bernard had always patiently told her. Staying was the best way of facing up to it, meeting the truth head-on, the truth being that Joe was gone. Joe was dead and it was high time she came to terms with that. They, or rather Bernard, had seen his body, although she had never questioned him about that, couldn't bear to be told that his face was smashed, preferring to think of him as unspoilt and sleeping.

She interrupted the morning's cleaning as she knew she would, taking his things out of the loft and just touching them, looking at them, vision cloudy from her tears. It still got to her. After all this time, it still got to her. Lifting things out of boxes, she knew it was time now to get rid of them. She had just stuffed things in any old how shortly after he died, unable to bear having anything of his on show. Masses of schoolbooks and revision books that she really ought to have disposed of at once. Stacking them up in piles, she came across a diary, a five-year diary somebody had given him for Christmas that year. Joe had never been the sort to keep a diary and she half-expected it to be empty as she flipped through.

To her surprise, he had written rather a lot that year, the year he died. There was his writing starting off very tidy, as you do in a brand new diary, but quickly resorting to its usual hard-to-read scrawl. Neatness mattered and she had told him that over and over. When they had heaps of papers to mark, an examiner could very quickly lose heart if they were faced with yet another hopelessly difficult-to-decipher essay. She needed to remind him about it because, unlike Stephen and Daniel, he was not academically gifted and would have to work very hard to achieve success.

And he had. To please her, he had pulled out all the stops and got the required grades and got the place he wanted on the course he wanted. The one she had helped him choose.

Starting to read, she paused, unwilling to go on. It was too painful and also, even though Joe was dead, it felt wrong to pry, to find out what her teenage son was thinking. But she couldn't possibly throw this out in case somebody else read it.

Darling Joe. Joe had not only looked like her, he had thought like her, too. He was going to succeed at doing all the things she had meant to do. He was going to do it for her. But, unlike her, he had always craved the outdoors, too; had that same glint in his eye as his brother when they talked about the stupid mountains.

And so, much against her better judgement, she had entrusted him to Daniel and Daniel should have looked after him. Wasn't he the big brother and wasn't that what big brothers did? Big brothers did not let little brothers slip over edges and fall to their death.

Downstairs, she heard the door slam and Daniel's footsteps and voice calling her.

'I'm up here,' she said, slipping the diary into the pocket of her cardigan, hearing him coming up followed by Bingo. 'Just tidying up,' she told him guiltily as he came in before she had time to clear Joe's things. 'I've been in the loft.'

'So I see,' he said easily. 'Want me to put it all back for you?'

'Yes. Just for the moment.' She stood aside as he collected it together silently. 'Don't tell me. I know I should throw it out,' she told him at last when he had finished. 'And I will. Soon. He would have been twenty-five you know. Next week. Next

Wednesday. He would have been married by now I'm sure.'

'I know.' Daniel tried a smile, hearing the gibe about being married. 'Hard to believe it's so long ago, isn't it?'

'It's not,' she said shortly. 'It's yesterday for me, Daniel.'

For a moment, standing there, he reminded her of the child he had once been, the one in the middle, the odd one, the one who had never quite gripped her in the way of the others. Stephen, her first born, was so bright, a joy, the delight of the school, faultless, no trouble, sailing effortlessly through life until he met that strange woman of his who dragged him off to Australia. She tried with that, tried to understand, but in the end it all boiled down to Jackie and, whilst she found her brittle, she was Stephen's choice and that was that. Joe was the little one and the love of her life, meaning more to her in some ways than Bernard, and this man standing before her, this man had allowed him to take a fatal tumble. What the hell had he been doing? They should have been roped together or something, although if that had been so, she might have lost both of them.

'I'm sorry, Mum. You shouldn't do this, it just upsets you,' Daniel muttered, turning away from her, dropping down and fussing over Bingo. 'When will Emily be here again?'

'Emily? You mean Miss Bellew? Why?'

'Just wondered,' he said with a shrug. 'She has a nice apartment over in Plymouth.'

'I imagine she would. There's a certain primness about her, don't you think?'

'Prim?' He thought for a moment of the dress she had been wearing at the dinner party, the way it clung to her body. 'I don't think I'd describe her as prim.'

'What's he like?' she asked. 'Her fiancé?'

'OK,' he replied. 'Good photographer.'

'I see. But not the man for her?' she said, catching the tone, aware she had known that all along. 'What did I tell you? What a waste. It's going to be a beautiful gown too. She'll look a dream.'

'She will.'

She looked at him steadily and he tried not to give anything away but suspected she knew anyway. 'She'll be here next week. Tuesday afternoon. She has a few days off, apparently. In fact, I'm toying with the idea of asking her to stay over. Your father's away so I'll be on my own.'

'You're getting a bit friendly with a client, aren't you?' Daniel grinned. 'You don't usually ask them to stay over.'

'No. I know that. But I think I'd like to give her the opportunity to talk to me.' She raised her eyebrows. 'Her mother lives in Kent and she needs somebody to talk to about this. Face to face. Somebody older. Somebody a little more detached. Me in fact.'

'Be careful,' he warned. 'She's going through a bit of a crisis I think. Don't upset her.'

'Difficult as it may be for you to believe,' she told him curtly, 'but I am actually rather a good listener. You'd better keep away,' she added. 'No sense in confusing the issue.'

'What do you mean?'

'Oh come on, Daniel. I'm your mother. Remember? And it's perfectly obvious that you've fallen for her.' She smiled as she caught the sudden defensive look. 'Go on. Admit it.'

He did not answer and she didn't press it, leaving him to look for the last of his precious books and going downstairs to start work on the dress.

The material was beautiful quality, soft and shining, and with carefully washed hands, she touched it, eyes closed, imagining the finished dress as she always did before she began work.

Measurements were made, transferred to her dummy.

The mock-up was ready.

She reached for her scissors.

Daniel preferred to work with children. He knew the adult company-based team-building courses were fast becoming the more important and most lucrative, an American concept the

Brits had latched onto, but he still liked working with kids. With the adults there was always this business of looking over their shoulders, seeing how other people reacted, and for the ones who genuinely hated the outdoors, this was nothing more than a thinly veiled torture.

He tried his best when it was his turn to lead the course to be sympathetic to their anxieties, trying to explain gently that it was – oh what a cliché – for their own good but that didn't stop these people, antagonistic and on edge, from hating him for putting them through it in the first place. Harvey did the marking, the grading, and it didn't bother him so much that he might very well be putting a lot of these people's jobs on the line. Leaders emerged over the week, sometimes unlikely people, and it hurt when work positions were virtually reversed, as they could be.

Sometimes, Daniel found himself secretly doubting the wisdom of all this. The kids' course was for fun, with no bitchiness, no chance of people being emotionally scarred forever by a lack of success. The kids enjoyed it and even those who found it tough generally ended up enjoying it in a fashion. He encouraged these kids like hell, the overweight ones in particular, and it was a joy to see the delight shining in their eyes when they achieved what they had thought was impossible. He never forced them into doing what they did not want but the encouragement usually worked and, if it didn't, if they were left feeling a failure, he would take time out to chat to them, to explain that people were good at different things and that, even though they couldn't face going onto the rope-bridge across the river, some of the others wouldn't be able to do things in later life that they would do.

In the end, it was all about building confidence.

Joe had been over-confident. Joe had been cavalier about safety, too. Joe had ridden his motorcycle without a helmet, of course, tackling the lanes with a careless abandon. It was a miracle he hadn't had an accident on them instead of the mountain, although what happened on the mountain had been no accident.

136

Talking briefly to his mother this morning about Joe had come as a surprise and, for once, there had been a touch of sympathy there for him. For a moment he had thought she might ask him to talk about it, for she never had, but the moment passed and he had brought up the delicate subject of Emily Bellew instead.

Were his feelings so very obvious? His mother was right. He had fallen for her in a big way and was starting to dream about her, so he ought to stay well away next Tuesday when she visited, but he knew he would not. What was the harm in it? He wasn't setting out to destroy her relationship because, to his mind, that was half-cocked already, but he needed to know what she thought about him, he needed to know that he had not misread those signals. To him, it felt like the electricity, that special spark, he and his climbing mates had talked about at dead of night when they were squashed into a box-tent on worryingly powdery snow. It had brought all emotions to the fore, confessions that they all knew would later never be talked of. Desperation talk. When it might very well be your last night on this earth, there was no subject that was taboo.

He had felt that bloody daft jolt the moment he saw her and, yes, he had caught his breath when she first looked his way; had known there and then that this was what they had been talking about. Meeting up with her the other evening had only strengthened what he felt for her and perhaps that was why he was so anti-Simon who, in all fairness, wasn't so bad after all.

Who was he kidding?

He treated Emily in a very off-hand, casual way and why the hell couldn't she see that? And he had caught him looking at Geraldine with more than a touch of interest. He could forget that. The genuine ice-maiden, that one. And, if he was looking at other women now, what did that say for their future happiness?

Oh God. What a mess. He dare not say any of this to Emily because he just knew she would bristle up with indignation, defend her man to the last.

137

Simon Newell was just a complete toad, that's all, but there were plenty of them around, for he had met more than enough of them on the corporate weeks at the Centre.

And toads never turned into princes, not in his book.

CHAPTER THIRTEEN

'Emily . . . it's Dad. Mum said to ring and leave a message if you weren't in and you aren't. She's had to go to your Aunt Louise's. Problem with Stella. She'll call when she gets there. Hope you're all right, princess. Ignore your mother. She gets a bit over-excited sometimes. Why didn't you just elope? Or, failing that, why didn't you just carry on living together? It wouldn't matter to me and it would save me the bother of giving a speech, which your mother is writing for me. Give me a ring if you want when you get in but not after 8 because there's a football match on TV. Oh, and don't worry about the speech, I shall just tear it up and say whatever pops into my head.'

Simon and his mother had arranged to meet on The Hoe the following weekend, which meant a lot of anxious waiting on both their parts before they knew what would happen. Heather contacting him had certainly put the stopper on any attempt at lovemaking that evening, with Simon shocked and tight-faced afterwards. Emily's excited questions once he had put the phone down went unanswered, but she had heard half the conversation and her heart sank at the coolness of his tone. Couldn't he unbend a little? Surely whatever was the matter between him and his mother could be resolved somehow and now she was here to help.

Emily could *hear* him thinking once they got into bed, hear his worried breathing and there was no joy in him whatsoever, no delight at hearing from his mother after all this time. She had expected she and Simon might talk more at breakfast next day but no . . . deliberate or not, he had to rush and, with him constantly clock-watching, it wasn't appropriate to instigate a serious discussion.

It seemed to Emily he still excluded her; he still wouldn't talk about it and that infuriated her because how on earth could she offer advice, give consolation, if she knew damn all about it?

However, she was off to Corinne's on Tuesday and with Simon away for a few days, she had accepted the surprise invitation to stay over. Why not? They would have the chance to talk and she needed to talk to somebody. She had tried talking to her mother on the phone, but the moment did not present itself, as she was in one of her famous huffs. Emily recognized the signs and ended up consoling *her*.

When it came to Simon and *his* mother though, the lines were not at all clear. Out of respect for their first meeting in goodness knows how long, Emily felt she ought not to be present herself. If it went well, and judging by Simon's manner that would be a miracle, then no doubt she would meet Heather in due course.

'You needn't worry, I won't be spying on you,' she told him, sensing his unease. 'I'm going shopping. Give me a call if you like and do for goodness sake invite her over. We won't make a big thing of it. Just a little supper for the three of us. I'd like to get to know her, Simon, and she must come to the wedding.'

There were so many questions to be answered, not least how on earth his mother had found him. And why? What did she want – Simon was of the opinion that she must want something from him.

That had annoyed her. 'Has it not occurred to you that she might just want to see you. She might have heard about you getting married. She must have heard because she knew my name. She asked if I was Emily. How did she know that?'

'It's not difficult. In my profession, I don't go out of my way to hide my name and I need to be available to contacts. So of course people can find out where I am.'

'Did you know where *she* was?'

'I knew where she was living ten years ago,' he said shortly. 'And then she moved. She put her new address on my birthday card once.'

'Which you promptly lost, of course?'

'No I did not lose it but I thought it best to let it go,' he told her, looking towards the spot he was to meet his mother. 'Off you go. I'll call you later when it's over.'

She watched him go, not exactly dragging his feet but very nearly. His whole demeanour certainly suggesting that he was not looking forward to this. She could shake him, but then harbouring grudges had never been one of her vices.

She crossed over to Dingles, wandering aimlessly through the store with her heart not in it, and afterwards, she did the rounds, popping in a café for lunch, grabbing a window table, hoping miraculously to catch a glimpse of this woman who, right or wrong, had so upset Simon. There had to be a good reason and, if there wasn't, then it was all down to him and she didn't want it to be like that.

The dress was tacked and pinned, her mother was ticking off this and that, the wedding ball was rolling and it seemed nothing could stop it. She had not spoken with Daniel Cooper since the disastrous dinner party. Geraldine had a word with her the following Monday telling her in no uncertain terms not to do that to her again.

'Sorry,' she said. 'I just thought you two might hit it off.'

'Why? You should know I don't go for the hunky type and did you ever meet a millionaire who ran an adventure centre and climbed mountains in his spare time?'

'Oh, I see. It's a millionaire you're after now then?' Emily said.

'Not necessarily,' she said with a smile. 'Figure of speech. I wouldn't say no but, whatever he earns, he's got to earn much more than me, probably nothing less than a six-figure sum.'

'Wow. You do set yourself high targets.'

'I'm aware of that. I told you he has to tick my boxes and Daniel Cooper didn't tick any of them. I found him incredibly boring, if you must know.'

'Boring? But he never got the chance to speak. Simon monopolized the conversation. If Daniel could have got a word in, you'd find he was very interesting. He's climbed all over the world.'

'You're quick to defend him,' Geraldine pointed out with a smile. 'Are you trying to make Simon jealous? Daniel obviously thinks you're pretty special. You should have seen his face when he looked at you.'

'That's silly,' she said, nevertheless feeling her heart thud at the unexpected comment. Was it so obvious? She knew herself, of course, had felt, if not seen the glances from him. 'I'm getting married to Simon.'

'Yes, you are,' Geraldine said drily.

She thought about that conversation as she sat in the café waiting for Simon to ring her. She did hope he would ring her and ask her to join them and her biggest hope was that, when she did, they would be all smiling and everything, whatever it was, would be forgotten.

A clean slate. And this time she would make very sure that Heather was not neglected in future.

'Thank you.' She smiled up at the waitress as she placed her meal before her. She had lost a few pounds over the last couple of weeks and Corinne had been quick to notice. It wasn't a problem, she told her for it could be tucked in or tucked up or whatever she might do to take account of it, but the inference was there nonetheless.

Steady as you go.

With that in mind, she ordered a hearty meal, telling herself that it was the worry that was doing it. She wished some days that she had never said yes to him, that they had just toddled along as they were. After all, there were times when she asked herself was she doing this purely to please her mother and, if that was so, then that was very dangerous.

'May I join you?'

She looked up as a middle-aged lady fiddled with the chair opposite, obviously expecting the answer to be in the affirmative.

'Of course.'

Politeness surfaced as Emily made room at the far from large table. It was a popular café and so it was hardly surprising that they were fast running out of tables.

'Sorry,' the woman said, dumping a heap of parcels on the floor. 'I have to sit down before I collapse.'

Emily smiled but hoped this wasn't going to develop into a conversation proper. She didn't mind talking to a stranger, it wasn't that, but it was just today of all days she could scarcely cope with her own feelings, let alone start to share them.

'Where on earth do you park?' the woman asked with a smile. 'Devil of a job, isn't it? And I hate multi-storeys.'

'I live in town so I can just walk in,' Emily told her, sympathising with a return smile.

'Lucky you. I was supposed to be meeting my son,' the woman continued, not picking up on her mood, 'but we've missed each other.'

'Oh.' She looked up, wondering for a minute if this was Heather. She hadn't a clue what Heather looked like although the woman opposite bore absolutely no resemblance to Simon.

'I've rung him and he's meeting me later,' she went on cheerfully. 'Lunch with him is always an effort. He's always in such a tearing hurry and I end up with indigestion. Anyway it gave me time to do a bit of shopping on my own. David's a blessed nuisance trailing round shops.'

Ah! Thank goodness for that. Somehow, knowing this wasn't

Heather after all, and they hadn't been caught up in a potentially embarrassing situation, eased things and she found herself caught up in the woman's chat, wonderful trivial stuff that required no effort.

She was the sort with a first-class honours in continuous conversation. Holidays. Her daughter's awful exam results. David's fabulous job. On and on it went, with the woman scarcely pausing for breath, although that did not stop her from demolishing her quiche and salad.

'Getting married in December? How lovely!' the woman said, after Emily, feeling she was making little contribution to the conversation, made the confession. 'I know it's none of my business, dear, but tell me, are you getting married in church?'

'Yes. Over in Kent. Near my mother's.'

'I'm so glad. I can't get into this business of being able to get married anywhere these days. I read about these divers getting married underwater recently. I ask you, is that completely mad or what? It makes a mockery of the whole business, if you ask me. Getting married in church on the other hand really concentrates your mind.'

'In what way?' Emily pushed her plate aside, having very nearly eaten the lot.

'Whether you're religious or not, it makes you realize what a serious thing you're doing,' the woman said, fingering her own wedding ring as she spoke. 'When you think how many people enter into it completely blind. . . .' She shook her head sadly. 'It doesn't bear thinking about.' She paused, as it occurred to her just what she was saying. 'Oh, sorry, I didn't mean you, dear. I'm sure you'll have thought about it very seriously before you make *your* vows.'

They had dessert and coffee and by the time they had finished they were, if not exactly good friends, comfortable companions at least. They smiled at each other as they parted company, the woman wishing her well in her new life, Emily in turn telling her that the daughter's exam results didn't necessarily mean it was the end of the world, although that was coming from somebody who had sailed through her exams without any problems.

Simon would smile about this when she told him later about meeting this woman and chatting to her, for, although he might be pushy in his job, it didn't spill over into his private life, which he preferred to keep to himself. You'd never, ever catch him engaging in a conversation with a perfect stranger.

Exiting into the street, it was then that she saw them. She could see the back of them, recognizing Simon, of course, at once and then looking at his mother. She was almost the same height, wearing a long mackintosh with a brightly coloured scarf slung about her shoulders but it was difficult to judge anything else from this angle other than she had striking strawberry-blonde hair.

Not quite sure what to do, her mind still on the conversation in the café with the stranger, Emily stood still a moment, causing somebody behind to knock into her with a mutter of 'sorrys' all round.

And then Simon turned and saw her.

There was a moment's hesitation before he put up his hand to acknowledge her and wave her to come forward to meet them. As she neared them, she saw that Simon had his hand on his mother's elbow, a gesture somehow comforting as Heather turned also to smile her way.

'Hi, darling, I was just about to ring you,' Simon said, his smile wary, eyes bright as he introduced them.

Heather was like her son, he was like her, whatever, but she had eyes too large for her face, a face that seemed to be caving in on itself and now she was closer, Emily saw that the mackintosh swamped her, draped over a painfully thin body. As they shook hands, the frailness of the touch transmitted at once, no strength at all in it, so apparent that Emily very nearly recoiled.

She knew just looking at her that there was something seriously wrong.

She knew this woman was dying.

She didn't need Simon to tell her.

CHAPTER FOURTEEN

'Emily . . . Mum. What a time we've had! Stella is stable, you'll be glad to know, and the crisis is over. She is determined to be fit for the wedding and your Aunt Louise is feeding her up with rice pudding and porridge. She's gained four pounds in a fortnight so it can't be bad. The unfortunate thing is I've also gained four pounds which is perfectly ridiculous. Now, about my hair, do you think I should go a shade darker, darling? Deep chestnut? I've asked your dad's opinion but he has no idea. If you'll think it would be a mistake, do say. I shan't be the least offended. After all, it's your day and not mine.

'I'll try again in an hour's time.

'Bye.'

'Talk to her,' Simon hissed at her as they strived for a moment's privacy in the kitchen. Heather was in the lounge resting with her feet propped up, looking as if the short journey here had taken its toll. 'I don't know what to say.'

'Well, neither do I,' Emily whispered, horror struck at the way things had turned out. 'What am I supposed to say? And why on earth didn't you warn me she was so ill?'

'Because I didn't know,' he said, which seemed on reflection to be a good answer. 'It came as a blow to me, too.'

'Sorry.' She pushed at her hair, tucking it behind her ears,

147

giving herself time to think. 'I must have looked so shocked when I saw her and I didn't have time to hide it. If I'd known, I would have been more prepared.'

'So that you could lie more easily? She's not the sort who wants people to pretend. She's straight, if nothing else. Always has been,' he added with a shake of his head. 'She's stubborn as hell.'

'Oh, come on, give her a chance. And you might look as if you are pleased to see her. True or not, it wouldn't hurt, Simon.'

'I'm not pleased to see her. I think she's a bloody nerve turning up like this. Is she trying to make me feel guilty?'

'Ssh. Don't let's fight, for goodness sake.' She gave him an exasperated look, trying hard to see his point of view and not succeeding. 'What's wrong with her exactly?'

'What do you think?' he said, running a hand through his hair. 'The big C, of course. It's only been seven months, but it's the virulent variety.'

'Oh, Simon, I'm so sorry.' She touched his arm but he sprang away, as if her touch was electric.

'No, *I'm* sorry for doing this to you. You don't deserve all this. Believe me, I had no idea. Not that it would have made a lot of difference,' he added, face tightening and eyes hardening in that way she hated. 'So it's tough luck but it happens. And she can't expect to walk back into my life just like that and for me to forget all that happened just because she's not got long to live. I mean, that's really hitting below the belt, don't you think?'

'Hey, come on, steady on.' Emily took a deep breath. 'Let me take the coffee through and I'll talk to her, but I don't want you hovering in here listening in. Go out. Leave it to me,' she finished, sounding more confident than she felt. She didn't know how to deal with this, and would just have to fly by the seat of her pants and try not to make too much of a hash of it. But first things first, and she determined to find out the history of all this, why they had fallen out and why Simon felt the way he so obviously did. Only then could she hope to help him get over it, come to terms with it, have some sort of late reconciliation with his mum. And, as Simon was in no mood to tell her the whole story, never had been, maybe never would be, then this was her opportunity to find out from his mother.

Something in the tilt of Heather's head and the dramatic blue of her eyes told her, as she went back into the lounge, that there was no mistake about this. This was his mother, like it or not. She was wearing trousers and top in a soft olive-green shade that suited her, but the trousers hung on her as if her legs were matchstick thin beneath them, and there was no substance to her, her skin pale and almost translucent, her eyes too large in her face, which was adopting a worryingly skeletal look. Once upon a time, she must have been a very attractive woman.

'You have a nice flat,' she said once they were settled. 'Central. Good view. Lovely bathrooms.'

'Yes, it's all finished to a high spec.,' Emily said, wishing it didn't sound as if they were negotiating a sale. 'It's convenient, but to me it has no soul, no character. It's like living in a show house.'

'We live in the show house, my husband and I,' Heather said with the slightest of smiles. 'I've always liked modern and Chris is happy to go along with what I like. We live up in Yorkshire and we lived for a while in a terraced cottage before we saw this new development quite near Harrogate. We bought the show house on site to save us the bother of doing it up. Chris is very busy.'

'What does he do?'

'Didn't Simon tell you? He's an architect. Doing very well indeed,' she added proudly. 'He's talented and ambitious. But a stay-at-home. We've never felt the need to move on.'

'You're probably right. You do begin to doubt your sanity because moving's such a hassle, but we always knew this was just a stop-gap. It isn't right for us,' Emily said, looking round the beautiful room. 'This is mostly Simon's choice of furniture and it will look so much better in an older house. I'd like something in the country. I have this dream . . .' She shrugged. 'But I don't know about Simon. I don't think he shares it.'

'Oh my. Have you talked about it?'

'Yes, but he doesn't listen. Not really listen. I think I'm getting somewhere, and then I realize that he won't budge an inch from what he thinks.'

'Why did I know that already?' Heather smiled at her. She had a nice smile like her son and it extended to her eyes, which were a warmer, deeper blue than Simon's. 'I'm stubborn too and I suppose that's why there's this barrier between us. Why is life always about compromise with the people we love?'

'I don't know if he's told you. We're getting married in December. Before Christmas.'

'He did tell me. Let me look properly at the ring,' she asked, admiring it as Emily held out her hand. 'You may have noticed, he doesn't communicate with me either,' she went on after a moment. 'He hasn't for years, not since I married Chris. That's what caused the upset, of course. Or perhaps it was the last straw.'

Emily nodded, as if she knew who this Chris was.

'How did you find Simon?' she asked.

'It wasn't too difficult,' Heather told her. 'I could have done it years ago. I wanted to but something held me back. I've followed his career closely. I know about the exhibitions, in fact I went to one once. It was ridiculous. I was scared stiff of accidentally bumping into him . . . my own son! Chris thought I was mad for going in the first place.' Her eyes filled up. 'He hasn't liked my doing this but, once he knew I was determined, he's helped all he can. The hardest part was whether or not to get in touch once I knew where he'd moved to. I knew he would be resentful, but it's something I have to do before I . . .' She bit her lip. 'I'm sure he's told you about my illness but the truth is I haven't got long, Emily. They're talking weeks now rather than months. I've had all the treatment I'm going to have.'

'Are you sure? Can't they do anything?'

'No. Chris has finally accepted it. He's been fantastic. He really is my rock. I know it's a cliché but it's true. You need somebody to be there for you when you're faced with this. I have no idea how I would have coped alone.'

'I'm sorry,' Emily said, knowing it was inadequate but not knowing what else to say. She didn't know this woman well enough yet to offer real comfort, but already she did feel sympathy for her at Simon's expense. Until she knew otherwise, until she had time to assess the situation, she found her fiancé's reaction hard to stomach. 'It must be very hard for you,' she went on, wishing she could come up with something a little more useful. 'I suppose you never know how you're going to cope until you're faced with it. I don't think I could.'

'Oh I don't know. Once you accept the truth, once you stop fighting it, it's easier,' Heather said taking a deep shuddering breath and looking away. 'He hasn't told you a thing about me, has he?'

'No. I always intended to find out,' she said quietly. 'But it never seemed the right moment and he was obviously not ready to talk. I know something happened that upset him but I don't know what. I have a happy relationship with my own mother . . .' she smiled. 'She's getting on my nerves about the wedding plans. She constantly leaves messages on my answerphone. She keeps on saying that it's my day when it's not. It's *her* day.'

Heather laughed. 'I've never had a daughter, but I think I understand. You must feel you're treading on eggs.'

'Exactly.'

'Are you ready for this?' The smile was slight. 'The whole story?'

'Only if you want to tell me.'

'I was barely eighteen when he was born,' Heather said at last, putting down her cup and moving her legs slowly and stiffly.

151

Emily couldn't help looking closely, noticing that even her shoes seemed too big, as if her feet had shrunk too. 'Usual story. I was stupid and I can't even be sure who the father was. I went to more than enough wild parties I can tell you.'

She looked up, half-smiled and Emily nodded encouragingly. There was something about Heather that she liked. Call it gut instinct, women's intuition, whatever. . . .

'Once I found out I was pregnant, I deliberately did nothing until it was too late for an abortion and then I insisted on keeping the baby, much against my parents' wishes. They were both very busy people and funds were tight, and I wouldn't consider adoption, so my mother came up with the idea of asking her sister to look after the baby when I went to college. Aunt Caroline has never married, and at the time she did scientific translation work from home and she was happy enough to supplement her income with what we could afford to pay her. It was the perfect solution because I didn't want to leave him with strangers and Aunt Caroline was family. In fact, she wanted children of her own. There'd been one brief unhappy marriage and I think she'd resigned herself to not having any. She was thrilled to have Simon to look after.'

Emily nodded into the pause that followed, trying to put herself in Heather's position. A single mum trying to find the best solution for her baby. So far, so good.

'I didn't go far to college, just fifty miles down the road, and I saw as much of him as I could, but letting Aunt Caroline look after him was the biggest mistake of my life.' Her eyes filled suddenly with tears and she blinked furiously. 'Perhaps I should have given up the idea of college, got a job and somehow looked after him myself. I would have managed. Other women do.'

'Tough decision,' Emily agreed, trying and failing to decide what she might have done. 'I'm sure it was the right one for you at the time.'

Heather smiled. 'Thanks. Aunt Caroline was well-meaning and

a lot more understanding than my mum and dad, but I think she was shaken by the responsibility we put on her. She'd read up on it, had a complete set of baby bibles but putting theory into practice was quite a challenge.'

'It must have made quite a change to her life.'

'It did. She'd got a little set in her ways and I wonder if Simon wasn't a disappointment to her. He was always a difficult little boy. She didn't have much patience with him, and I once arrived there unexpectedly when she was in the middle of giving him a good telling-off. She was embarrassed when she saw me standing there, but the damage was done,' she said, shaking her head as if to rid herself of that thought. 'She said she wouldn't dream of smacking him but I never quite trusted her after that and whenever I visited, I wanted to take him away, but it was impossible. I finally took him back when he was four, just when he started school because it was easier then to sort out other arrangements, but it was too late by then, too late for us to form a proper bond. It was a long time before he stopped talking about Caroline. The truth was I wasn't there for him when he was very small and I should have been.'

'He never told me anything about it,' Emily said. 'I wish he had. He's certainly never mentioned an Aunt Caroline.'

'He wouldn't, would he? Those years are best forgotten. I've scarcely spoken to her since.'

'He should have told me about her, about you. It wouldn't have made any difference to how I feel about him.'

'It shouldn't,' she said sharply. 'His past should have no bearing on how you feel for him.'

Perhaps not. But his past was surely part of him and she had a right to know because it would help her to understand him more, and help her to help him get over whatever it was that was still bugging him.

'But his not talking about it, not even to me, especially not to me. . . .' Emily struggled to find the right words. 'It's almost an insult. I mean, if he can't talk to me, tell me about it, then who can he talk to? He can't bottle it all up for ever. You can't put a stopper on your past, can you? Not completely.'

'He's ashamed of me,' Heather told her candidly. 'That's why he hasn't told you about me. He can't bring himself to forgive me.'

'For what? Because you weren't married? Because you passed him over to your aunt to look after? Oh, come on, he's got to grow up. We can't all be born very neatly into a happily married partnership.' Emily clicked her tongue in exasperation.

'It's only partly that. Remember I got him back when he was four and we were together then, just the two of us. What he really couldn't come to terms with was my marrying. He can't get his head round my marrying Chris.'

'But surely that's no reason to shut you out of his life as he has?' Emily said, fully aware she was taking Heather's side on this, aware too that Heather recognized she was. 'He can be very pig-headed sometimes. Don't tell me this rift was caused by that. If you wanted to marry Chris then he should resign himself to it, no matter what he thinks. Not only resign himself to it but wish you well at that,' she finished stoutly.

'I can tell you've never been put in that position yourself,' Heather said, lifting a weary hand to smooth her hair. It scarcely needed it, for it was immaculate, blonde and shiny. 'If I tell you that Chris was his best friend at university, perhaps you'll understand a little more. Simon introduced us. The problem is Chris is eighteen years my junior, Emily. He came to visit one summer with Simon and we fell in love. I wasn't always as haggard as this . . .' she said, waving her hand in despair. 'I had my own hair then. This is a wig.'

'Oh.' She had finally guessed as much but didn't know what to say. Luckily, Heather was in full confessional flow and just carried on.

'I had lovely hair, blonde but a prettier colour than this. I was only thirty seven and the irritating thing is that Simon and I were beginning to get it together at last. It wasn't the normal mother/son relationship, far from it, it was always awkward, but I was working so hard at it, trying to understand him, trying to make him love me.'

Emily wanted to tell her that you couldn't do that, love just happened, but she stayed silent for it seemed cruel to say it out loud.

'I was proud he did so well at school and I kept trying to tell him that,' Heather carried on. 'He wouldn't talk to me though, never would and then this thing with Chris just killed it. He really hated me for it. Chris's parents were very kind. They were puzzled and a bit amused by the age gap but they did their best to understand. We tried to have a baby, a child of our own, but it didn't happen.' She sniffed. 'It doesn't matter. And it's much too late now. Chris and Simon haven't spoken since then. I have to say it's mutual animosity. Chris despises him for acting like he did, for making me miserable.'

'I see,' Emily said as a silence fell.

'I don't want his sympathy.' Heather pulled herself up, frowning suddenly, swinging her legs off the footrest and wincing as she did so. 'But I have to make the effort. I want things left neat and tidy and I want us to be friends at least, if that's possible. That's all I want. And I need to know . . .' she looked solidly at Emily, 'I know it's a bit late for me to be acting the concerned mother but it's very important to me. I need to know he's going to be looked after when I'm gone. I knew he had a girlfriend although I didn't know you were intending to get married, but I wanted to meet you.'

'Looked after?' Emily laughed, trying to lighten the moment. 'I don't exactly look after him. It's more a partnership. I suppose we look after each other.'

'Of course you do and that's how it should be. I don't see you as the sort of girl who'll wait on him hand and foot. I wouldn't want that.' She smiled too. 'I'm so pleased I met you because I like you and I know you love Simon. I don't think I'll be around for the wedding . . .'

'Oh, do please come. My mother would love to meet you.'

'I didn't mean that. I was being realistic because I'll be gone by then or, if I am still hanging on, I'll be in no fit state to attend a wedding.'

'We could bring it forward,' Emily said desperately, upset with herself for misunderstanding. 'It can be done. We can just have a quiet wedding.'

'What? And spoil your mother's plans?' Heather shook her head. 'Absolutely not. You get married in December as you plan to do. I wouldn't dream of anything else!' She paused, gulped. 'Promise me you'll do your best to help him through it, Emily. I think he'll take it much harder than you think. Or he thinks. I'm talking about my dying,' she finished, just to make it perfectly plain. 'Help him. Be there for him. That's all. I'm so glad he found you and knowing you will be there with him makes me feel much better about it all. I can rest easy. Do you see?'

This was all getting very heavy and if they didn't watch it, they would both end up in tears. But they had to carry it through to its conclusion, Heather needed the reassurance and so Emily went to sit beside her, reaching for her hand and saying the words Heather was willing her to say.

'I *will* be there for him, Heather. Don't you worry about that,' she said and at that moment she genuinely believed what she was saying.

'Good. I can rest easy now.' Heather turned away, eyes blurring with her tears. It seemed as if she was going to carry on and reduce them both to quivering wrecks but thankfully she got a grip on herself. 'I could murder a cup of tea,' she said instead.

Relieved, Emily went to put on the kettle.

CHAPTER FIFTEEN

'Emily . . . message timed at six forty-three. I'm tearing my hair out, darling. I've threatened to sue Angela. It looks nothing like the colour on the chart she showed me. And I did say at one point would she check because it seemed to have been on a long time but she was fluttering around with somebody else and ignored me. I nearly died when I saw it. The fact is it's a bit vibrant. Your father says it looks nice but you know him. Anyway, it's only a trial. It will fade in a couple of months and I can try something else for the wedding. What's this I've heard about Simon having a mother? Thank God for that. But do ask her to consult on our choice of outfit. Will you be in by seven? I'll try then.

'Bye, darling.'

Corinne was dog-walking, giving the old boy a treat by taking him in the car to one of his old favourite tramping grounds by the river. It was a popular spot for visitors but quiet this afternoon, the picnic tables deserted. The summer was long gone and the cool air of autumn had settled in with a vengeance. And now, the morning clouds had gathered in a great grumble of grey, and rain threatened.

'Where are we, Bingo boy?' she asked him in her cheery-best voice, hearing his tail thump in delight as he recognized the car park. She paused a minute when she had stilled the engine, thinking briefly about how long she had been doing this, how they, she and Joe, often used to come here with a much younger and bouncier Bingo.

She had to help the old dog out of the car and felt a tug at her heart as she did so, remembering the way he used to leap in and out without any effort. He ran off in an imitation of puppy madness as she unclipped his lead although, after the initial crazed outburst, his pace rapidly slowed to a very respectable shuffle. It suited her, for she was happy to stroll by the riverbank, taking the lower, easier path, even if it was muddier as water drained into it. She was equipped for the uneven terrain with her walking boots and, because it threatened to pour down any minute, she had a hat plonked on her head.

'Mrs Cooper? Corinne, isn't it?'

She spun round, surprised because she hardly ever met anybody on her walks, aside from other dog owners with whom she shared a sort of dog-speak, meaning they spoke not to each other but rather to the respective dogs.

'Cuthbert!' she smiled as he approached, scarcely recognizable in wet-weather gear. 'What on earth are you doing here?'

'I'm recharging my batteries, taking a break from house hunting,' he told her.

'Oh, I see. Bernard didn't say you were looking for a house in this area,' she said, having assumed he would be looking in the north of the county. Far be it from her to remind him that commuting on Devon roads was something else.

'Bernard doesn't know. We don't see much of each other. Anyway . . .' he took in her appearance with a quick look, no doubt noting that she had quickly removed the hat and run urgent fingers through her hair, 'I thought some fresh air might make the decision-making a bit easier. It's a tough one because I've just seen a place I really like.'

'Why is it tough? Is it too expensive?'

He nodded. 'Off the scale. Can't think why I viewed it.

Nuisance, isn't it? I'm going to let them know tomorrow. Have a big think tonight and come back to them. Of course I know already what I'm going to do.'

'You're going to go for it,' she told him firmly. 'What other choice is there? Never mind the finances, Cuthbert. You have a good job with prospects so you should be a very good bet.'

'Thanks for that,' he said. 'Nice to get approval for doing something completely mad. It's an enormous place for a single guy. All in all, it's a stupid decision. Tell me it's stupid, Corinne.'

'Not at all. You have to think of the future,' she told him, wishing she didn't sound so matron-like and sensible. 'When you get married and have lots of children, you'll have a ready-made home for them. You'll be a great catch for some lucky girl, Cuthbert.'

'Thanks again,' he said. 'As a matter of fact . . .'

His grin said it all.

'You've met somebody,' she said in delight. 'How wonderful. Who is she and what does she do?'

'Steady,' he warned. 'I'm not sure she'll have me yet. She told me at the start that when it comes to men, she's terribly picky.'

'I thought I was,' she said with a quick smile. 'And then I went and married Bernard. Must have taken leave of my senses.'

'You are a fibber, Corinne,' he said, returning her smile. 'I've never seen two people so suited to each other.'

'Come on . . . how can that be? Just look at him. If you didn't know better, you'd say he was an absent-minded college professor, wouldn't you? I've been trying to get him to be more stylish for thirty years.' She paused, but there was no point in pretending she was younger than she was. He could count for goodness sake and he knew she had sons of a certain age. 'And still he wears those awful ties when he has an assortment of beautiful ones purchased, of course, from you know where. What must people think? I did think of having a ceremonial burning, throwing the lot of them in the fire, but I couldn't bring myself to do it. He's such a child in many ways.'

'There's more to a man than style,' he said lightly. 'He's well thought of, you know. He might be a big cheese in the company, but he's always got time for a word with the juniors. They respect him for that.'

'I know. Marian thinks the sun shines out of him.' She glanced at him. 'Sorry. I shouldn't have said that but the damned woman does have a crush on him. Can't think why.'

'There you go again. If anything happened to Bernard, you'd be devastated, wouldn't you?'

She quietened, nodded. Of course she would and how perceptive of him to see that. She couldn't stop herself doing this, doing dearest Bernard down, talking about him to complete strangers and embarrassing them. Fortunately, Cuthbert could see right through her.

'We lost our youngest son,' she said as, by common consent, they slowed their pace, pausing at a bend in the river. A rustle above them proved to be a squirrel scurrying like a rat possessed along the branch. They both looked up but said nothing. At their side, Bingo was walking sedately and she knew he had probably had enough now and they must head back. 'Our son Joe. People know about it but they don't usually mention it these days. It was seven years ago and I suppose they think we might have got over it.'

'God, I didn't know. I'm so sorry,' he said, digging his hands deep into his pockets. 'What an awful thing. Do you want to talk about it?'

'Do you mind?' she looked at him as they started back. 'I don't often. Sometimes I talk to my cleaner when we're having coffee. She's actually a terrible cleaner but she's a wonderful listener and very sympathetic. But I can't talk to Bernard or Daniel about it. Bernard because I don't want to upset him and Daniel because . . . well, because it was his fault that his brother died.'

'Oh . . .'

'Daniel climbs. Amongst other things, he's a mountaineer.'

'Really? People like that must be dedicated I suppose. I mean it might sound exciting but it's no picnic, I expect up there. . . .' He waved a hand to illustrate his point. 'What happened?' he then said, face suddenly serious.

'Daniel dragged Joe along on one of his weekends,' she said, the memory reluctant to surface. 'It was meant to be a treat for him because he had just finished a summer of awful exams and was looking forward to taking up his place at university. . . .' She paused but, at her side, Cuthbert was silent. 'They were simply trekking along a stony path, not particularly hazardous ground, but there was a fair old drop at the turn in the path and Joe just slipped. They weren't roped together. As far as I'm concerned, if there was a drop big enough to kill you then they damned well ought to have been, but then I don't understand anything, do I? I'm just a mum after all.'

'Accidents happen,' Cuthbert said in a level voice. 'Sorry, I know it's hard but they do. Why blame Daniel?'

'Because I have to blame somebody,' she said. 'And he's the only one to blame. He should have looked after him better. He was his brother, for God's sake.'

'Yes, but what good does it do to keep on blaming him? What do you think that does to him? Shouldn't you let it go, Corinne?'

She glanced sharply at him. 'What the hell do you know about it?'

'Nothing.'

'You haven't been talking to Bernard, have you?' she asked. 'Because it gets to him sometimes, the way I treat Daniel.'

'I am completely impartial,' he said, trying another smile although it was a little subdued this time. 'Just trying to see things from a neutral point of view. I don't know Daniel, but I do know Bernard and I knew there was something that bothers him, apart from the fact that he thinks I'm going to sneak the chief executive's job when Mr Malley retires. If I was, would I be going to the trouble of buying a house here? I'd be thinking of London, wouldn't I?'

'But Bernard isn't interested in Malley's job,' she said with a laugh. 'Far too much responsibility when he's not far away from retiring himself. Why should he lumber himself with that, especially when there's a slump in trading?'

'Ah! That's what I tell myself. You'd better have a word with him about that.'

The rain started then, great big drops, and he quickened his pace. Corinne plopped her hat on again, suddenly not caring how she looked, calling to Bingo who had found an interesting scent.

They parted at the car but she sat awhile before driving off, contrasting this meeting with their last. Then she had been a bit tiddly and flirty, but this morning she had behaved with great sobriety, like the grandmother she was, and seen him for what he was, a young man who was simply trying to be friendly and not about to seduce her.

Damn.

'I'm pleased you can stay,' Corinne told her, leading her up the stairs onto a wide, red-carpeted landing. 'By the time we've done the fitting and had a chat it will be getting late and . . .' she paused. 'Enough of excuses. I just needed company with Bernard being away.'

'So did I,' Emily said. 'You'd think I'd be used to it after all this time but I'm not and I don't think I ever will be.'

'You're in here,' Corinne said, opening the door. 'Is it all right for you?'

Emily recognized the doubt in her voice, but there was no need, for the room was quite charming, if surprisingly small for such a grand house. She expressed her delight, dumping her bag down and going across to the window to look out to the garden. The trees were at their splendid autumnal best, leaves of gold and brown and deepest red.

'It won't be long before they start to come down in earnest,'
Corinne said, behind her. 'It's such a bore, but at the same time I
think autumn has to be my favourite time of year. I hope you
don't mind but Daniel's coming over this evening for a meal.
Cooking it for us, in fact, if you can bear that.'

She felt her heart thud, knew why and was suddenly and hopelessly confused. After all that had happened these past few days,
she really didn't need this. She thought of the conversation she
had had with Heather and the comfort Simon's mother felt in
knowing that she would be there to look after him when she was
gone. She had promised she would and it meant she had to screw
the lid on all the silly little doubts that had been surfacing and
bubbling upwards these last few months, ever since she had said
yes to marriage in fact. Having somebody else relying on you,
counting on your word, somebody who wouldn't be here for very
long, was sobering.

'We'll work on the dress a while when you've freshened up,'
Corinne said, pointing out where the bathroom was. 'And then
we can relax before Daniel gets here. I have no idea what he'll be
cooking. He can be very exotic or very plain depending on his
mood.'

The relaxing took place in the formal sitting-room, the dress
tucked away for the moment in Corinne's workroom. It was
beautiful, would fit like a dream, and the prettily edged jacket
would make it very special.

'The nights are drawing in,' Corinne remarked, switching on
table lamps, although she left the curtains undrawn. 'I look
forward to winter. I like it when you can shut yourselves in. I love
the snow, although we don't get much of it here and I even like
the rain. Heat depresses me, it always has.'

The sound of a car interrupted them and they saw the lights
approaching and disappearing as Daniel drove round the side.
Nervously, Emily flicked at her hair. It was a new style, a little
shorter than she had wanted, and she wasn't sure about it, but

there was time for it to grow longer again before the wedding. She was wearing a favourite long skirt and a sweater and Corinne was in one of her quirky colour combinations of emerald green and peach, a patchwork skirt and frilly top and masses of jingly bracelets.

'I haven't seen Daniel for a while, since my dinner party,' she commented, trying to keep her voice level. 'It didn't go brilliantly well.'

'That's the way with blind dates.' Corinne smiled. 'He didn't say much about it but I just read between the lines.'

'Simon didn't help. I'm afraid he can be difficult with new people,' Emily went on, determined to try to set things straight. 'Sometimes people find him abrasive at first until they get to know him. It's just his way. I suppose it's the job. Seeing the sort of things he sees it's bound to get to you. Sometimes he wants to talk about it, every last awful detail, and other times he just clams up.'

'You needn't explain. People find my Bernard totally incomprehensible,' Corinne said. 'He twitters when he's nervous and he hates meeting new people. But he's also very candid. He knows straight off whether or not he likes somebody and if he doesn't . . .' she shuddered. 'He makes no damned attempt with them. I think perhaps Daniel is like his father.'

'It wasn't that exactly. I think he did his best but Geraldine, my colleague, is not an outdoor type at all and I can't think now why I ever imagined they would hit it off. They didn't. She was quite scathing about his job, in fact, which made me squirm. She's not usually like that.'

'Don't worry. It wouldn't have bothered Daniel. Water off a duck's back. Ah, talk of the devil . . .'

Sitting on the sofa, she heard his footsteps crossing the hall and then he was in the room.

And her heart fluttered for all the world as it always did to the heroines in romantic novels. And worse, she felt distinctly embarrassed. She wasn't like this normally, so what was it all about? This man was doing things to her, at a distance, things that used to happen once upon a time with Simon.

'Hi, there.' He smiled. 'Not interrupting, I hope?'

'No, we've finished the fitting,' Corinne told him, acknowledging his presence with a barely perceptible nod. 'I've warned Emily that you've offered to cook dinner for us. What is it or are we to be surprised?'

'Pork steaks with an apple and herb sauce. And a fruit pie with clotted cream. Good for the arteries,' he said with a grin. 'Pretty basic stuff. You can help me if you like.'

Corinne gave a little snort. 'Like hell. I am off to do some gardening. I feel an urge to commune with nature. Perhaps you might entertain Emily?'

'I'll help you,' Emily said at once, standing up and following him through to the kitchen.

'There's no rush. Coffee first I think,' he said, taking off his jacket and pushing up the sleeves of his sweater. 'You sit here,' he went on, solicitously pulling out a chair for her. 'Do you want to peel some vegetables?'

'Not particularly, but I will,' she told him with a smile. 'This is a rare treat for me having a man cook for me. Simon does nothing in the kitchen.'

'Probably thinks it's not a man's job,' he said, handing her the vegetables with a smile.

'No. He's not like that,' she said, anxious to defend him, although in fact Daniel wasn't far wrong on that count. 'We decided at the outset that we should share the housework with us both working. It's only fair.'

'I see. Very commendable.' He grinned. 'And does that actually work? The division of labour?'

'Well, no . . .' she admitted, wondering when was the last time Simon had done anything round the house and then, when he did, it was to a chorus of great grumbles. She didn't mind, not truly, for that was generally the way of the world and it was certainly that way with her own parents, but it irked a little that Daniel seemed to have the measure of Simon. She felt uncomfortable, too, criticizing her fiancé like this and knew she would have jumped guiltily if he had suddenly appeared.

'I don't have a problem with domestic stuff. When you are up a mountain,' Daniel went on cheerfully. 'It's all hands to the wheel work-wise and you really learn about working as a team. I like working with people and that's why we reckon we can do these courses, the ones your fiancé and others are so scathing about, because me and Harvey have experienced team work at first hand. You're only as strong as the weakest member of your team and on a climb, you can't afford to carry somebody who isn't going to pull his weight at the last. I know it's not so much a matter of life and death in your line . . .'

She laughed. 'Don't you believe it! As a matter of fact, I do see your point about the team-building exercise although I still don't like the idea. I think it's being unfair to those of us who are naturally bad at sport and suchlike. And surely it's become something of a gimmick for a company to send its senior management on such courses? I have to say I think Simon's right to be wary of them. Sorry and all that.'

'You're not a bit sorry,' he said, still managing to smile. 'Thanks for being honest though. Simon's a lucky man.'

'Why? Because I'm honest?'

'That's part of it,' he said, fussing around now with dishes and knives.

She fluttered around too, not entirely sure whether or not she had just been handed an enormous compliment. She would try to analyse it later just as, later, she would go through this whole innocuous conversation piece by piece, seeing his face, listening to his words.

Watching him watching her.

'Before we go back in . . .' he said suddenly, 'I'd like to tell you something just in case Mum behaves a bit oddly tomorrow.'

'What is it?'

'It would have been my brother Joe's birthday tomorrow,' he said, his face puckering with emotion. 'It might be seven years since he died but it doesn't get any easier, never mind what people say. Especially for me, because Mum's convinced it was my fault he died.'

'Car accident?' she asked.

'Climbing. He fell. A helluva long way. It was quick and, we can only hope, painless, in that he probably lost consciousness before he hit the ground.'

She felt a chill hit her, shivered. 'I'm so sorry, Daniel. I had no idea.'

'That's OK,' he said, although his face said differently.

Sympathy welled up and she wanted to touch his shoulder, have him lean into her for a moment, but she could not bring herself to do it, not yet.

'How awful for you and how awful that she blames you for an accident.'

'The thing is, it wasn't an accident . . .' He stopped, turned away and she prompted him gently.

'Go on.'

He shook his head. 'It's nothing,' he said. 'And I shouldn't be bothering you with it. Can't think why I am.'

'Can't you?'

He looked at her a moment, smiled slightly. 'After what happened after your dinner party, I'm not sure it was a good idea you coming here, Emily.'

'Nothing happened,' she said heatedly. 'I don't know what you mean.'

'Oh, yes, you do.'

There was no point in denying it further. She might as well have a note pinned to her chest saying, 'I wouldn't say no if you suggested taking me to bed here and now.'

'This is very awkward, Daniel. I'm not sure about anything anymore and the awful thing is that Simon's mother has suddenly arrived on the scene. They've not spoken for years,' she went on, regretting starting on this but wanting to tell him now she had. 'And she turned up out of the blue and the fact is she's dying. She's only got weeks to live.'

'My God. How do you cope with that?' he asked.

'The thing is I promised her . . .' she gulped, felt the tears building up, 'I promised her I would look after him. Look after Simon, I mean, and now I wish I hadn't promised because how on earth can I go back on my word to a woman who's dying?'

'Are you intending to do that?' he asked gently.

'Oh, I don't know . . .' Impatiently, she pushed at her hair.

'You've had your hair cut,' he said, voice still gentle. 'It suits you.'

'Thanks. Simon prefers it longer.'

'If you want to talk about it, I'm here anytime.'

'My haircut. . . ?' she asked, deliberately obtuse, daring to look straight at him.

'You and Simon,' he said and in his sigh there was such a wealth of emotion that she wanted to curl up in his arms there and then and have him hold her tight.

'Thanks again, but everything's fine, really it is,' she said firmly, turning from him to hide her face, closing her eyes a moment but still seeing him standing there looking at her, his expression puzzled. She wanted to say more, but it seemed the moment had passed and, intentionally or not, he swiftly changed the subject.

Standing today in the mock-up for her bridal gown, she had known that the wedding itself was now a mockery. The moment had gone, they had waited too long, they had been happy as they were and it was all a terrible mistake. She knew that for sure but with her mother steaming ahead with the arrangements, just about to change to fifth gear, how could she put a stop to it?

Remembering her promise to Heather, she knew she would not be stopping it either.

Silly fears. Once they were married she would laugh at herself.

CHAPTER SIXTEEN

'Emily, darling, it's me. Your mother. What's this nonsense about Simon refusing to wear a tie? Is he mad? Of course he must wear one or at the least a cravat. In fact that may be rather nice. We really can't have the men turning up in just any old thing and if you like I'll put out some feelers. The choice of hire clothes for the men is simply splendid these days and they needn't necessarily end up looking like tailor's dummies. The difficulty is your father, poor soul. What with his gammy leg and his awkward arms, such long arms, he'll be a devil to fit off the peg. This is seriously worrying me and it's all very well saying we have ages yet. The days are ticking off and November will be here before we know it and then it's the skid path to the day itself. My nerves are shattered. Anyway, give me a call when you get in. Where on earth do you get to all the time?

'Bye.'

Before he went to London for a meeting with Malley, Bernard consulted Marian about what he should do re Joe's birthday.

'Do you think I should let it go this time?' he asked, stopping her in her tracks as she spun round after leaving a cup of coffee and a chocolate digestive on his desk. 'Do you think Corinne will still expect me to make something of it? If I don't, will she be upset? Or, on the other hand, if I do, will that remind her of something she might now want to forget?'

'She's always appreciated the flowers, Bernard,' Marian said firmly, taking a seat, unasked, on the chair opposite, her spectacles swinging from a slim silver chain round her neck. 'And you know as well as I do that she will never forget. Surely you of all people can gauge her mood? You really don't need me to tell you.'

Oh, but he did. Sometimes it was as if he couldn't do a damned thing right where Corinne was concerned. He thought at one time he could read her like a book, but times had bloody well changed with a vengeance when they lost Joe. Now he could only hazard a guess and mostly he was wrong.

He looked across at Marian, at her puffy face, her darkish hair pulled back severely these days and held in place with a vicious-looking hair accessory. She was not getting any younger and it was time she found herself a man and stopped this ridiculous nonsense of believing herself in love with him. It wasn't as if he had ever done anything to encourage the dratted woman. He sipped his coffee, barely warm, and waited for her to come up with something.

'If you want me to get the flowers and the card as usual then I will,' she said at last. 'Perhaps we can review the position next year?'

She was so brisk and, although he liked that in her, it didn't help on this occasion. He wanted sympathy but sympathy with some proper input. He wanted to know her real opinion.

'Yes, but what shall I do?' he asked, worried he was coming over as pathetic. Whatever he did, he risked doing the wrong thing. He had noticed the tension building up in Corinne these last few days and it was a pity that he wouldn't be there this year to console her, but this meeting was very nearly a summons, something he couldn't get out of, not unless he had a sudden understandable heart attack brought on by the extreme sodding stress. 'I don't mean this to sound callous, Marian, but maybe it

171

is time we brought it to a halt. Moved on. If only she would ditch all the stuff she keeps up in the loft, cast it aside. What's the point of keeping it?'

'She lost her son,' Marian reminded him gently. 'Oh, come on, Bernard. I can't imagine what it's like of course, not having any children of my own but I wouldn't take the chance of upsetting her on that day of all days. Let me buy the card today and you can sign it and then I shall make sure a nice bouquet is delivered to her on his birthday with your usual message. How about that?'

'Daniel lost his brother, too. Don't forget that,' he said, glancing at the clock and realizing he had to get a move on. 'Go ahead then,' he finished with a sigh, fluttering around for some money. He operated almost entirely with credit cards but Corinne usually made sure he had what she called loose change in his wallet. 'Get some flowers if you think that's the right thing to do.'

'Any ideas on what kind?'

'Good God, no . . .' he said. 'Pink. She likes pink.'

'We always do pink.'

'Do we?' Mystified as to why they were discussing this when flowers were simply flowers, he slipped a note out. 'Will ten pounds be enough?'

She gave him a pained look. 'Twenty at least, please, if I'm to get a decent bunch. They add a delivery charge, too.'

Bloody florists.

Reluctantly he peeled off another two.

'Bernard always remembers,' Corinne told her at breakfast next morning. 'He sends me flowers today. I expect they will arrive shortly.'

Anniversary? It took Emily a moment to remember what Daniel had told her about it being Joe's birthday.

'How very thoughtful,' she said, awkward because she wasn't sure how much she should admit to knowing about it.

Corinne smiled slightly. 'I'm sorry, I should explain. It's my youngest son's birthday today. My late son. I suppose Daniel told you about the accident. Or at least his version of events?'

They were taking breakfast in the old conservatory, which was filled with a mix of odd chairs covered in pretty fabrics. The floor was black-and-white and Corinne seemed to have made an effort here with the plants. Emily, who usually had coffee and toast, had felt obliged to have the cooked breakfast that Corinne seemed keen to provide.

His version of events?

Reaching for a glass of orange juice, Emily glanced across the table at her, taking in her mood. She was tired herself because she had slept badly and she knew why she had slept badly at that.

As Corinne lapsed into a comfortable silence, she found herself thinking about last night. They had dinner in the splendour of the dining room, the food had been very good and they had both congratulated the chef. They had chatted cheerfully about Daniel's travels, about Corinne's childhood in Norfolk, about the children when they were small and yes, Joe was mentioned in passing even though Emily had noticed the shadow that immediately passed over both their faces. And then Corinne, making a supreme effort, had told them indiscreet tales about some of her brides, omitting names of course.

'Sorry,' she said with a rueful smile. 'I love them all, but it's just hilarious the way some girls let it get to them. Your wedding day is supposed to be the happiest day of your life but I'd like to take bets on that one.'

'Are you trying to put her off?' Daniel said.

'I sometimes wish . . .' Emily sighed, glancing round the softly lit room. 'Sometimes I wish we'd just had a quickie wedding at the registry office, grabbed a couple of people off the street as witnesses and just got on with it. My mother would have been deprived of wearing a big hat but she would have got over it.'

'Don't you believe it,' Corinne told her with a glance at her son. 'I believe that her daughter's wedding is the wedding that a mother truly enjoys. Of course, not having had a daughter myself . . .' Her voice trailed away and she flicked absently at something unseen on the folds of her skirt.

Daniel had left shortly after that, pleading he had things to do and he made his goodbyes, kissing his mother on the cheek and simply smiling his goodbye to Emily.

Very aware of him as he closed the door on the two of them, Emily had seen the knowing look on Corinne's face, but thankfully she had made no comment.

But it seemed this morning at breakfast, all the bitterness she felt towards Daniel had resurfaced and she was in no mood, today of all days, to try to disguise it.

'Corinne . . .' Emily said, refusing another cup of tea with a smile. 'Please tell me to mind my own business but . . .'

'He was Joe's big brother,' Corinne said, knowing precisely what she was getting at. 'And as such he ought to have looked after him. Daniel's an experienced climber, for goodness sake, and surely he could have had the sense to realize that Joe wasn't. Joe was a beginner to the sport and he should have looked after him. Don't you see? He didn't do that and he . . . Daniel . . . let us all down.'

'He feels very badly about it,' Emily told her, not knowing why she said that, but knowing it to be true. 'And it hurts him that you won't forgive him.'

'Did he ask you to say this?'

'No. Absolutely no,' she said fiercely, shaking her head. 'And don't dare tell him I said it. It's none of my business.'

'You're right. It isn't,' Corinne huffed before glancing out of the window as a white van pulled up outside. 'Here they are. He's predictable if nothing else. He never forgets or rather that secretary of his never forgets. Marian chooses the flowers. She's very predictable too. Pink usually.'

Emily thought it ungracious of her to be so dismissive, both of the flowers themselves, which true to form was a large bunch of various pink flowers, and of Bernard's gesture. What was the poor man to do? It was all too easy to be dismissive of him like this, but she would do it once too often.

For the first time, she wondered if she had chosen the wrong woman to make her wedding dress.

She took a walk in the grounds following breakfast, delaying the moment she had to return home and face up to things. She knew that Simon was having doubts but, like her, he was slow at voicing them. They had been together a while now and it was hard to admit the truth to each other and to themselves. Their lovemaking had changed. It was no longer spontaneous. Difficult to pinpoint exactly how it was different, but it was and last time it had happened, they had been at the last unable to meet each other's eyes.

It was chill, a low mist was steaming over the trees in the valley and she shivered under the clouds, looking up at the trees as the summer leaves shrivelled and crisped. Some were already lying at her feet reminding her that the seasons just went their own sweet way and soon enough it would be late autumn and then winter and with winter, her wedding. . . .

How effortlessly she had sailed through her younger years. No problems with exams, getting the job she wanted, relishing for a while her life in London, meeting Simon and the delights of it all.

And now . . . it was all falling apart, just as surely as the leaves were falling off the trees. And she couldn't put it together again.

There was no sensible alternative.

She was going to have to do it.

She was going to have to come clean and break it off.

Emily had the distinct feeling that Geraldine Grainger was avoiding her. She put it down to the near disaster of the dinner party and she determined that in future she would leave well alone. Let Geraldine find her own man for goodness sake, and what a foolish idea it had been to imagine that she would hit it off with Daniel.

Geraldine was not Daniel's type. She wasn't sure who would be – other than herself, of course, for that had been made abundantly clear over the last few days. Staying there had been a colossal mistake and she couldn't think why she had subjected herself to it. If she had done it purely as a personal test then it had failed miserably on all counts. It had done nothing to assuage her doubts and, coming home to Simon, she had felt it necessary to clam up about it, to sweep his questions aside and concentrate on the two of them and them alone.

Simon was not at his best, either, but she put that down to pressure of work. On his return, he had immediately started work compiling a new portfolio for another exhibition of his pictures and for some reason it seemed to be affecting him deeply. Very likely this thing with his mother was getting to him more than he cared to admit. Heather was now confined to bed, at home, and the end was expected soon. Emily felt he ought to be there, but he insisted she did not want him there so that was that. With this hanging over him, how could she break the news that she wanted to end their engagement? She couldn't be so cruel.

So, what with one thing and another, she could hardly cope with a strained atmosphere at work and, glancing towards Geraldine, she vowed to get to the bottom of it. After all, her intentions at that doomed dinner party had been honourable, even if it had backfired, and it really wasn't worthy of Geraldine to be offended by it. Not only to be offended but to keep the damned huffiness up. It was unlike her and it was high time it was forgotten.

'Fancy lunch?' she asked, stopping by her desk.

'Sorry . . .' Geraldine looked up and smiled brightly, too brightly. 'I'm up to my eyes in it. I'm off to check some paintings that have turned up in an attic this afternoon so I'll have to work through lunch. Angharad's getting me a sandwich in. She's so attentive, like a waitress taking everybody's orders today.'

'About Angharad . . .' Emily sighed. 'I don't want to be

awkward but I think this astrology thing is getting out of hand. Little Nicola is very upset at what she's been told. I think we should warn Angharad that if she hasn't anything positive to say then perhaps it might be better if she doesn't say anything at all.'

'*We* should warn her?' Geraldine asked, her determined smile slipping. 'It isn't compulsory to buy a chart, Emily. She's been spot on with me,' she added. 'She uses her discretion and if she thinks you can't cope with the truth, then she omits it.'

'It's all a load of nonsense,' Emily said, annoyed at the way Geraldine was reacting. 'Spot on with you, eh? Does that mean you've met the man of your dreams, then?'

She might have just hit the bull's eyes as Geraldine flushed.

'I'm sorry,' she said quickly, smiling to rectify the unsavoury question.

Geraldine smiled back, but there was a wariness about her and Emily wondered just what she had done to warrant such a reaction. Good heavens, she had only been trying to help. Well, stuff it, if she was going to be like that.

Feeling like a child who had overstepped the mark, Emily slid away.

'Geraldine Grainger is being a bit awkward,' she told Simon that evening. She had made a special effort with their meal, trying in vain to cheer them both up as they waited for news of Heather, but it had been a pointless exercise, for he merely picked at the food, mind obviously miles away.

'Awkward?' He raised his fork, frowned. 'In what way?'

She shrugged. 'Very off me, for some reason. The dinner party, I suppose, but that was ages ago and you'd think she'd be big enough to let it go, wouldn't you? I said I was sorry for trying to palm her off with Daniel. What more can I do?'

'Forget it.'

'Look . . .' she pushed her plate aside, reached for the wine and refilled their glasses. She had determined this afternoon that she

177

was giving this one more chance. It had meant something once and this might be just a blip. It was foolish to throw something away on a whim. She had loved him once and she could love him again. Cold feet, that's all it was, the kind of pre-wedding jitters all brides had. Hadn't Belinda confessed as much? And Yvonne? Although of course with her track record, poor Yvonne had been quite right to have jitters.

Simon looked at her over his glass. 'Look what?' he asked with some suspicion. 'You're planning something, aren't you?'

'Why don't we go up to Harrogate to see your mother?' she said, ploughing on, even as she caught his expression. 'I know it won't be easy but if you don't see her before . . . well, you know . . . you'll only regret it afterwards. And you ought to make your peace with Chris.'

'I can't. Too much was said. He won't forgive what I said.'

'He might. He was the one who found you for her and he wouldn't have gone to that trouble if he was still miffed with you.'

'A bit more than miffed.' Simon grinned suddenly, but his eyes were cold. 'Thanks for trying but I don't see what can be gained by my seeing her. We've said our goodbyes. She doesn't want me to have to see it.'

'All right. Be like that. But honestly, Simon, you have to learn to give a little.'

'Keep out of it,' he said, voice sharp. 'It's between me and her. Not you.'

'But it is my problem too,' she told him. 'I'm very nearly your wife, Simon.'

'Not yet,' he said and the words were sharp as an ice-edge.

It was very final.

Daniel wouldn't treat her like this and, more and more, she was comparing the two of them. She could do it no longer. They would not make love again. That night, she had to pretend a dreadful tummy-ache – a headache just seemed too corny – to prevent it happening. She knew she hadn't fooled him for a minute but funnily enough she had the strangest feeling as he turned away from her that he might be relieved.

Lying beside him but keeping carefully to her side of the bed, she stared into the darkness for a long, long time before finally drifting off into a troubled sleep.

CHAPTER SEVENTEEN

'Emily, Mum here. What a to-do about Simon's mother. I had no idea until you rang that she was, that the poor lady was . . . oh dear, I don't know what to say. Do you want to bring everything forward? I know it will mean a much more subdued affair but what can we do under the circumstances? I feel absolutely numb. You're not to worry about me or the arrangements. Everything can be cancelled just with a phone call and we'll only lose a few measly deposits. It will be wonderful for Heather to see her only son married. Everyone will understand, even Stella, although I dread to think how she'll take it. It's the one thing that's keeping her from going under. She needs a good talking to, if you ask me. However, needs must on this occasion and you can get married at the bedside if necessary. I'm standing by tomorrow, ready to make all the phone calls so do let me know asap.

'Bye, sweetheart and don't worry.'

Bernard had some free time before his afternoon meeting with Malley and took the opportunity to do some flat hunting. Bloody ludicrous prices. They could, however, get a two-bedroom two-bathroom apartment in a nice area, with all the perks that Corinne yearned for, near the shops, good restaurants and galleries, round the corner from a tube station, and still have some left over, *if* they got a good price for their house, which he was quite certain they would.

He knew what this meeting was about. It was about Malley's plans for his successor. It ought to have been sorted out months ago so that the staff knew where they stood, but that was Malley. Leave everything to the last minute, keep people on their toes, keep *him* on his toes. Malley was power mad. He was just holding onto the reins for as long as he could, but he would have to let go soon so that the new chap could pick them up. There was no reason for it to go to an outsider, not when they had such a capable bunch ready and willing, tongues hanging out for the job.

He dismissed the opposition. It had to be him. He was due the job. Simple. He had swallowed his pride on more than one occasion, buckled down to take on some of Malley's more outlandish ideas, ideas he had instinctively known would never work. That man flew the entire business by the seat of his pants. Ducking and diving. Weaving and floundering. How the hell he got away with it, with dubious sales expectations and so on, was a complete mystery given the state of the retail trade just now. They were all up against it. Competition was tough and you had to learn to be ruthless. Kill that competition and not be afraid to use all the tricks in the book.

He had a few ideas of his own that would bring the shops back into line, soothe the men and the women who shopped at Pacmans. Never underestimate the ladies, Corinne told him, they have a lot of clout as to what their men buy. So, it was on his agenda to make the shops more lady-friendly. He planned sitting areas with piles of women's magazines for them to browse over, sipping coffee whilst their menfolk were sorted out. He knew space on the sales floor was precious per foot, and it would meet with raised eyebrows, but he would argue that this would boost their sales no end.

Nervously waiting to be allowed into the inner domain, Bernard tried to appear calm. A lot was hanging on this so-called little chat. Corinne thought he was determined to live out his time at the old house and would be delighted and surprised if he suddenly presented her with a promotion, *the* promotion, and a chance to live in the city. It was a long time since he had done something to surprise her.

He could just see her face and, although he had been dying to tell her about today, about what it might mean, he had kept quiet.

Who else was there for this job? Who could do it better than him?

Nobody.

Once he got it, he could then start to groom his successor and he wouldn't be keeping him in suspense like this. He had his eyes on Cuthbert.

'Mr Cooper?' The secretary answered the buzz of the intercom. 'You may go in now, sir.'

He nodded, stood up and straightened his tie, his mouth suddenly dry from anxiety.

Malley had been wallowing in his own self-importance for too long.

Malley needed to go and get on with his watercolours.

'How long have you been with us, Bernard?'

He told him, although his file was on the old sod's desk so he could have answered the question himself.

'Nearly as long as me,' Malley said with satisfaction. 'And you'll be following me into retirement before too long. How's dear Catherine?'

'Corinne, actually. Very well, thank you.' Bernard said, fingering his tie and looking with disdain at Malley's scarlet one. If it wasn't scarlet it would be bright yellow or even shocking pink. The new wider-styled silk range they had bought in for the younger man. Extraordinary.

'Charming woman, your wife,' Malley said. 'Cuthbert Innes is getting married. Did you know?'

'No,' Bernard said. 'Good God, that's quick. Where did he find her? At the last count, he was still looking.'

'Whirlwind romance, I suppose,' Malley said, shaking his head in bewilderment. 'Know nothing about it at all. Women have always been a mystery to me. Anyway, I'm pleased the fellow's settling down. She's an academic by the way. Computer buff or buffess . . .' He grinned at his own joke. 'Fiery lady apparently, able to hold her own. She'll be an asset to him. Young and attractive. He's shown me a photograph. She'll look good hanging on his arm.'

Bernard gave a grunt. What the hell was he supposed to say to that?

'How are we doing, Bernard? Will we have to issue a profits warning this next quarter?'

You should know, Bernard thought, giving him a quick off-the-cuff run-down of the projected figures. It could be worse but then it could be better.

'As I thought,' Malley said with a sigh, gazing out of the window onto the city. 'I don't want to close a single shop. Thin end of the wedge. But we might have to consider losing some of the smaller outlets. I never liked the idea of those little mini-shops in arcades. Sending out the wrong image.'

Bernard nodded gravely, refraining from pointing out that the idea, not unanimously supported by the board, had been Malley's.

'I shall be retiring soon,' Malley went on, eyebrows raised as if he was making a surprise announcement. 'And somebody will have to step into my shoes. Who will that be, Bernard?'

It was a glorious autumnal day outside, the sky wide and high, a day when London was looking at its best and the advantages of living here seemed to outweigh all the problems as Bernard glanced out of the window, wondering what he was supposed to say to that. Better be honest, he supposed.

'Me,' he said. 'I am ready to take it on . . . sir,' he added, never quite sure what the hell to call him. He had been asked, years ago, to call him Dickie but he couldn't bring himself to do that.

'Thought so.' Malley nodded sagely. 'You've been shadowing me for years, haven't you, Bernard? Know the ins and outs of the job. But you're getting on a bit. No sooner would you be in then you'd be out, if you get my drift? And then the whole caboodle will start all over again. It's unsettling both for the workforce and the city. Is Cuthbert ready for it, do you think? Do we need somebody with verve? A youngster?'

Hang on.

'He needs time,' Bernard said, fixing his eyes firmly on the lapels of Malley's suit. Last winter's range. Fine tweed. Bloody good quality. 'Pleasant enough chap, of course, and he has some experience but . . .'

'He's young and adaptable and his new wife is a city girl apparently. If I gave it to you, it would mean moving,' Malley said. 'You can't handle it from where you are now. You need to be here, in the thick of it . . .' He waved a hand vaguely towards the window. 'We need to keep an eye on the opposition too. And we need to appoint a new designer for the casuals. I think the last one was taking the piss, don't you? Nonsensical ideas. Anyway, Cuthbert's got contacts there. One of them has come up with a portfolio of eye-catching stuff and if we don't snatch him up, somebody else will. Nothing too extreme but nothing dull about it either. Middle-of-the-road with punch, that's what he called it.'

He was watching Bernard closely as he spoke, waiting for a reaction. Well, if he thought he was going to break down in tears and beg for the job, he was mistaken.

'We're keen to up sticks,' he said quietly. 'Corinne particularly. She's bored with country life. To be honest, it's always been my thing rather than hers. If we were to move here then we'd stay on when I retired. There wouldn't be any opposition to moving from my wife,' he added, just to drum it in, realizing he was beginning to sound desperate. 'However . . . if you think you need young blood, then I won't deny Cuthbert's a good chap.'

'It's not my decision entirely,' Malley said, drumming his short squat fingers on the desk, the crisp white cuffs of his shirt peeping out from his sleeves, neat gold cuff-links showing. Natty dresser aside from the lurid ties. 'It will have to go to the board of course for a final decision but they'll be happy to go along with my recommendation. They're anxious for stability, getting things back on an even keel, as it were. Once the decision is made, we'll make an official announcement and it will make the financial pages of course. We'll take the opportunity of outlining our new sales strategy at the same time. It will all be very positive and should up the share price.'

Bernard made approving noises, wondering when the bastard was going to say it.

Malley glanced at his watch. 'Coffee, Bernard?'

Bernard smiled. He could see he was in for a long session. Malley was going to make him sweat this one out.

Corinne fluffed out the material before smoothing it, glancing up and blinking away her concentration. She needed glasses for the close work she suspected, which was a pain, but only to be expected at her great age.

Poor Emily was having awful trouble with the bridesmaids, but then she could have told her as much. Adult bridesmaids were akin to lighted matches near a bonfire. They knew what suited them and, unlike children, would not take kindly to being stuffed into things they did not like. Or if they did succumb for the sake of harmony, then on the day itself, they generally displayed a childish ill-humour, making their dresses look ten times worse.

She and Bernard had just had two little attendants at their wedding. The boy who had displayed a roguish charm, even at seven years old, was now no doubt still dispensing the charm doing something in the City and the sweet little girl was now a formidable headmistress of a private school over in Norfolk.

She and Bernard. . . .

Corinne sighed. Another year gone and perhaps it was time she told Bernard to forget the flowers on Joe's birthday. She would still remember it, of course, but it was time she got through it in her own way without a reminder from him. She was beginning to find the gesture irksome.

Look to the future, even if it meant resigning herself to staying here forever. It was time for a few concessions on her part.

She was still debating whether or not to read Joe's diary. She'd always been a stickler for good manners and would never dream of reading her children's private diaries, but this was surely different.

The problem was she worried about what might be there. She thought she knew Joe as well as any mother knew her child and she worried that she might discover he did not love her.

Stephen had rung the other afternoon all the way from Australia to announce that they were to have another baby. They were, he was at pains to tell her, absolutely delighted. Although she offered her surprised congratulations, she couldn't help her own disappointment that it would be another baby she would never bond with because she was too far away. What a dratted nuisance! She had never been particularly good with her own babies, apart from Joe, but she would have liked the chance to fuss and spoil her grandchildren. She would have to wait for Daniel and the rate he was going it might be forever. He kept choosing the wrong girls. Amanda, when she thought about it, had never been the right one and now Emily . . . she was the right girl but she was not available.

She smiled a little, rubbing at her eyes, feeling the smooth silk on her lap, the silk of the gown that Emily would be wearing come December. The girl had worried eyes, ever more worried in the time she had known her, and watching the two of them together at dinner that evening, she had known with an absolute certainty that, if ever two people were meant for each other, they were.

She wondered if she ought to tell Bernard, but he would be both surprised and useless and wouldn't have any sensible ideas. But how could she carry on with this sham? Wasn't it her duty to speak to Emily? Perhaps if she could come up with another situation where the two of them were thrown together, they might in turn see sense. But she couldn't keep on inviting Emily to stay over, for that would look odd.

What Bernard was up to in London she had no idea. He was very likely in collusion with Malley about the succession. Goodness, this was becoming a nightmare, and she wondered if Cuthbert was speaking the truth when he said Bernard had his sights on the big job. News to her. So far as she was aware, he was simply biding his time, writing his dratted book that she wasn't supposed to know about yet, and longing for the moment he could push aside his financial reports and take up his armoury for his silly re-enactments, a little boy playing soldiers.

Unable to concentrate on the job in hand, she was just debating whether or not to take a break and make herself a coffee when she heard a car coming up the drive and saw it was Daniel.

As he stepped out, saw her, waved, she could not stop that little shiver of irritation that always happened whenever she set sight on her second son. She would tell him Stephen's news, and already she was starting to wonder if he might accompany her to Australia when the child arrived. Bernard would not go on such a long flight and she did not fancy the trip alone. And, if she was going to do something about her feelings towards Daniel, a trip to Australia together might be just the very thing to bring about a sort of peace and reconciliation.

She had seen the hurt look in his eyes, the one she usually chose to ignore, and she remembered with irritation what Cuthbert had said about it. Goodness, he had been rather shirty about her attitude and most definitely had seemed to be on the side of Daniel.

It had irked her terribly at the time but later, calming down, she saw that perhaps after all it had taken a stranger to tell her the truth.

CHAPTER EIGHTEEN

'Emily ... Dad speaking. Your mother said to pass on the message. She's had to shoot off to your Aunt Louise's. Crisis. Stella's taken some pills and been carted off to hospital again. Nick-of-time business, but they think she'll pull through. A cry for help, they say. Aunt Louise won't have it that she was trying to kill herself. It didn't help the poor girl when your mother told her that you might have to rush things, have a quiet wedding because of Simon's mother. Awful news. Poor woman. Your mother means it when she says not to worry. She's hovering on the end of the phone waiting to cancel everything. You do what you think best.

'Bye, sweetheart. Look after yourself.'

Chris informed her of Heather's death over the phone. Emily took the call, Simon having been called away on an urgent assignment, and after expressing her condolences, she said she would make sure Simon knew.

'The funeral's on Thursday, if he's interested,' Chris went on to say, his voice ultra-calm as he fought to control it. 'She wanted family flowers only. She liked yellow flowers. Anything yellow.'

'I'm so sorry, but Simon's not back until Saturday,' Emily told him, knowing already that he would not be coming back for it. 'But I will come. I'll take some time off, no problem. If you could give me the directions . . .'

189

Emily was dreading it. She wouldn't know anybody and, with Simon not here, she felt she would have to keep on apologising for that and making excuses. It had been difficult getting hold of him and then she hadn't known what to say, how to break the news. She had not known what to expect either, whether he would be upset or not. His voice gave nothing away but, as expected, he refused to return home for the funeral. Now that Heather was gone, what was the point? They had made up their differences, sort of, and parted on reasonably good terms. What more could he be expected to do?

'Why the hell you feel you have to be there is beyond me,' he told her, voice tight with irritation. 'You don't know Chris. You don't need to stand in for me. Chris knows the score.'

'I want to be there for Heather,' she told him. 'It may sound daft, but there it is. If I don't go, I'll regret it.'

'OK. Sorry. Of course you must go. She would like you to be there,' he said and she heard the sigh, wondering how he would react once she had replaced the receiver. She had a sudden urge to hold him to her, to offer comfort.

'I love you,' she said, twisting the cord of the phone as she waited for his answer, aware she hadn't said it for a very long time, aware also that she was just saying it because he had lost his mother and sounded suddenly like a little boy.

'Take care,' he said. 'Call me when you get back.'

As she replaced the receiver, it took a minute to sink in that he had not said he loved her, too.

Chris's directions were clear and she had no trouble finding the house, where a small group of people, suitably low-voiced, had gathered.

'You didn't wear black. Good,' Chris said, greeting her with a kiss and introducing her to the assembled strangers. He was a hefty man, roughly the same age as Simon but looking and sounding much older, the strain of the past few months apparent.

Emily scarcely had time to mingle before the hearse arrived and they stood up solemnly as the undertakers came in to speak to Chris. Murmured voices in the hall and then, as they piled in some comical confusion into various cars for the journey to the crematorium, the heavens opened. There was a good turn out, she was pleased to see, and some of the principal mourners were wearing black. She had chosen a warm burgundy coat as the weather was getting colder as autumn drew on. Comfortable black boots because Belinda had told her that there was always a lot of unexpected walking about at funerals and heels could be excruciating.

They sang 'All things bright and beautiful' and the duty minister, who had not known Heather said a few kindly words as he had done for the previous funeral and would do for the next. As the coffin slipped through the curtains, Emily felt unexpected tears welling up for the woman she had scarcely known.

She was utterly hopeless at events like this. She followed the other mourners outside into the cold afternoon, the rain settling into a drizzle, autumn well and truly settled in now, and found herself examining the floral tributes, including the one she and Simon had sent. She didn't have much time to dwell on them because the next funeral was following hot on the heels and everyone was forced to shake their umbrellas and retreat hurriedly to their cars for the trip back to Heather's home.

She vowed she would stay the minimum amount of time that she could decently allow, say her goodbyes to Chris and scoot off to report back to Simon. Suddenly, standing there, as some woman who seemed to have taken charge distributed plates of this and that, she felt so angry that Simon was not here. Heather's home, the show house, was grander than she had expected, the elegant drawing-room overlooking a pretty, if damp, garden. On the sideboard, beside the napkins and cutlery, there was a photograph in a silver frame of an attractive and healthy looking

Heather, a woman she had never known, holding hands with Chris.

'Simon couldn't make it, then?' a woman at her side inquired. She had removed a small black hat and her greyish blonde hair was flattened down, but her discreet make-up still looked good and there were no smudges of mascara, so she had obviously managed to keep control of her feelings. She had a smiley face, uncomfortable with the occasion and the necessity for a more sober exterior. In the event, the smile won through. 'I understand from Chris you're Simon's fiancée?'

'That's right. Emily Bellew. Nice to meet you.'

'I'm Caroline Shriver,' she said, as they shook hands. 'Heather's aunt. Such a sad business, isn't it? Poor dear, Chris says she was terribly brave at the last. I didn't visit but then I'm not sure she would have wanted that. I wouldn't have thought she had it in her, to be honest, but I suppose how you face up to your own death is the ultimate test.'

Emily nodded, wondering why she should be more upset apparently than anybody else here, with the possible exception of Chris who, underneath a brave attempt to tough it out, was obviously heartbroken.

'Simon's overseas and these things take such a time to arrange so I told him to stay put,' she said, feeling she had to make some effort to explain, deciding also that she might as well take some of the blame for his absence. 'Otherwise he would have been here. They met, you know?' she added, in case Caroline was not aware of the current state of affairs. 'She came to our flat for dinner and we had a nice chat, the two of us. A heart to heart in fact.'

'I see. Did she mention me?'

'Yes.' Emily felt a blush come on. 'She said you looked after Simon when he was little.'

'I did.' The smile remained fixed but the eyes lost it for a moment. 'He came to me when he was a few weeks old and

Heather went to college. I work from home so it fitted in nicely and I adored having him. I used to do my work in the morning and then we would go off in the afternoon to the park and I would push the pram and people would look in and say how lovely he was and I used to . . .' She paused, gave a little laugh. 'I used to pretend he was mine. It was easier than all the explaining. And then, after a while, it felt like he *was* mine. Heather was not the maternal type. She used to get along at the weekend and spend time with him but he was already getting to know me more and I think it broke her heart that he preferred to sit on my knee and let me give him his bottle.'

'I see.' They had progressed into a little corner of the room and sat down, facing each other across a small table, their collection of nibbles untouched.

'And then one day, when he was three, she heard me shouting at him and she was horrified, practically accused me of abusing him.' Caroline gave a short laugh. 'What nonsense. The fact was I always thought – and I still do – that if a child is doing something that could physically harm him then yelling at him will give him such a shock that he jolly well won't do that again. He'd picked up a marble from somewhere and stuffed it in his ear and I'd just that minute rescued him when Heather walked in. She wouldn't listen to an explanation.'

'I see. It sounded a bit different the way she said it.'

'She told you then? You see how important it was to her. Simon grew into a lovely little boy but, after that incident, Heather was never happy at my looking after him. She wanted . . .' She glanced round but nobody was listening in, 'she wanted it all and she resented me and the influence I was having on him in the end. One day she just waltzed in and took him away. Just like that. Said she'd be looking after him herself from then on and she did in a fashion. It upset me dreadfully at the time but there was nothing I could do. It was just a family arrangement and nothing was in writing. I had no claim on him whatsoever. I just parcelled up all his things . . .' she paused a minute, looked away. 'And posted them to her. We never talked about it after that and she didn't want me to see him either, which I could never understand. I didn't think it was fair to the little boy to cut him off from me completely. How do you explain to a child? But it was what she wanted and I thought it best not to interfere. After all, she was his mother. I always sent him a card and presents on his birthday and at Christmas, but I don't know if she ever passed them on to him. But I've kept track of what Simon's been up to. I was very fond of him.'

This was not quite the version Heather had presented to her and it was awkward to be discussing her like this, criticising in fact, when they had only just returned from the funeral. 'If you'll excuse me . . .' Emily said, softening her impending departure with a smile, but not keen to pursue this any further. 'I must have a quick word with Chris and then I have a long drive. It takes ages,' she went on in a flurry. 'Across Birmingham and down the M5 and then it's quite a trek down the A38 to Plymouth. I shall break the journey, of course, as it's just me driving, probably half way down the M5 and then just before it ends at Exeter . . .' She stopped, realizing she was twittering on about nothing.

Caroline nodded, managing to seem interested. 'When's the wedding?'

It was an abrupt question. Was she expecting an invitation? And why on earth hadn't Simon thought of asking her, this woman who had played such an important role in his young life?

She told her the date, explaining hastily that the invitations had not yet been sent out, blaming her mother.

'My apologies in advance,' Caroline said, seeming to assume she would be receiving one. 'But I feel it would be best if I don't attend.'

'If that's how you feel then I'll tell Simon,' Emily said, smiling with relief as Chris butted in, asking if they'd like to sign the card.

The card was a huge one and Chris wanted everybody who had attended the funeral to sign it with a comment. Rather like a comments book in a B&B. Uncomfortable with it, but unable to come up with a good enough excuse not to sign, Emily found herself sitting at the little desk, the card open in front of her, pen in hand.

The card was blank so far, so it fell to her to start the ball rolling, to come up with something suitable when she didn't feel she knew Heather at all, even less so after her conversation with Caroline.

Simon should be doing this, damn him. But then, hadn't she insisted on coming along. Chris was rounding people up and a little respectful queue was forming so she signed her name with a flourish, adding Simon's, saying that Heather had been such a sweet, kind lady and how dearly she would be missed.

There.

Duty done.

She collared Chris a few minutes later, regretting that she would be first to make a move. To her surprise, he hugged her close and, sensing the depth of his grief, she hugged him too.

'Simon sends his love,' she told him, whispering into his ear. 'He will miss her, you know. I know they were only just reconciled but . . .'

'Let's not go into that,' Chris said, moving to hold her at arm's length. 'It was nice of you to come, Emily. Don't bother to send me a wedding invitation, but I wish you both well. I can't get my head round the fact that, by refusing to accept how we felt about each other, he made Heather very unhappy.'

'I'm sorry,' she said, touching his arm. 'Truly sorry. I'm sure it was never intentional.'

'Maybe not,' he said with a faint smile and she knew he was just saying that to make her feel better.

'I'll keep in touch,' she said lightly, desperate now to leave, desperate to have time alone to think this through.

On the way home, she found herself thinking more and more about this man whom she was to marry in a few months' time. Simon's problems were deep-rooted, as had been proved today, and surely she could find a way to help him through them.

She was becoming Miss Dithery where this whole business was concerned and if it wasn't for the fact she had promised his mother she would look after him, she would have called it a day by now. Oh God, she couldn't go through with it, with marriage, for a reason like that.

She needed to talk to somebody fast.

Not her mother.

Nor Corinne because she was too close to Daniel.

Certainly not to Daniel for she knew she would end up in his arms being consoled and where the hell would that lead?

Geraldine . . . she had been a bit prickly of late – very likely the ticking all the right boxes thing – but she would be perfect.

Not too close a friend but close enough.

She would spill the entire can of beans, swear Geraldine to secrecy and see if the two of them couldn't come up with a sensible solution.

One where she got away scot-free, where her mother was not too upset and where Simon did not lose face.

CHAPTER NINETEEN

'Emily, what an awful shock to hear about poor, dear Heather. How very sad and do pass on our deepest sympathy to Simon. However, looking on the bright side, it does mean that we can go ahead as planned with all the arrangements. Frankly, darling, although I didn't want to say as much, it would have been hell on earth cancelling when everything is coming together so wonderfully well. Stella is absolutely fine. I'm sure she never meant to kill herself, but it gave her the shock she needed to get her act together. Aunt Louise is going to watch her like a hawk from now on, so there won't be any more nonsense.

'The cake, darling. Have you come to any decisions on that? Your father and I had a wonderful three-tiered wedding cake with silver pillars and all the paraphernalia but Bernice had a chocolate cake of all things, so anything goes these days. Have a think and let me know. Miss Millet has agreed to make it, whatever your choice, but I should be giving her some ideas and not springing things on her at the last minute. We must forget about her past because it's what she can do with icing that matters.

'Again, our sincere condolences to poor Simon. Tell him it was for the best.

'Bye.'

Simon had left a message on the machine saying that he would be unavoidably delayed by a couple of days but she could probably get him on his mobile.

Probably?

She was annoyed because she felt exhausted after the drive back from the funeral, and she had thought he would be back the following day. She was annoyed also because of all the excuses she had made on his behalf, especially to Chris, who had seen through them anyway.

Geraldine had taken a few days off work too, so she hadn't been able to speak to her, to try to get some other sane point of view on this. Geraldine understood her and she knew Simon vaguely. She would reassure her and tell her that all these anxieties were normal. And she had to remember that Simon had not had the best of starts, effectively abandoned by his mother and then, just when he was learning to love Aunt Caroline, that said mother had whipped him away and denied him ever seeing Caroline again.

All this according to the blessed Caroline, of course, and Heather was no longer around to ask her why she had done it.

It would take a day or two to recover from the long journey and the next day she left work early because Clive had caught her dozing at her desk, shopped briefly for food and went back home.

It felt very empty and alone and she frowned as she dropped her shopping bags on the kitchen bench, deciding on a hot shower to revive her and, with nobody likely to disturb her, she could then relax in front of the television watching some mind-soothing soap.

It was seven o'clock by the time she was showered and changed into her towelling gown and she had just finished a comforting meal of tomato pasta and chocolate ice-cream when the buzzer sounded.

'Hi, Emily. It's me, Daniel.'

Of course it was. She would recognize the voice anywhere and felt her heart give a little jolt of surprise.

'Daniel! What are you doing here?'

'Just passing,' he said. 'It seemed daft not to give you a call. I wondered if you and Simon might like to join me for a quick drink?'

'Simon's away,' she said, knowing her voice sounded strange. 'But I'd like a drink with you. Look, if you hang on there, I can be with you in ten minutes.'

'OK.'

Frantically she flew into the bedroom, finding something casual to wear. Her hair was curly and a bit damp from the shower and she didn't have time to do a good make-up. Oh, what the hell. She struggled into newly washed jeans, a sweater, finally easing herself into a jacket and, giving up on the hair, pulled a beret over it.

He would have to lump it. He ought to have given her warning.

With a final despairing look at herself in the mirror, she splashed herself with perfume and headed for the lift.

Daniel was not just passing. He had spent the time since he had last seen her just thinking and dreaming about her and this morning, after Harvey had finally asked what the hell was wrong with him, he had made a decision.

Enough of this creeping round on eggs business. He was going to tell her how he felt and stuff the consequences.

Driving into the city, he was taking a chance on Simon being away. He was away a helluva lot, so the chances were in his favour. He had his fingers crossed when he pressed the buzzer. If Simon had answered, then he would have had to honour the invitation for the two of them and never mind what Simon might make of it. He had felt like hammering the air when he heard her say he was away and then the breathless request that he hang around for ten minutes. An invitation up to the apartment was what he had really hoped for, but you couldn't have everything. A drink followed by a meal, perhaps, if she hadn't eaten already and then, maybe then, she might invite him back.

What then?

Well, that depended very much on her but, if he had read the signals properly, she was every bit as desperate for him as he was for her.

And here she was.

'Sorry . . .' Emily exploded from the door, almost unrecognizable in a short heavy jacket and a pink beret. 'I'm having a bad hair day,' she said, catching his glance. 'Don't say it. This is awful, isn't it? Fashion victim I'm afraid.'

'You look like a French spy,' he said with a grin.

'Not intentional. Anyway, how are you?'

'Fine. You?'

'Great. Just great. Or rather . . .' she hesitated just a moment. 'To be honest, I'm shattered. I was going to have an early night.'

'Sorry. You should have said. It was only an idea to have a drink. Do you want to eat afterwards?'

'I've eaten. I think. What are you doing in Plymouth?'

'Just seeing somebody about something,' he said, keeping the lie as vague as he could.

She gave him a quick bemused glance, but did not probe further. 'I'm just back from Simon's mother's funeral,' she explained instead. 'And you can imagine how that was.'

'Oh, I see. You poor thing. I've been to more than enough of them.' He shuddered. 'Best mates mainly. Climbing friends.'

And Joe's of course. A vision flooded his head, of his mother leaning heavily onto his father, managing to keep the tears at bay. Stephen had been upset and shown it, his father grim-faced and he . . . well, he had stood in church looking at the casket and not been able to put aside those last moments of his brother's life.

The pub was crowded and warm and they had to weave their way through the crowd.

'I hope Simon won't mind you being here with me,' he said when at last he managed to get hold of some drinks. 'White wine and soda?' He handed it to her and squeezed beside her on the bench.

'I don't think you mind very much what Simon thinks,' she said, taking a handful of peanuts and popping a couple into her mouth. 'In fact, I don't believe you were just passing at all.'

'Ah. Guilty as charged,' he said, pulling a wry face. 'Am I so transparent?'

She nodded and he searched her tired face for the truth and found it in her look.

There was no going back.

'What are we to do?' she asked gently. 'I don't want to hurt Simon, especially not now, just when his mother's died. And you know I promised her I would be there for him. How can I just abandon him?'

He reached over and held her hand, feeling her little fingers close round his, feeling so protective of her.

'I love you,' he mouthed and that made her smile.

'You don't know me, Daniel,' she said. 'We've not known each other very long and it's much too soon to be talking like this.'

'Why is it?' he asked. 'I've never understood this thing about timing. When I'm climbing I often have to make quick decisions. Make-or-break ones. Life or death ones at that. And I just do it. I don't start agonizing about the pros and cons of it.'

'Your mother said something like that. About the vicar asking if she loved your father and looking very relieved when she said she did. That was all there was to it.'

'Exactly. It's the same with us. I don't know about you but I knew as soon as I saw you that you were for me.'

He was keeping his voice low, for this intimate conversation was not one he wished others to hear, but nobody was listening anyway and the music that was blaring from speakers changed as if he had requested it to a more suitable romantic mood. A crooner of old singing 'In the Still of the Night'.

'I knew too,' she said with a big sigh. She took a swig of her wine, her cheeks flushed, eyes bright and shining. She looked fantastic, even with the daft hat.

'That's it then. Let's get out of here,' he said, pushing his half-finished drink aside.

She made no protest, following him outside, still holding his hand and once they were in the street, they made their way back to her flat.

He tightened his grip on her hand as they waited for the lift. A woman emerged, smiled at them and walked off, a little white dog tucked under her arm.

'We're not supposed to have animals,' Emily said as the door slid behind them. 'But I think some people take advantage. I don't mind but . . .'

He shushed her, kissing her then, kissing her long and hard. Wound his arms round her, pulling her close so that he could feel her body beneath the many layers of clothing.

'It's long been a fantasy of mine,' he said slowly, drawing away and looking at her newly kissed face, at the love in her shining eyes. 'This lift thing . . .'

'Mine too,' she giggled.

'Do you think we dare?' he asked, reaching for the button to stop the lift in its tracks.

But there were already protesting voices outside and, with a grin and a little pat on her bottom, he let her go.

He kissed her again once they were in the flat but before it all got too much for them, she disentangled herself, taking off the beret and running her fingers through her hair.

'I'll make a coffee,' she said. 'We have to talk.'

He didn't want to talk. He wanted to make love to her there and then. He had dreamed about this moment, but she was right, or it didn't seem right to do it here, in Simon's flat, in Simon's bed. Bloody hell, he wanted to though.

'Don't . . .' she whispered, as he followed her into the kitchen, gently lifting her hair and planting a little kiss on the back of her neck. 'Oh, please don't. Not yet. I can't bear it.'

'OK.' He knew it wasn't a rebuff and she was just being sensible before they got carried away. 'There's going to be a helluva stink, isn't there?'

'You bet. My mum will go spare. The last time I spoke to her I did hint that something was wrong.' She smiled as she recalled the turn the conversation had taken, her mother assuming that she was pregnant and deciding that it wouldn't matter too much because she would scarcely show and anyway, her father was desperate to buy a train-set. Boy or girl it wouldn't matter. 'She did ask if there was somebody else and I said no.'

'Liar.'

'I know. I did love Simon once,' she said, sitting down with him at the kitchen table. 'But I should have realized we've been gradually pulling apart. But I didn't know then what I know now. I didn't know about his childhood, because he would never talk about it. His mother left him with an aunt who more or less brought him up for four years. And then Heather suddenly got an attack of conscience and decided she wanted him for herself and she just took him away. I don't think Aunt Caroline ever forgave her for that. She seemed a nice woman, but then so did Heather. I'm getting two conflicting views here and I don't know what to believe. But, whatever happened, whoever's right, just think of the effect on a small boy. No wonder he acts as he does sometimes.'

'You're making excuses for him,' he told her. 'We've all got something in the past that we might prefer to forget about . . .'

'I'm sorry, I've reminded you of your brother,' she said, sensitive to his sudden change of mood.

'Sweetheart . . .' He smiled at the word and her reaction. 'Before we go any further, I have to tell you something. Something that I haven't told anybody before.'

'That sounds ominous.'

'Are you sure you're up for it? It's a bit of a nightmare.'

'Go on.'

'Well then. Here goes,' he said with a rueful smile. 'Joe was always pestering me to take him for a proper climb. I always knew he had the potential to be good at it but he was only a beginner and I was very aware of that. So, I had been careful and we'd been on a few decent walks together, nothing too arduous but he had it in his blood . . .' He paused a minute, remembering the keen look in his brother's eyes. 'I decided I'd start to break him in gently. He'd finished his exams and this was going to be a treat. I would take him up to the Lake District and we would do a few climbs together. Not serious mountaineering, not with Joe, just a bit of strenuous fell walking.'

Emily nodded encouragingly as he battled for a moment with a sudden strong emotion. Bloody hell, it still did it, every time he brought it back to mind, which was why he had tried over the years to forget it.

'We set off to do this walk. It's a good day's walk, seven miles or so and the route follows a rocky ridge to the top. It's an elevation of two thousand feet plus all the way so it makes you feel good. It promised to be a glorious day, one of those days that sticks in your head,' he said, closing his eyes a moment and almost feeling the morning sun on his face. It wasn't an easy place to get to but he liked it because of that and he had done the climb a few times before and never met a single soul, which was fine from the solitude angle but tough if you landed yourself in trouble as it had turned out. 'We'd set off at eight o'clock so that we could get a good run at it and take our time.'

Emily was very still, looking at him, hardly daring to breathe, afraid to spoil the moment and bring him back to the present. But she need not have feared for, talking about it like this for the first time ever, he was transported back as if it were yesterday.

'There are two peaks to scale and we stopped at the first summit for a break. You get a fantastic view from there of the way ahead. That's what it's all about . . .' he continued. 'The air up there, the sky. It's almost a spiritual experience and it seemed to get to Joe too for he started to talk about the exams and his girl-friend, who had just dumped him. Mum hadn't liked her so she shed no tears, but Joe was pretty devastated. I knew he was, and I was waiting for him to talk about it.'

'First love . . .' Emily smiled at some memory.

'Exactly. And then there was his course at university, the one he'd had to work so hard for. He said that he'd only gone for it because of Mum. She wanted him to do it and he didn't want to disappoint her. So, he was worried about that too.'

Emily sighed. If she ever had children, one thing was sure, she would never ever try to make them do things that she had always wanted to do and never done.

'It was an eye-opener for me. I hadn't realized he was so fed up. We didn't talk much about things like that. But, up there, you feel so at one with nature but so insignificant at the same time, up there he talked to me and I listened. He was getting emotional though and I didn't want it to affect our progress so I bustled him along. It wasn't a hard climb,' he added, turning to look at her. 'It was more a toughish walk. Any fit guy could do it without a problem.'

She nodded, prompting as he fell silent. 'What happened, Daniel?'

'He just flipped,' he said, needing to get this over with now he had started. He looked at this woman whom he loved, felt her sympathy, and finally said the one thing that he had kept to himself all these years. 'We got up to this part near the second summit where the rocks form a sort of staircase. Even though it's wide enough, you've got to take some care there because just at one point there's a terrifying drop on one side and that's where it happened. He didn't fall. He went off deliberately, Emily.'

The shock banged into her and she recoiled from it, looking as if she had been physically hit.

'He picked his spot and I think he knew the fall would very likely kill him,' Daniel said, closing his eyes again as the memory swung and levelled in his head. 'He was behind me. He called out to me and I turned round and then he looked at me, said sorry and just walked off the edge.'

His voice caught then and she was there in a flash, at his side, taking him in her arms and holding him close, murmuring little words of comfort as he fought to regain his composure. He hadn't thought it would affect him so badly, telling her this, but it was as much relief as anything else, getting it out of his system at last, telling the truth, the whole truth and nothing but the truth.

'And of course you didn't feel you could tell your mother,' Emily said after a while, stroking his face. 'Oh Daniel, how awful for you.'

'I still can't understand why he did it,' he said. 'We all get rejected and life doesn't always fall into place as easily as that. But we don't kill ourselves, do we?'

'Some people do,' she said. 'I don't understand it, either, but I think you should have told your mother the truth. Better that than her blaming you for it. She'll cope. In fact, I think she'll be relieved too. You must tell her or, if you don't feel you can, then I will.'

'No.' he said, more sharply than he intended. 'I don't want you to do that. Why tell her? So that she can pin the blame on herself rather than me? I think I'd rather she blames me than that.'

Driving home that evening, having reluctantly said his goodbyes to Emily, fortified with a final lingering kiss that made leaving her all the more difficult, he found his heart lighter because at last somebody else was sharing his burden.

He still doubted that he would tell his mother but he found himself turning off at Dapplestone. It was late but he knew his father hung around until midnight so it was not too late and he needed to speak to him now before he lost his nerve.

CHAPTER TWENTY

'Emily . . . Mum here, leaving a message. Your father is making no attempt at all to write his speech. He says he'll do it off-the-cuff. I ask you. I've bought him a little book to help out but it doesn't seem to be helping at all and he won't look at the speech I've written. I thought we might include some funny little anecdotes about when you were little. Do you remember the time you dressed up as a fairy and forgot your knickers? Aunt Jean has bought you a Dyson cleaner and Mrs Foster next door has ordered you some bathroom scales from the Argos catalogue. They sound awfully complicated and, as well as your weight, they measure your body fat and your body water content. Anyway, the thought's there, isn't it? I hope you've got over your little worries, darling. As I say, we all have them and it's as well to get them over with sooner rather than later.

'Speak to you later.'

'Your mobile was switched off,' Emily said, accepting a kiss on the cheek.

'Sorry. Bad reception anyway.'

'Where were you?'

She sighed, picking up the jacket he had thrown onto the hall table and hanging it up. The guilt she had been feeling these last few days was all the more acute now that Simon was back.

Although her heart said otherwise, she had rung Daniel to ask that they didn't see each other for a while, a cooling-off period to see how things panned out. She just wanted to be quite sure that she wasn't suffering from a sort of temporary relapse into emotional insanity, the result of Simon being away from her. But now that he was back with her, the feelings that had been creeping up about him were intensified.

Quite simply, the reaction she normally had, the delight in seeing him again, was no longer there. She had to tell him the truth. Daniel was right. She couldn't marry Simon just because she had promised his mum she would. Foolishly though, she wished Heather was around so that she could explain as much.

'Where have I been? Where haven't I been?' he said in answer to her question. 'All over the place.' He plumped down on the sofa and reached for the remote. 'I'd rather not talk about it. I'm knackered.'

'Do you want to know about your mother's funeral?' she asked, sitting opposite as the television blared into life. It was a cookery programme and they watched a moment in silence. 'Because if you are remotely interested, I will tell you all about it.'

'Look , . .' he flicked a switch and the sound turned down but still the cooking went on. 'I told you we said our goodbyes. There was no bloody need for you to go, but if you wanted to act the martyr then so be it, but don't drag me into it and don't try to make me feel guilty. I don't want to know about it and if you think I'm going to get in touch with Chris you can forget it.'

'He was upset,' she said, trying to ignore the frantic goings on in the TV kitchen. 'He loved her. He loved her a lot. And I met Aunt Caroline. She loved you a lot too.'

'She never came to see me, not once,' he said, his eyes a cold blue. 'I know mother didn't want her to, but she could have made the effort.'

'Oh, for heaven's sake,' Emily said, irritation bubbling over. 'If only you'd talked, the three of you. Caroline loved you, your mother did, and you loved them both. Why make such a big issue of it? Why spend a lifetime in a stupid huff?'

'Emily . . . I think we should just put all this behind us,' he said with a quick smile that brought no warmth to his eyes. And then he said something that took her completely by surprise. 'I've been having second thoughts about the wedding.'

'Second thoughts?' she echoed, the words startling her into silence for a minute. 'What do you mean?'

'It's the tie business,' he interrupted, his smile suddenly beaming. 'What the hell! To please my lady, I will wear one.'

She was working with Michael next day and it didn't take him long to come up with his news.

'Angharad was right,' he told her. 'I've come into money.'

'Congratulations,' she said, matching his smile. 'Well done.'

'I know you're dying to ask how much but you're far too polite and too English to ask,' he went on cheerfully. 'Not enough to make a difference to my life, that's for sure. But since I've never even won a raffle prize before it was a real surprise.' He looked round, leaned towards her, lowering his voice. 'One hundred pounds on Premium Bonds. I only have twenty of the things, had them since I was a teenager, so when you consider the odds. . . .'

She took the point and saw him chatting with Angharad when she arrived. Chatting and giving her a little kiss. Angharad seemed delighted and, giving a little wave, headed her way.

'How are *you*, Emily?' she said with feeling.

'Fine, thanks. Shouldn't I be?' she said, regretting her sharp reply at once. 'Sorry. Things are a bit . . .'

'Why don't you come over to see me sometime?' Angharad said gently. 'Just for a coffee and a chat.'

'I'd like that. Maybe we could have that private session you mentioned?' Emily asked, before she could stop herself. It was Michael's win that had done it, nothing spectacular, but there was no getting away from the fact that Angharad had been right.

'Of course. Give me a few days. I need to consult your chart anyway before I see you to see what positions the planets are in.' She made a tutting sound. 'People think I can just pull things off out of the blue. They don't realize the time it takes or the concentration it requires.'

'I'm very grateful to you for taking the trouble' Emily said, at a complete loss as to why she was doing this, horribly aware too that she was forking out fifteen pounds for the pleasure of listening to a load of twaddle. 'Will Friday after work be all right?'

'Yes.' Angharad gave her a close look. 'I can't change the stars you know. I can't make bad news good.'

'I know that.' Emily saw Clive heading purposefully her way and wound things up. 'Drop me your directions on my desk if you will. Thanks.'

Angharad's cottage was about as awkward to get to as it could possibly be. Once over the Devon/Cornwall border, heading towards Gunnislake, the road swept downwards to the river in a series of terrifying bends, over a narrow bridge and then up and up.

Angharad had warned her not to miss the sharp turn or she would have to drive for another ten miles or so before there was anywhere safe to turn round, so Emily made damned sure she didn't.

She wondered how Angharad could face this journey every single day but a quick glance at the cottage and the pretty garden and the views over the river valley was surely the reason, even though it was dark now and the views Angharad had told her about were invisible. She could feel them though, if that were possible, as she stepped out of her car and got her bearings. The nights were drawing in fast as winter approached and she had noticed a sharp tang in the air first thing.

Angharad was at the door to usher her through to a cosy sitting room, where a log fire blazed in an inglenook fireplace. Logs sat in a wicker basket on the hearth on one side and on the other lay a pale ginger cat in grave danger of singeing his or her fur. The sofa was cinnamon-coloured with orange and red cushions piled on it and there were a lot of lively plants grouped together in one corner. A lavender fragrance hung in the air and it had an instantly calming effect.

'Sit down,' Angharad said, almost shy here in her own home. 'It's funny that we've known each other so long, Emily, and this is the first time you've visited.'

Emily nodded, embarrassed that it had taken something like this, something she needed, before it had occurred. There had been invitations casually flung her way but, as in the way of casual invitations it was never quite clear if they were meant to be taken up. For the first time, she wondered if Angharad was a little lonely.

'I'm sorry about that,' she said. 'We must do it more often and you must visit me although . . .' She pulled a face as she sat down. 'I'm sure you are about to tell me that I won't be long at my present address.'

Angharad laughed. 'I'm not a fortune teller,' she said. 'All I can do is equip you with the facts and then you do what you think best.'

There was a short silence. Emily wondered what to say, how to say it, because so far, other than throwing the hint at her mother, she hadn't told anybody else about her doubts. Admitting it to Angharad would be admitting it to the world.

'I once did some astrology charts for a company,' Angharad said at last, noticing her hesitation. 'Before I joined Greys. It was a small company and the managing director was a friend of mine. She was taking on new staff, a couple of people, and desperately worried that she might make a dreadful mistake because they needed to fit in. So, she passed on their applications and asked me to do a character analysis. All very confidential, of course. But I was able to tell her that as she was a Scorpio she would get on very well with people with a heavy water influence in their chart, that's the Cancerians and Pisceans. I can tell from a chart if a person is emotionally stable or otherwise, and how they'll react in a difficult situation.'

'Can you? I can see that being very useful,' Emily said, reluctant to admit to any doubts because Angharad seemed so certain.

'It is. People in the corporate world are using alternative methods like astrology more and more, and it's much more accurate than an in-depth interview. People can lie their socks off at an interview, but they cannot change their charts. It works personally for me too. I always ask a man what his star sign is and it's prevented me from getting into a hopeless relationship more than once.' She looked directly at Emily. 'When's your fiancé's birthday?'

The question took her by surprise but it was of course no surprise when Angharad smiled slightly at the answer.

'I see. Fire and water clash terribly. It rarely works.'

'Is that what you saw in my chart?' Emily asked. 'A clash of personalities? Did you know my love life was running into trouble?'

Angharad nodded. 'Absolutely. I've watched you over these last few months but you wouldn't have thanked me for telling you and no, it doesn't make me feel good. I'm sad for you.'

Over a cup of coffee, they chatted some more and by the end of it Emily was convinced that there was *something* in it. Angharad had told her nothing she didn't know already, but maybe she had just been looking for confirmation of what she knew already.

Fire and water.

A terrible clash of personalities.

Simon and herself.

CHAPTER TWENTY-ONE

'Emily . . . Mum here. You sounded very down, darling, when I last spoke to you and we really can't have that. You have to buck up. All these arrangements are enough to send anybody off into a downward spiral but we just have to keep focused as they keep saying. Can we fix a date for you and Simon to come over? There are so many things we need to discuss face-to-face and it's ages since we've seen you I've very nearly forgotten what you look like. Joke, darling!

'Mrs Evans wants to know if you would like some matching suitcases?

'Have you any idea where Simon's taking you for your honeymoon? I'd try to find out if I were you because surprises have a nasty habit of being just that.

'Anyway, do ring and we can juggle our diaries because mine fills up so quickly.

'Love to Simon.

'Bye.'

Corinne was in bed when she heard Daniel's car arriving. She was reading a new biography, propped up with pillows, the room softly lit. She had drawn the curtains, not because they were overlooked but because it was cosier that way.

Bernard was acting very strangely. He had come back from

London and seemed reluctant to answer her questions about what had happened. She presumed therefore that he did not wish her to know and the only thing she could think of was that Cuthbert had spoken the truth. Bernard had wanted to be considered for Dickie's job when he went and once again he had been passed over.

What a company! To pass on Bernard with all his experience was utterly ridiculous and she half-hoped the new man – whoever he might be – would make a real dog's dinner out of it. That would show them what a ghastly mistake they had made.

She tried to make it up to him, finding herself not annoyed this time but indignant on her poor husband's behalf. She would not mention the dreaded words *top job* unless he did. There was a tingle of regret on her own part, too, for it would have been nice – dammit, it would have been fabulous – to be the chief executive's wife. The job demanded a wife, unless the new person was a woman, in which case it would demand a husband.

Corinne put down her book, hearing voices as Bernard let Daniel in. It was odd that Daniel should be calling so late but a bit of father–son bonding would not come amiss, and she would leave them to it. Let them hammer it out, whatever it was. She found, however, that she was not the least sleepy but not in the mood for carrying on with the chapter, either, for the book was proving to be rather plodding. Reaching across to the little bedside table, she opened the drawer and lifted Joe's diary out. She ought to have thrown it out without looking at it. If she did look at it, it would surely upset her yet again.

Or would it?

It was hard to face but grief did heal and seven years on, she knew her grief had peaked and was on the downslide now. Of course, she still thought of him, but mostly happy thoughts these days. That was the way it was with grief. It became bearable eventually.

So, perhaps it was time she laid the ghost once and for all.

She wondered what they were talking about downstairs. Very likely, Bernard would be telling Daniel about the job that had once again flown out of the window. It might take a few days for him to pluck up the courage to tell her, but when he did she had worked out how she would react. He needn't worry. This time she was going to place the blame squarely at dopey Dickie's door.

With a sigh, she opened Joe's diary, smoothed the page lovingly for a moment before starting to read.

'Have you told Mum yet?' Daniel asked, accepting a glass of beer and settling back on the sofa in his dad's study. He had interrupted his father doing some work on his book, the lamp on the desk sending a glow over the massed papers.

'No.' Bernard smiled. 'Not yet. I'm waiting for the right moment, Daniel. I have to do it before word gets around, of course and I'm not sure I can trust Marian, for instance not to let the cat out of the bag. She's going to miss me.'

Daniel smiled too. Who would have thought it? He had always known his dad was damned good at his job and it was nice to think that somebody else thought so too. A couple of years heading the company would be a great way to go out and his mum would be thrilled for at last she would get her way and the move to London she had craved for so long.

'Congratulations!' he said, raising his glass.

'Thanks. What have you been up to?' Bernard asked him. 'You look pleased with yourself. Don't tell me you're off to the Himalayas again? That won't go down well with your mother.'

'No. It's all a bit delicate,' Daniel said, putting his glass down before deciding it might be best to just come straight out with it. 'You've never met Emily Bellew, have you dad?'

He shook his head. 'One of your mother's clients I believe. I've heard her mention the name. What about her?'

'We've . . . me and Emily . . . we've. . . .'

'Spit it out,' his dad said with a grin. 'Don't tell me you've gone and fallen for the girl.'

'That's it. And the best thing, Dad, is that she feels the same way. It's just great, isn't it? Tricky, of course, because she was going to get married in December to this guy called Simon.'

Bernard whistled. 'Bloody hell, Daniel, you don't half make your life complicated. Has she told her fiancé?'

'Not yet. She's going to have to. I'm sorry for that but. . . .'

'You mustn't be. It will be for the best. Your mother likes the girl. She's mentioned her once or twice and that means she likes her. Had her over to stay in fact.'

'I've told Emily what happened the day Joe died,' Daniel went on, hearing his father draw a sharp breath. 'I'm going to tell you and then we'll decide whether or not to tell mother.'

Bernard sat down heavily on the desk chair. Out in the hall, the grandfather clock whirred and started on its chimes. Daniel waited until the last chime died away and then he started to speak.

'I'm driving over.' Daniel's voice over the line was clear and determined. 'We'll see him together just in case he starts getting awkward.'

'He won't,' Emily said wearily. 'He's being very nice to me since he got back this time. He's even agreed to wear a tie at the wedding.'

'There isn't going to be one,' Daniel said. 'Or at least you're not marrying Simon.'

'Is that a proposal?' she asked, looking out of the apartment window onto the lights below.

'Sorry. I meant to do it by the book. On my knees and everything. Scrub it and I'll propose properly later.'

'I can't scrub it,' she said, smiling at the phone. 'I'm not sure is the answer. We'll just see how it goes. I can't face the thought of all this again.'

'OK. Whatever. So long as we're together,' he said easily. 'The

217

proposal stands and you can let me know when you're ready.'

'When's your birthday? Do you know your star sign?'

He told her, mystified as he heard a little whoop of delight. He had no idea what was so special about his birthday but it had struck a big chord with Emily.

'Are you serious about driving over?' she asked. 'Because if you are then I want him to know before you get here. And it would be better if I moved out, don't you think? I shan't want to stay and he won't want me here, either.'

'I wouldn't dream of letting you stay there a minute longer. Get your bags packed,' Daniel said. 'And then you can come back with me. I've already sorted it with Harvey and he's OK about you staying until we can get sorted out with a place of our own.'

Emily sat in the dark, waiting.

She sat in the smart leather chair, the one she had chosen, thinking how she would break the news. She had done it a couple of times before, broken off a relationship, but this time it was harder. After five years more or less, it was *very* hard, for they had had good times at the beginning and yes, she had imagined they would live happily ever after. She supposed she had hoped they would marry eventually, even if the proposal had come as a surprise and she wondered if she ought to have taken heed of her immediate lukewarm reaction. That was the gut feeling, wasn't it, and that ought to have told her something.

Poor Simon.

She could not blame him entirely for this but then she couldn't blame herself either. It was just a steady drifting away. When had they last had a quiet evening in together and done normal happy things?

There would be such heartbreak as a result of this. Her mother would dissolve completely and as to Yvonne and Stella . . . well, she hoped she wouldn't be held responsible for Stella. But they would get over it and when her mother had calmed down – her dad would help her out here – she would see it was much better to do it now.

Her answerphone was flickering away and she suspected another frantic message from her mother, but she was in no mood this evening for a heart-to-heart. She would have to go over to Kent when she had told Simon because she needed to speak to her mother face-to-face.

Simon's key in the door roused her and she sat up straight.

'Why are you sitting in the dark?' he asked, switching lamps on as he came through. 'Were you asleep?'

'No. Just thinking.' She put down her cold cup of coffee. 'Do you want a drink?'

'No,' he said briskly, sitting on the sofa opposite and placing his arm the length of it. There had been a time when she would have curled up there beside him but not now.

'Simon . . . we have to talk,' she said, fingering her engagement ring to remind her what this was all about.

He laughed but it was a bitter sound. 'I think I know what this is about. Things were going great between us, weren't they, up until a few weeks ago and then it all went belly up.'

'You could say that,' she said, almost in a whisper. 'I'm sorry.'

'No, I'm sorry,' he said, his smile nervous. 'Hell, I never meant to hurt you, not in a million years. But these things happen. I made a promise to my mother that I would look after you and it's hard to break that promise now she's gone. It makes me feel mean as hell but I can't go on pretending. It's not fair to you.'

'*You* made a promise to your mother?' she asked. 'So did I. I promised the same, or rather that I would look after you.'

'I see. She really had the pair of us sussed, didn't she?'

'Are *you* pulling out of this?' Emily asked, feeling stupid as it dawned what he was on about.

'Yes.' He looked at her straight, determined as ever. 'I have tried to do the right thing by you. And at first I thought I could do

219

it, go through with it, but I can't. Geraldine feels terrible about it but what can we do?'

'Geraldine? Not Geraldine Grainger?'

He nodded and everything fell into place. No wonder Geraldine had been a bit off with her, guilty feelings no doubt.

'Have you and she. . . ?'

'Just recently,' he said quickly. 'After I realized that your heart wasn't in it any more. I got hold of Geraldine to talk to her about it and well . . .' He shrugged. 'It just happened.'

'But you don't tick her boxes,' she said, not able to take it in. 'And she's not your type either. How on earth. . . ?'

'I know.' He was watching her warily. 'Don't tell me. I don't tick any of her damned boxes and I don't go for tall blondes. But . . .' He tried a tentative smile. 'Are you going to be all right about this?'

'Yes.' She laughed her relief. 'You could say that. Geraldine's done me an enormous favour, Simon. I was just working up to having the same conversation with you.'

'Don't tell me you've met somebody else, too?' he asked, his astonishment a little insulting. 'Good God, this is bloody convenient all round then.'

'It's Daniel,' she told him. 'And don't you dare say anything against him.'

'Daniel?' His amazement showed. 'The climbing guy?'

She nodded. 'The very one.'

There was a short amazed silence and then he smiled, a smile she remembered from way back.

'The best of luck then,' he said.

'You too.'

Was that it? Was that all there was to it?

Not daring to look at him, she slipped the ring off her finger and placed it carefully on the table. For a moment, the emotional upheaval of the last few weeks caught up with her and her eyes misted for what had been, for what might have been, but then she thought of Daniel and put it behind her.

Saying only what was necessary, Simon helped her with her bags. They had things to discuss, financial stuff mainly, but they would do it later and, by the time Daniel arrived to take her away, she and Simon were almost comically behaving in a very polite, restrained manner.

He didn't quite hand her over but it felt like that.

'Are you all right, sweetheart?' Daniel asked in the lift on the way down.

She found it hard to speak so instead she reached for his hand and held it.

She would be fine.

She knew it.

'I'm sorry. I will pay you of course for the work you have already done,' Emily said, standing nervously in the doorway of Corinne's workroom.

'Nonsense. And do come in and sit down,' Corinne said, knowing now why she had slowed right down with the dress. She had known this would happen. In fact, she had pricked her finger and a tiny spot of blood had appeared on it the other day and that was a sure sign of distress. It never happened unless the dress was never to be worn. It had happened only twice before and each time it had been a cancellation at the last minute.

'Daniel's here,' Emily went on, perching on the chair. 'The thing is . . .'

Corinne laughed. 'I know. Don't bother explaining. You and Daniel have become an item. Isn't that what they call it these days? And about time too, my dear. You must be mad. He'll be off on those damned expeditions of his and you mustn't think you can stop him.'

'I know that.' She sighed. 'I'm not going to get my nine-to-fiver, am I? My nice cosy man.'

'No. But then there's no such thing as the perfect man. Look at

Bernard. Although I have to say, he has redeemed himself rather well. He's got the top job at Pacmans,' she added. 'And we shall be moving to London as soon as we sell up.'

'Congratulations, Daniel told me what happened with Joe,' Emily said, tucking a strand of hair behind her ear. Hesitantly, she continued, 'He doesn't want you to know the truth but I think you should. He doesn't want me to tell you so, if I do, it has to be just between the two of us.'

'I know what happened,' Corinne said quietly, going across to the window and looking out. The temperature had plummeted and there had been a sharp frost first thing. The leaves were gone, the trees stark against the grey sky. 'I know what happened,' she repeated. 'Joe wrote about his feelings in his diary. It finally made sense. So you don't have to tell me. It makes me see Daniel in a different light, of course, and I don't know how I'm going to make it up to him. All these years . . .' She sighed but kept her composure, determined not to break down.

'He loves you,' Emily told her. 'That's all that matters, isn't it?'

'What a to-do this is going to cause,' Corinne said, coming back to sit opposite Emily. 'I take it you have broken the news to everybody?'

'I've told Simon,' Emily said with a small smile. 'He was very relieved.'

'Oh?' Corinne raised her eyebrows. 'And your mother?'

'Ah . . .' Emily dared at last to look at the mountain of creamy material lying in a sad crumpled heap in the corner. 'I still have to do that. Daniel's coming with me over to Kent to meet everybody and we'll of course have to break the news then.'

'Poor you.' Corinne said with feeling. 'How about a glass of champagne to celebrate? Two things. You and Daniel and me and Bernard.'

Daniel had spoken of the cottage at the Centre so scathingly that she was pleasantly surprised that it wasn't so bad. It was basic, true, but charming also and, with a few little special touches, Emily knew she could make it feel like home. The other cottage, what she thought of as *her* cottage, was still on the market. Later, perhaps, she might persuade Daniel to look at it.

'It will do until we get something else, won't it?' he said anxiously as she wandered round.

'Of course it will. It's fine,' she said, peeping into the bedroom that was dominated by a large, old-fashioned iron bedstead covered with a spectacular quilt.

'Mother made it,' he explained. 'She used up her odds and ends.'

'Wow.' Emily went in, touched the soft silkiness of it and sighed. 'What a view!' she said, looking out of the small deep-silled window onto fields and in the distance the sea. 'She was proved right in the end,' she said, almost to herself.

'Who was?'

'Angharad. A girl I work with,' she said, not bothering to go into further details. 'How far is it to the beach?'

'Stone's throw,' Daniel said, coming up behind her and putting his hands round her waist before drawing her round and firmly into his arms. 'It will be a longer journey for you to work.'

What did that matter? What did anything matter other than that they were together?

Daniel manoeuvred her onto the side of the bed and gently removed her shoes, cupping her feet in his hands and soothing away the last of her worries. Outside, the wind rattled against the window and a flurry of rain shot against it but inside, it was warm and cosy, feeling suspiciously like home.

From downstairs, they heard the phone ringing but, absorbed as they were, they let it ring.

'Emily . . . what on earth is going on? I spoke to Simon who informs me that you've left him and gone to live with somebody called Daniel and he's given me this number for you. I do hope I have it right because he flustered me rather, although he seems to be taking it very well. This is Mrs Bellew, by the way leaving a message for her daughter Emily. Are we cancelling the wedding or what? I'm so worked up about it, darling, that in some ways I would welcome it. You've sounded so down recently that I was beginning to have serious doubts myself about whether you were doing the right thing.

'The Manor has changed hands and the menu has gone completely down the pan. Would you believe it, the nerve of these people?

'Fantastic news about Stella. She's met this man. Isn't that amazing? Anyway, he's quite a bit older but very sweet and they're getting married in the spring. I do hope he knows what he's taking on. The thing is that with your Aunt Louise being so utterly hopeless at organizing, I expect I'll be called upon again to do it. What a palaver! However, if I'm asked then I shall say yes. After all, it's family. Stella would love it if you would be bridesmaid, darling. You'll have to say yes or she'll be off again.

'Look forward to seeing you on Saturday and we can have a lovely chat.

'Your father says you are not to worry. I can say this now but he never quite took to Simon. We shall make this Daniel of yours most welcome. Is he vegetarian, by the way, because I am doing a roast on Sunday?

'Take care. Bye, darling.'